AMERICAN HEAVEN

AMERICAN HEAVEN

A NOVEL BY MAXINE CHERNOFF

COFFEE HOUSE PRESS :: MINNEAPOLIS

Front cover: "Bird's-eye view at night of Michigan Ave., looking South." Photograph by Stephen Deutch, used with permission from the Chicago Historical society.

Cover design by Jinger Peissig.

Dust jacket photograph by Jennifer Arra.

Parts of *American Heaven* have appeared in slightly different form as stories in the following magazines: "Chopin" in *SFSU Review,* "Irena" in *Magazine* and *2B Quarterly,* "Best Boy" in *Chicago Review,* and "The Whole Truth" in *ACM.* The author wishes to thank the editors.

Coffee House Press is supported in part by a grant provided by the Minnesota State Arts Board, through an appropriation by the Minnesota State Legislature and a grant from the National Endowment for the Arts, a federal agency. Additional support has been provided by the Lila Wallace-Reader's Digest Fund; The McKnight Foundation; Lannan Foundation; Target Stores, Dayton's, and Mervyn's by the Dayton Hudson Foundation; General Mills Foundation; St. Paul Companies; Honeywell Foundation; Beverly J. and John A. Rollwagen Fund of The Minneapolis Foundation; Star Tribune/Cowles Media Company; and The Andrew W. Mellon Foundation.

Coffee House Press books are available to the trade through our primary distributor, Consortium Book Sales & Distribution, 1045 Westgate Drive, Saint Paul, MN 55114. For personal orders, catalogs or other information, write to: Coffee House Press
27 North Fourth Street, Suite 400, Minneapolis, MN 55401

Library of Congress CIP Data
Chernoff, Maxine, 1952–
    American heaven / Maxine Chernoff
        p. cm.
    ISBN 1-56689-041-1 (hard)
    1. Polish Americans–Illinois–Chicago–Fiction. 2. Grandfathers–Illinois–Chicago–Fiction. 3. Gangsters–Illinois–Chicago–Fiction. 4. Women–Illinois–Chicago–Fiction. I. Title.
PS3553.H35644   1966
813'.54–dc20   96-2563
                                                                   CIP

10 9 8 7 6 5 4 3 2 1

The author wishes to thank the Illinois Arts Council, a state agency, for a Literary Fellowship in 1994, and San Francisco State University for a faculty development grant in spring 1995.

Thanks to Art Lange, Dominic Pacyga, and Jadwiga Wroblewska for help in researching the book.

Thanks to Paul Hoover and Koren, Philip, and Julian for their love and support.

In memory of Joe Brainard and Eleanor Risteen Gordon

PART ONE

CHAPTER ONE

SHE LIKES TO LOOK OUT HER WINDOW at the cars scurrying home from work. They look so small from the 29th floor. Americans have many cars. Yes, this strange parade of traffic is called *rush hour*. She gets out her American English book and reads idioms, practicing in the big oval mirror over the blonde dresser that has three empty drawers. It is comical that her worldly possessions fit into one half of the large bureau that Mr. Waters has provided. She has three fine hand-knit sweaters and several flowered silk scarves that she bought in Italy. Before she came to Chicago, she had stayed for several days at the Italian seashore in a town full of emigrés awaiting flights. It had a beautiful but rocky beach like Albania's, and she was surprised to see people who were not poor walking barefoot through the town casually carrying their shoes. They are relaxing, she had told herself again and again. She would never have walked barefoot in Warsaw nor gone out on the street half-dressed. She has saved a few smooth stones and shells from the beach. They are in the top drawer, where she keeps her meager jewelry. Local merchants were friendly, although most of her fellow emigrés had so little money that all they could do was buy food. Last night's dinner would be part of her picnic lunch for the next day: left-over bread and cheese and sometimes hard-boiled eggs and pasta with no sauce, her Italian diet. And in the benign sun of Italy, she had cried big loopy tears, for what she didn't know. And struggled through Joseph Conrad, whom she really didn't like, because he, after all, had left Poland, too.

"What would you like to eat?" Mr. Waters had asked when he took her to a steak house owned by an American sports figure, whose name was unfamiliar. The paraphernalia of football lined the dark paneled walls and a thousand photographs of the optimistic faces of athletic American men, men too carefree to be of much interest to her. "That's Walter—" somebody, Mr. Waters had said of a handsome black man at the bar. She had raised her eyebrows in pretended recognition, but what had startled her more was the size of the steak overwhelming her plate—how would she ever eat it?—and the kindness of her old man, who must have known she knew nothing, that words couldn't even express what she didn't know. Mr. Waters had ordered his usual Dewars with two splashes of water, the way she made it for him at home, and she had ordered red wine. "Give her the best," Mr. Waters had said and toasted her. "To Irena, who lives in America."

Now she can lie down and close her eyes. She'll fall asleep and dream in Polish, which is flawless. Words will float like chiffon in the sky of her dream. The grass will be green in brown old Warsaw. And then she'll wake up and practice her idioms again. "I am pleased to make your acquaintance," she says in the mirror. "I am of the opinion—" or is it "in the opinion"—that, what? That Americans are very generous or rather condescending to immigrants like herself. After all, she was a mathematician in Poland. She knows universal, unchanging signs in a language deeper than language: calculus and probability, proofs approaching infinity. Nobody in this high-rise understands math better. Yet nothing is truer than the newness she feels in America, where her hair color is apricot, like the abundant fruit she's bought in the grocery, and her eyes are aquamarine—if she understands the dictionary definition.

She dabs at her large, intelligent, maybe aquamarine eyes with her palm, and thinks about her old apartment in Warsaw with its massive dark wood furniture and noisy radiator that rarely worked. She thinks about Joszef's full lips and his wonderful musk that makes her feel sad and angry at the course of human events, a phrase from the Declaration of Independence of America, her new country. The course of human events has left him in her old city and her on the shore of an endless Midwestern lake surrounded by architecture that is too tall and too bright. "Even the pollution looks clean," she has written Joszef in her fine hand. And she thinks of Warsaw, where everything, including the sky, is older and richer than in Chicago.

In an hour she'll walk into Mr. Waters' sleek "Euro-kitchen" and fix him his old man's dinner accompanied by his Scotch with two splashes of water. Her old man is polite and serene. He never calls her unless it's absolutely necessary, and then with a deference she expected he might ask—demand—of her. At 5:30 they'll sit down in the kitchen at the small Danish-modern table. He'll turn on Channel 7, and Peter Jennings, who resembles her Joszef, only smoother and less complicated and knowing English, will tell them the news of the day. Sometimes Mr. Waters will be quiet or shake his head in regret, which is what he did while they sat together her third week in America and watched Los Angeles burn. Other times he'll ask her how she spent her afternoon. She'll cover her mouth for a second, maybe, she thinks, he can see she's embarrassed, and tell him that she was learning English as usual. "I think you do fine, Irena," he'll say and pat her arm paternally. He'll look at her with his kindly, red-veined eyes and suggest with his look not quite of pity that they both need more than either can bear to imagine. At these moments, she thinks of Joszef, who moves quickly and rarely touches her, and of her father, with his triangular face and gentle brow, dead for six years. She'll serve him his usual: mashed potatoes and a chicken breast, the size of her fist, and diced carrots and

Jello. She'll cut his meat into tiny thin strips and think about the cat she left behind in Warsaw, her baby, who'd eat tiny bits of chicken liver from her hand, his scratchy little tongue wetting her palm. Joszef would scoff at her tenderness towards Chopin. And in the course of human events, or is it *curse*, Joszef has him now.

Mr. Waters pays her for being as kind to him as the owner of a loved housepet. She feeds him and walks him and on mornings when he is particularly stiff, helps him out of bed and into his shower and lays out his clothes, which include brightly colored sports coats in soft wools, and old, large-patterned ties, which Mr. Waters has trouble knotting by himself. She has learned to knot his ties and fold his silk handkerchiefs like origami designs into his pocket. She laces his shiny black oxfords and hands him his cane, whose top is wood—embroidered—she knows that's not the word—in Africa.

When the weather is warm, as it is this October, she takes him by the arm or pushes him in his chair down Oak Street beach. Sometimes they sit under a white canopy in a flower garden named after a rich Chicago woman and admire the profusion of flowers in America. They laugh because she only knows their names in Polish, and he doesn't know the English translation for any flowers except roses, daisies, and orchids, which are nowhere in sight. After sketching one for her quickly on paper, he'd told her that they'll visit Hawaii some day and see purple orchids. When he smiles at her, his gums are surprising pink and healthy looking. Maybe they are artificial. He flirts coyly on this shimmering October day near the Drake Hotel, a building that is shorter and duller and very appealing because it might be in Warsaw. Mr. Waters raises his face to the sun and says that his favorite summer month in Chicago is October, and they laugh. He once lived on the Left Bank in Paris, he tells her, as they eat thin cucumber and fat-free mayonnaise sandwiches on crustless bread and drink clever little packets of sugary juice designed for schoolchildren.

He is funny, her old black man with the white shock of hair that he covers with a colorful hat like a patterned fez. He is dapper and handsome, and she's proud to accompany him. They laugh at overweight joggers and young couples so in love at 11:34 in the morning. He tells her lots of stories about his life, and once when a Miss McPartland was in town, Irena helped him take a cab to a radio station. He talked on the air about the days when he was the pianist in a jazz band that Irena had never heard of. There is a black baby grand in one corner of the apartment—it has the best view of the beach—which he never plays. He wasn't as famous as some musicians like Mr. Charlie Parker, whose music she'd heard in Warsaw, but she could tell by the songs the woman chose and the way she talked with solicitousness, though there was much that Irena couldn't understand, that her old man had been truly impressive. Through age he had become a crippled, gentlemanly former musician with swollen ankles and a failing heart. Through the course of human events, she has assumed a new station in life: lady-in-waiting (which isn't what it is called, but she can never remember in English what it is called) to a former great man, not Mr. Charlie Parker.

Sometimes when they'd strolled along the beach that summer, he'd seen young girls in very small bathing suits, younger than Irena by maybe fifteen years, and he'd said, her kind old man, "My Irena is fairer by far." Sometimes at night she'd try not to think of Joszef, who was often cruel in dreams and denied her his attention even when they shared the same dream room. Dreams are more honest than memories, which we select and beautify like a garden, she'd thought. And she'd tried to remember the words of a song that Miss McPartland played that slow Sunday in June. They were beautiful American words. One phrase was unusual, a joke at the expense of love for all its triviality: *"I wear my heart on my sleeve,"* the words said. She wondered if there was an American idiom, *"I wear my heart in my sleeve."*

Thursdays are her favorite day. She takes whatever book she

is currently reading and her list of idioms and collects Mr. Waters' wash and hers. She combines them in a white mesh pillowcase with a drawstring, a special invention for laundry, fills a small coin purse from India that is shaped like a swan with a curled neck, takes her bottles of detergent and fabric softener, and proceeds to the second floor of the building, where the commissary and laundry rooms are located. She would never buy detergent in the commissary, which bilks old people who are trapped in the building. Instead, she walks down to Walgreens at the corner of Michigan and Chicago and buys what's on sale. Mr. Waters has said that they can send out the laundry, but she likes the calming effect of separating colors from whites, listening to the peaceful hum of the dependable American motor, adding blue perfumed fabric softener, and then standing with her legs warming against the vibrating machine as her laundry spins dry. Mr. Waters has even bought her an ironing board with a pad featuring a row of yellow ducklings following their mother, and a bright blue iron with twelve settings. She keeps the equipment in her room and irons his shirts with care every Friday. She doesn't suppose that the building management, which posts endless rules on every unadorned surface of the building, would consent to her hanging Mr. Waters' shirts on his balcony to dry. Cotton smells so good, like it's full of life, when the sun warms it.

Sometimes other attendants are in the laundry room. She has a nodding acquaintance with a heavy black woman in a short white uniform, whose dress pulls open at her waist and whose nylons end at her knees. Today she sees a Hispanic woman in a dark blue jogging suit, with glamorous auburn hair piled high on her head. The other visitor to the laundry room looks like a resident of the building. She is a tall brunette, who wears an expensive fisherman's knit sweater and a scrubbed denim skirt along with fashionable cowboy boots. Her nails are manicured. Perhaps she is a lawyer, and this is yet another minor holiday for the American pantheon of heroes, like the Columbus celebration last week. Perhaps this woman is a young wife, whose small child is sleeping upstairs under her nanny's watchful eye. When Irena walks Mr. Waters, she sees many women like this American pushing their babies in finely quilted French and German prams the size of ocean liners. Their babies are not plump like European infants. The residual fear of hunger doesn't make Americans obsessively feed their children, as her married friends in Warsaw do. These babies are lean and look as if they participate in baby calisthenics. She would have liked to have a child with Joszef, but he was too serious about himself to consider children. When she took him to visit Margarit and her curly-haired son Andrej, Joszef was unimpressed with the boy's wise little head and sympathetic eyes.

Irena observes this American mother or lawyer open a thick book with a serious cover and turn to a page well past the middle. Maybe she is a doctor or a scientist. Irena can't believe her good fortune to have perhaps found another mathematician in the laundry room of her building on a Thursday afternoon. But if this woman were a scientist of any type, would Irena know enough English to demonstrate her command? She checks her American idiom list for verb phrases. She looks "around" the room again, and watches this woman settle into a molded plastic chair, the color of salmon, and close her eyes.

Noticing the woman's keys on the washing machine that she's finished loading, Irena walks gingerly across the room to gather up the prize. Now she moves toward the dozing American lawyer, mother, or scientist. Maybe in America women can be all three simultaneously!

"Please excuse me," Irena begins, "but I have found these."

Opening her eyes, the woman stretches her arm lazily, almost seductively, towards Irena's palm.

"Thanks," she says casually, and looks at Irena with small brown eyes.

Irena is afraid that these eyes will close again before she has made the desired impact. "I, too, am sometimes losing things,"

Irena confesses. And she refrains from covering her mouth with her hand, though she feels tempted.

"Are you from somewhere else?" the woman asks politely.

"Poland," Irena smiles, self-consciously, displaying slightly crooked teeth in this land of perfect dentition.

"I guess everyone's from somewhere else. I'm from Albany."

"Albany?" Irena pronounces slowly.

"New York state."

"I come from Warsaw to city of Chicago because some friends live on North Side."

"You live in this building with your friends?"

"No, with Mr. Harrison Waters. He is man I care for. Very good man." Irena smiles as in a commercial. Everyone in America smiles, even when they're angry.

"So we have the same profession," the woman says without elaborating, and points her small brown eyes toward the floor.

This knowledge makes Irena slightly giddy. "You do not live here?" she asks to confirm that she's understood.

"I do live here, but I don't *own* here."

"You are not married woman?"

"I am not married woman," the American smiles ironically. She surveys the floor or maybe her boots again.

"I am sorry to be invading you."

"I live in 24B with Jack Kaufman." She hesitates, as if Irena is supposed to respond to the name. "He's very ill."

"My Mr. Waters is also ill with bad heart. How long have you been here?"

"Ever since I left Albany. Two-and-a-half, almost three years."

"In Poland I was mathematician." There. She's said it. Like a brilliant diadem of knowledge, the words perch between them.

"Excuse me," the American says. "My wash is ready."

How disappointing that she didn't respond, Irena thinks, as she watches the woman cross the room. Her shoulders are broad, as if she might have once been a swimmer.

Maybe later today Irena will wheel Mr. Waters to the pool and help him in. Once or twice a week, she encourages him to exercise. With the sun so bright over the rooftop solarium, this might be the day to persuade him to dangle his spindly legs in the water and kick them a little for good measure. First in the apartment, she'll trim his coarse toenails and make sure he feels comfortable in his terry robe and the new trunks he chose last month, maroon with yellow parrots. Irena had been quite shocked at their boldness. Old men should wear black or gray, she thinks. He had convinced her to buy a new bathing suit too, a tasteful royal blue tank suit pleated in the bodice— and not too revealing. It says "Lord and Taylor" on a discreet seam. Today she'll swim a few laps in the small bluish green pool and think about her friend from Albany with the big shoulders and tentative eyes, to whom it doesn't matter that Irena's a mathematician.

Back at her dryer folding her last laundry, Irena hears the woman's voice. "I never introduced myself," she is saying. "I'm Elizabeth O'Conner."

"I am Irena Bozinska."

"We'll have to talk again," Elizabeth O'Conner suggests before she turns away from Irena and walks toward a dryer.

Irena is tempted to pursue her, but Joszef used to accuse her of following him. Not in the street but in their own small apartment, Irena would, indeed, accompany Joszef from corner to corner. "Like a dog wanting to be fed," Joszef once said, thinking he was being funny. How could she have loved such a hard man, she wonders, as she watches from behind as Elizabeth O'Conner stoops and tosses all of her unsorted laundry into an expensive-looking willow basket.

Back in her apartment, Irena finds Mr. Waters napping in his chair. His head is down on his chest, which contains the badly pumping heart, and newspapers are scattered around him. Mr. Harrison Waters subscribes to five daily newspapers: *The Chicago Defender*, *The Chicago Tribune*, *The Chicago Sun-Times*, *The New York Times*, *The International Herald Tribune*. He is lucky, Irena thinks, that his wife's family had enough money to keep him in such comfort. He told her the name of the hair products his father-in-law had invented, but it meant nothing to Irena—so many new words slip out unrecognized. On the street she sees old men with nothing, not even a kind hand at their elbows when curbs are high and traffic unpredictable. By late afternoon, Harrison and his oxblood leather chair are usually buried in sections of newsprint. Irena bends to put her ear close enough to hear his breathing. Her one fear in working for an old man who is ill is finding him dead.

She thinks of two times that death surprised her. When she was a child, her canary died while she was at school. Irena found his stiff body at the bottom of the cage. She held him in her palm—he weighed no more than a tissue—before carrying him into the garden, where she dug a small hole and covered him in dirt and weeds. A few days later, she noticed that something had dug him up.

When she found her father dead in a little country retreat where he had gone to finally write his book about political corruption, she hadn't been completely shocked. She assumed, as many friends had warned her, that he'd be watched by government operatives. Imagine working on the surveillance team for a slightly mad professor of chemistry, who had taken to clandestine political action in his old age. Had one of the paid cowards accosted him with a poisoned syringe in his country wayside? Where were the signs of struggle or violence? His real cause of death—a massive stroke some twelve hours before her arrival—had saddened her more than this imagined one. And the useless relics of her devotion: she had been bringing him a bouquet of wildflowers that day, thinking that he had probably never received such a gift, and some black market cocoa, which she later shared with Joszef. While his ground was still fresh, she'd resolved to leave the country that buried fine men like her father. She wouldn't tolerate a place where telling the truth was a crime. Her desire to leave had first been a joke among friends. Repeating that joke had hardened it to a vow.

I'm in Chicago now, she tells her father in a hushed reverent whisper whenever she can't sleep. *It's better for us,* she confides, though it isn't always clear how this is true.

Now she checks Mr. Waters' breathing whenever she finds him asleep. At night she welcomes the sound that always disrupts her sleep, of his crooked progress down the hallway to the bathroom. Sometimes she hears his swollen feet slapping the parquet floor. At other times his hands brush the wall. She holds her breath while she hears the slow stream of urine and the flush, before his steps retrace themselves and silence resumes.

The two times he has been ill since April had been quite unextraordinary. She has accompanied him by taxi to a Michigan Avenue office, where a celebrated cardiologist in seersucker and a bow tie entertains a wealthy clientele. His office is lined with soothing photos of marine life, none too vigorous for the assembled patients with their enlarged hearts: mostly jellyfish and anemone, and an occasional seahorse suspended in sunlight. Mr. Waters hates going to the doctor. "They killed Gwen, you know," he told Irena, who was afraid to ask more. Gwen was Mr. Waters' wife, the smiling, full-faced woman whose photo sat on the piano. Gwen might naturally be doing what Irena is paid to do, had she survived whatever it was that killed her. Irena is sorry that Mr. Waters' wife is dead and that no child resulted from the union. But she will do her best to keep her old man breathing.

Now she sits near his feet and randomly picks up a section of the newspaper. She notes that the bidding scandal—the city's lost millions of dollars due to one small, balding man— is still front-page news. Once again, the red-faced mayor is pictured behind a podium denouncing fraud, promising to weed out the offenders, who have betrayed the trust of all Chicagoans. Irena likes this American newspaper, which, naively as herself, seems to take its corruption seriously.

Again and again, her friends, who hadn't understood her desire to leave Poland, had argued with her. She was foolish, headstrong, simple. Didn't she understand that corruption, in fact, is an assumption of control anywhere in the world? "Why make it so hard on yourself?" Urszula had asked. "Turn your head the other way, as the rest of us do. You think you are helping your father by leaving your country, but you are only hurting yourself, Irena. And in America, my dear friend, it will be the same corruption, only consensual. Instead of being raped by it, you will be screwing it. You'll choose your favorite criminal at the voting booth. You should emigrate to heaven," Urszula had continued before intoning the official list of American transgressions from ordinary to extraordinary. Maybe Irena should send Urszula this refreshing newspaper as proof of her sound judgment. Then Urszula could understand that a desire for truth could pervade a whole culture, that here men and women, good people, are rewarded for their honesty.

On the subject of the scandal, however, Mr. Waters had seemed closer in sympathy to Urszula. "Typical Chicago story," he'd sighed. "Everything's for sale here. Everyone can be had for a price. Can that be news?" To which Irena had only shrugged in resignation, not wanting to be insubordinate to her boss and protector.

Maybe it's Irena's feeling of intimacy with the inanimate world, solid and real to her as the familiar faces of friends, that provokes her protective impulse. She had always admired the integrity of solitary pencils, books, pillars, staircases. After she had become a serious scholar, numbers, too, took on more than a provisional existence. They were as real as cathedrals, as solid as the earth. She wants to think the best of the horizontal, black-and-white, gleaming, water filtration plant, which she can see from her high-rise window near its neighbor, the tallest all-apartment building on earth. In changing locations, one can change the level of candor. In small ways with Mr. Waters, she is already more honest. She had told him, for instance, that his swim trunks were rather bright. This small step toward disclosure of her views will begin a trend. In America she'll demand the full story. Perhaps she'll even report a scandal someday and be rewarded for her efforts.

Though there is never a large job section on weekdays, she combs the classifieds for positions available. Data entry is popular, but there are rarely jobs for mathematicians. Perhaps when she knows more English, she can find something suitable. Meanwhile, she'll straighten up the apartment, dust but not vacuum because Mr. Waters is napping, and start dinner. She has promised him that she'll serve something Polish soon, and yesterday she had walked more than a mile to get a bus to Milwaukee Avenue, the Polish Riviera, her friend on the North Side call it, to purchase ingredients for pirogi. Tonight they'll eat pirogi stuffed with chopped meat and onions and potatoes. She has made three compromises, one to convenience and two to Mr. Waters' heart: she has bought ready-made dough but refrained from kraut and sour cream. Instead, there will be plain yogurt and a bottle of Polish vodka flavored with fragrant grasses named after a Polish version of the American buffalo. She will offer it to Mr. Waters as a gift, though she suspects that he would secretly prefer his Dewars. She has also read in an article about the governor's heart problem that it might be a good idea for Mr. Waters to take a single aspirin a day. She has clipped the article with the beautiful diagram of the governor's clogged, Y-shaped artery to show Mr. Waters at dinner. As she warms the vegetable oil, not lard, for the pirogi, she keeps glimpsing the full-color heart diagram out of the corner of her eye. She thinks about her Joszef with his pale blue eyes, fine light brown hair, and well-trimmed beard, and lets out a nearly inaudible cry when the hot oil skitters in the pan, spitting a drop at her cheek. There are telephones, she thinks, and large satellites in space for the times when one misses a person so sorely that she can't even cook a pirogi. Maybe after dinner, she'll go to the public phone in the lobby and ask the international operator how to place her call to Warsaw.

She hears papers shuffling in the next room. Mr. Waters will be stirring, and soon she'll hear him say, "Irena, are you in there?" Then he'll sit at the kitchen table in his tie and shirt-sleeves, put on the news, and quietly and patiently as a child, watch her cook. She remembers how her mother used to fry sausage and potatoes while Irena recited her multiplication tables. The old kitchen heated up and stayed filled as a sealed jar with the greasy smoke of dinner. Often her father was away at the university, so she and her mother would sit in happy silence, sharing the robust tastes. The calm of her new life, with the smell of cooking the apex of pleasure, is similar. "It's like being a child again—or a nun," she had written Joszef, who had interpreted her comment on simplicity as a reference to her celibacy. "Don't save yourself for me!" he had responded, always cavalier and slightly eager to be cruel.

But now it occurs to her that her kind employer might want applesauce with his pirogi as well. Why hadn't she thought of applesauce yesterday? She is going to have to give his money to the robbers in the commissary, his beautiful American money with its surrealistic eye embedded in a pyramid and its platitude about God. It makes her angry to picture the bland face of the clerk accepting this somehow divine currency, perpetrating a fraud with something as basic as applesauce. Maybe there is room in the headlines for this story too.

"Will you be wanting applesauce with Polish dinner?" Irena asks when Mr. Waters enters the kitchen.

"Whatever, Irena. You just give me what you please."

"There should be applesauce, I think. I will get and return."

"Whatever, Irena," he yawns, then turns his attention to Peter Jennings, whose formidable head is outlined next to a graph of economic indicators.

On the way to the door of the food store, Irena pauses to read the instructions for international calls on the phone. There are so many listed that she will have to take her idiom spiral to write them down and study them if she is really going to call Joszef some day. Maybe the difficulty of the operation is a sign that it shouldn't be attempted. She gazes another moment at the phone, then, marching into the commissary, selects the smallest jar of applesauce that she can find, $2.29, and sneers at the clerk as he rings up her sale.

But heading toward her before Irena can prepare her opti-mistic American face is Elizabeth O'Conner, who has filled a miniature shopping cart with items. Irena knows that the small package of coffee on top of her pile alone costs $7.99.

"Hello, again," says Elizabeth O'Conner.

"Hello also," says Irena.

"I always come down here before dinner."

"It is very convenient," Irena adds. Elizabeth O'Conner's old man must be very foolish to allow such behavior—or very rich. "But too expensive, I think," Irena adds quickly, gather-ing courage.

"Money is no object," Elizabeth O'Conner laughs brightly. Irena notices that her sturdy wrist is sporting a thick gold braid of a bracelet studded with green gems—could they be emeralds?

"I must go," Irena says belatedly. "Dinner is prepared but one ingredient I still need."

"Well, good dining," Elizabeth O'Conner adds. "See you around."

There are two types of people, Irena thinks in the musical elevator. To some, everything is a joke because they think they are too good for life. Pain especially makes them laugh because they are too good for pain. Joszef and Elizabeth O'Conner are of this type, and those American athletes with their smug faces, whose signed photos lined the restaurant wall. To the rest of the world, to those who know how fragile the heart of an old man is and how much applesauce is really worth, nothing is very funny. She and Mr. Waters, and maybe Peter Jennings with his handsome brow and sad economic figures, are of this kind. No, she will not call Joszef, who would remind her of how unneces-sary she is. They had agreed to be free of each other when Irena left Poland, but for real freedom from Joszef, she is going to have to steel herself and act as she did during Lent as a child. *I will give this up because I love it so,* she told her mother about a bar of Swiss chocolate she had hoarded since Christmas. *I do not need it,* she told her mother. But she hadn't felt as hollow then as she does now, unlocking Mr. Waters' door and saying with false cheer, "We are ready to eat now. May I pour you some wonderful vodka from my country?" to her sweet old man.

"Do you maybe know Mr. Kaufman?" Irena asks after dinner.

"Jack Kaufman? Everyone knows Jack Kaufman. He's about as infamous as they come, Irena. And he lives in this building."

"I meet his Miss O'Conner in the grocery. She is caring for him."

"He's a politician of sorts. But maybe in your country you'd just call him a gangster."

"He is like Mr. Al Capone?"

"Not quite Al Capone. He made a fortune in real estate in pretty shady ways. He was a poor boy from the West Side like me. But during the Depression he bought up lots of fore-closed property—property the bank owned—for pennies—and now he owns about all that the eye can see." Mr. Waters gestures broadly with his hand. "I'd say he's as close to a king as you get in Chicago. And he didn't come by all of this with his brains, though I've heard he does have a good head. It was his connections. He could make people nervous. He could have someone make a call and get a leg broken if he had to, so people just let him have his way. Your voice would quiver if Jack Kaufman was on the phone."

"His helper, I am afraid, is not very smart lady. She buys too many items at commissary. She fills whole cart with this and with that."

"He probably owns the commissary too. He owns lots of things—theaters, parking lots, restaurants, apartment build-ings, bars."

"He is richest man in Chicago?"

"I wouldn't be surprised, Irena, if his mattress weren't stuffed with thousand dollar bills, as well as a couple of lock boxes somewhere else. He's been in and out of trouble with the authorities for years, but he probably owns them too. Nothing sticks to the man."

"So no one can hurt him?"

"Plenty of people could hurt him, but why would they want to? Why get your sugar daddy arrested?"

"Please, what means sugar daddy?"

"The one who gives you sweets. The one who supports you in a big way. The one who butters your bread. I bet a few clubs I played in were owned by him too, Irena. One for sure, where the bouncers, the men who kept order, packed weapons. So technically he was my employer once or twice," Mr. Waters chuckles.

"I'll tell you, though. I prefer his type to the thugs of today. These college boys with their clean shirts and conservative ties and good morals going and robbing banks left and right and buying companies just to ruin them. At least with Kaufman it was personal. He was a poor kid. People were mean to him. He got tough and showed them all. Bet there was a little light in his eye while he did it."

"His helper seems maybe strange. I think she is teasing my English a little."

"She and her sugar daddy will have me to answer to if that keeps up, Irena," Mr. Waters smiles. He picks up his four post-dinner pills, which Irena serves him nightly in a Dutch spoon rest, and swallows them one by one.

"My head is full of vodka and pharmaceuticals and thoughts, Irena. Once I played for Kaufman and a lady friend at a little club on Lake Street. We dinosaurs were both pretty young then. I think I'll take me to bed."

"So you meet this Mr. Kaufman?"

"He gave me a little diamond stickpin. I still have it somewhere if I'm not mistaken. He probably got it off a corpse."

"A man who has died?"

"Just a little joke, Irena. Jack was a little ugly guy with bad skin. He ran around trying to buy the world, but he never did me any harm. I tell you, Irena, that woman who works for him doesn't have an easy job. Men like him have giant egos, big as that," he says pointing to the piano. "They need lots of attention. He probably runs her ragged. Though life with Kaufman wouldn't be dull, Irena. I can promise you that. He knows where all the bodies are buried."

Should she write Joszef a letter about Elizabeth O'Conner and her short and proud gangster? No, she thinks, grinning and submerging her hands in the soapy water to scrub a pan before placing it in the dishwasher. She'll wait until tomorrow and then decide whether to tell Joszef. Maybe she'll mention nothing at all. And she prolongs the moment of pleasure, thinking how he, a connoisseur of American corruption, lover of James Cagney and George Raft films, will have to live for several more weeks without knowing of Irena's fantastic news discovery, a shady sugar daddy right in her building on Lake Shore Drive.

CHAPTER TWO

OO BAD, Essie, that your heart stopped before mine. There was a little prayer I used to say at all the funerals we attended, business and otherwise. "Let me go first, God. Amen." But who's to question how these things work? It would break your heart anyway, to see how the world's changed. Frank Sinatra is old and sick and Johnny Carson's retired. Woody Allen, a nice Jewish boy, was fooling around with a step-daughter, for heaven's sake. Where's the finesse? Where's the charm, Ess? Remember how Crosby would croon, *Ba Ba Ba Boo,* and your heart would tick more softly for a minute?

People just don't get it these days. Everything's lousy, ugly. I watch a lot of TV, Ess. You have to shake your ass and talk in rhyme. And the rhymes are simple. Anyone could think of them: class, ass, bad ass, not Cole Porter. And they have nothing to say about love, these bums.

Get this, Ess. Communism is kaput. No more gonifs in the Kremlin. They took the statue of Lenin and tore it down just like that. Still Chinese gonifs, but they're older than me. Soon they'll all be dead, and their kids will be laughing and buying Gucci bags and BMWs and making French soufflés.

Only our own local variety of gonif is left, but these guys are nothing compared to me in my prime. They can't even take payoffs right. There's a pretty little headline all week about an unimportant guy I know—third-rate Ziggy Floekorn's son— who rigged bids like crazy with the Water Reclamation Department. Millions of dollars are missing, the mayor is screaming, and little Eddie's here twice now moaning to me. "I'll see what I can do," I told him, but he's going to drown, no matter what.

Where does a little schnook like him get the idea of playing solo? You get married when you go into business, in sickness and in health, but this little guy wants to be his own bride. The organization might have set it up; they're always looking for opportunities, and they're smooth—but not at the Water Reclamation Department, which they already own. But this sorry little fucker sees too many movies and thinks it's as simple as shaving to make a big play like this. And then he comes crying to me and flashing some money in my face while I'm lying in bed here with a needle in my arm. I'm supposed to save his butt, Essie, because his father used to cheat me at cards. The whole time he made the deal he was talking right into a wire some bald asshole has taped to his hairy chest. With the technical side of things so sophisticated today, you have to be smart as a whip. You can't fuck around or you're screwed, even if you know Jack Kaufman. Even if he cares. But who thinks straight anymore? And why should Jack Kaufman care?

Not even the mayor is as bright as his dad. He always looks like someone's roughed him up and mussed his hair. He looks like he keeps a bully as a valet. I saw him once when the city council was voting on a zoning ordinance. The aldermen are yakking, and he's not even pretending that he's listening. His lips are open and his tongue is hanging out, and he's balancing on his knuckles like an ape. Is that a way to run a city? I tell you. His dad wasn't so smart to begin with, but he knew how to put himself together. There was always a nice hankie in his pocket, and his hair was lacquered real neat. And his mouth was closed. His shirts always looked like he wore them only once. Fresh and white as snow. I tell you, Essie, appearance counts. He used to call me Jackie, like Jackie Gleason. He's dead too, Essie, for years, and Lucille Ball and her good friend Ethel Mertz. I always liked her better. Maybe Milton Berle is still alive somewhere, at least I haven't heard he's not.

All the waste, Essie. Handsome young people dying from AIDS and drugs and you name it. People bumping each other off on street corners like during Prohibition. But all of them are black kids, Ess, kids who have nothing. We had fathers to slap us on the ear and show us how to grow up fast. They made us take care of ourselves real good before they worked their butts off and got sick and died. I remember Pa polishing apples and unloading potatoes for Mr. Bruno's produce store. He got eleven dollars a week and sometimes less, and his hands were always dirty.

I remember Joey saying to me, "I'm not going to be like Pa." And he wasn't, Essie. He was the first Jew at his fancy country club with the Scottish name and the shiny pastel golf carts and the palm trees. He made it big, my little lawyer brother with the runny ear.

But these kids now have no fathers. Maybe their mothers try, but it's not the same. What can a mother teach a kid about the street? What can she tell you to do with a guy who grabs your balls and won't let go? So the kids sell a few drugs and buy these fancy jackets that say "Raiders" and think they're making it. Then *bang*. Some punk shooter Wres, and that's it. There's no tradition for them to come up in, no one looking out for them and greasing their path a little. Where's the promise, the upward mobility? I could teach them a thing or two about thinking big, Essie. I found the right guys, I listened close, and the rest is history. I'd like to help a few of these black kids really learn how to make it. Maybe I'll call Nadel and see about starting a foundation or something to help them out.

Over one thing and one thing only I could cry. Roy never calls or tries to see his father. I've got bundles for him. I could make him a rich man, but he thinks he's too good for me and stays away. I could give him a company with an office like the Taj Mahal on the top floor of the Hancock. I could teach him things I bet he doesn't know he doesn't know. Meanwhile, his kids go to their fancy private schools courtesy of me. Get this. The younger one is practical—she wants to be some kind of Greek scholar. But not so much as a call from Roy. Sometimes Susan phones for a minute from her car. That ring on her hand? I put it there. But Roy loved you, Essie, so don't feel sad about it. It's just an old man's dissatisfaction.

I mostly lie in bed these days and take my painkillers and doze. Sometimes the strangest things come to mind. A man's mind, I think, is like a pool. Everything that's ever happened is in it at some depth. Some of it's hidden under a rock or a shadow of one, but it's all there. Maybe someone said that already. It seems like someone's said just about everything. Was it Freud or some other intellectual Jew? Sometimes I think about all the smart people Hitler killed—what a waste—and the dumb ones too.

Then I list the things I remember. I can still see Ma's round face and her little red curls like Cs on her forehead. I can see her coming for me when we sold papers, bringing me and Joey a hot sandwich wrapped in waxpaper. I can remember sleeping on Navy Pier on nights when it was hot as Hades. The breeze would come off of the lake, and the kids would run around having fun, and the air smelled fresh and no one worried about what they read in the papers. The papers brought problems from other places. They were exotic. Here, everyone took care of each other. "Get down from that tree," you'd schry at someone else's kid as soon as your own. Strangers weren't strangers. It goes without saying that I see you all the time like you were alive with your dark shiny eyes. Then I make inventories of all the things I know, the practical stuff: how to make money left and right, how to inject painkillers in my own thigh, how to mix a perfect dry martini straight up, how to call the right guy for the right job, how the small little bone in the neck cracks when it gets twisted too far. Forget I told you that, Ess, though they can't get wives to testify against husbands. How a big fat lying son of a bitch, 250 pounds at the least, towering over me like Goliath, has a small little fragile bone like a wedding ring hidden in his fat neck that can snap when his brakes go out. Always test your machinery, I say. I could have told him that, Essie, if he didn't stab me in the back. If he didn't dangle me like meat on a hook. But the sharks weren't hungry that day. And you never even knew the extent of the trouble, because I didn't want to scare you.

My girl keeps me entertained best she can, Essie, but it's nothing like you. She talks refined and has a small little face that looks sad. Is she sad for me, I wonder, or just sad, period? It kind of touches me how her voice is so soft now and then, how she seems to have lost her energy, like something just squeezed it out of her. Maybe she's sick too. I worry about her at night, Essie. Why is someone so good involved with an old man's tubes and shots and shit and piss? She seems too good to read me the editorials and sports scores and hold my hand when the pain gets so bad that I want to bawl. I keep asking myself why she's doing this and not riding around in some fancy limo with some consultant. That's what people are these days, consultants. No one makes anything or buys or sells a thing. They just consult about all the things they don't make or sell or buy. Well, that's not quite fair. They do make computers.

By the way, Essie, computers are so small now you can hold one in your lap. It weighs seven pounds like a new baby. There are computers that play solitaire. You would have loved it. And imagine what I could have done with a piece of machinery like that. It would have eliminated lots of middle men, the guys who are good for carrying your chewing gum and fucking things up at every turn.

This Elizabeth won't tell me much about herself. She says it would be boring, and sometimes I think that's the trouble with society today. Kids just don't tell stories anymore. Maybe because of TV they don't understand that they can just make things up. I used to play with a stick and dirt. I'd be a pirate or whatever. Kids today are surrounded with fancy toys. But they don't play anymore. This Elizabeth doesn't have a story to tell in her head. She wouldn't know a story if she saw one. But I tell her lots of things, Essie, so maybe she'll learn. Sometimes I tell her about my business associates. What can it hurt now? When and if she sings like a canary, I'll be covered in sod. I even told her a few of my aliases. I bet you never even knew I had them, Essie. I was always Jack to you, and that was how it should have been, your own Jack. What did you need with Jake Dubrow?

Remember when you were young and pretty as a little chicken? You'd put that white powder on your face to look like a ghost, frighten your teachers to death, and get out of school early. I'd come for you, my own Queen Esther, in that big hearse from Allegretto's funeral home. Remember little Allegretto with the acne? His nose looked like a penis. And they say Jews have noses. Remember how I gave you flowers that had gotten lost on the way to the cemetery? Beautiful wreaths and bouquets of white roses. Would the dead people miss them? We used to just jump on each other whenever we had the chance. Remember at your Bubi's house in her sun room while she chopped eggs and onions in her favorite European bowl three rooms away? I always think of eggs and onions when I think of sex. But people nowadays think they invented fucking. Well, I got news for them. We fucked all the time. We were just careful. Nobody made babies they didn't need back then.

Now, people have MTV to tell them what to do next. They don't know how to close their eyes and hear what music is saying. They lack imagination. They're stupid or something. It's true. But sometimes my heart still goes out to them like I'm a little god or someone looking down from above, like I have the right. Elizabeth tells me about a girl she's met, a little Polish girl in the commissary, afraid to buy applesauce. She's come all the way here from another world where people wear cardboard shoes and eat crap. Like Ma and Pa did way back when in steerage. She's living sky-high in this fancy building on this beautiful, rolling lake afraid to pay two bucks for a jar of something. Why are people afraid, Essie? You do what you can and you die. That's it. They write your name on some stone and if you're lucky there's someone to read it.

I remember when I was in the service, not some politician's crapola version of this I recently heard on the news, by the way. The real version, where I stood on the deck in the middle of the Pacific, a little Jewish boy sailor in the Philippines, and thought about you, Essie. You were pregnant with Roy, and we had some property already. I'd say we were well off, so you would have been a rich widow if something had gone wrong over there. I thought about a song again and again and told myself that even if my voice stinks I'll sing Essie a song when I got home. Well, I never sang it after all. Know what that song was? "I'll See You in My Dreams." There was wonderful music then, like composers had gotten together and planned to make people cry forever. The kind of crying I did when I first saw Roy and when I buried you.

I like to think who'll be at my funeral. Maybe the whole Chicago Crime Commission, some members of the best clubs, a few politicians and judges, the real estate division of s & G, and a few other old-timers I helped along the way. Maybe some grateful widows, too. Not everyone loves their husbands like you did me. I'll tell Elizabeth that there should be music at my funeral. Something serious and loud. Then you'll hear me coming, Essie.

Wouldn't it be nice if there were something after this? Like stepping out of the back door into a park instead of an alley when yesterday an alley was there? That's how I keep picturing heaven, like Lincoln Park near the Shakespeare statue on a sunny day in October. It's funny that I think I'd go to heaven. But why in the fuck not? I was a good businessman. I kept my shoes polished. I never cheated poor people, only gonifs who deserved it. I figure America must still own some property somewhere, maybe in the clouds. In American heaven you don't have to have been good, just smart. Henry Kissinger, for example. He can go to American heaven. I'd hate to think who lives in other countries' heavens. But I figure. It must be zoned this way so that Khadafy can get into his place and Castro into his and Kissinger into his and me into mine. Otherwise, it wouldn't be fair, and someone would complain. Now don't get me wrong, Essie. Some people can't go at all, no matter who says what. Forget Hitler even in German heaven and that asshole who tried to hang me out to dry. Sorry, American heaven is closed, they told that fucker when he rang. He had to get his fat ass to hell. But Ess, I want to talk about heaven a little more. If I have the privilege of meeting you there, we'll get Allegretto to drive us to our favorite place out in Humboldt Park near the boathouse like it was then, and we'll lie down on the falling leaves and wail like banshees with joy. I'll sing you that song I thought of in the Pacific, or maybe I'll surprise you with a new one. There's always that possibility.

CHAPTER THREE

"I AM CALLING maybe Poland today," Irena tells Mr. Waters.
"Your mother or your sweetheart?" he asks, flirting
politely—in a European way—as Irena finishes knotting
his tie. She likes this brown tie full of little songbirds with
their beaks open. She holds his camel-hair sports coat up
behind him. Painfully, he fishes for the first sleeve, which is
lined in camel-colored silk. The old dry hand finds the opening and slides in. Then she steers his other arm toward the
waiting sleeve. "There we go," he says, coaxing it in slowly,
with effort. Maybe old people shrink, Irena thinks, so that
their clothes can pose less resistance. The challenge of pants
legs, zippers, buttons, shoestrings and sleeves is certainly dis-
couraging to Mr. Waters. "I am calling maybe Joszef, the man
I know there. To my mother I write only letters. She is atheist
about long distance."

Mr. Water chuckles. Irena appreciates how she can make
him happy. He doesn't know how hard she works to find
words that equal jokes. Often, in her effort to form full sentences before she speaks, it feels as if someone is pinching her
brain. But being entertaining is like keeping a promise to Mr.
Waters not to disappoint him.

"You must miss your Joszef," Mr. Waters groans, as he seats

himself on the edge of his bed, holding his shoe in his hand. "I remember separation, love, all those things. Sometimes they come back to me like music, but they're a part of ancient history, Irena. Gwen and me—" and Mr. Waters mildly curses as the hand with the shoe fumbles to reach the foot.

"I will help you," Irena says softly. She watches him stare downward, imagining how humiliating it must be to be daunted by a black shoe.

"Here's the damn thing," he says, handing it over. "Gwen and me missed each other like hell when I went on the road. Then we fought each other like heck when I got home. And she had a big family. They'd gang up on me, all her bullying sisters, and take her side. That's why living in Paris was so terrific. We were free from every human problem on this earth." Irena kneels on the carpet and guides his foot into the opening. "I'm stiff as a board today."

"I cannot imagine you to be fighting like heck."

"It was simple, Irena. We were selfish people, wanting our own way more than we wanted each other."

"I cannot imagine you to be selfish."

"Let's say we were strong-willed. Most of it was foolish. If I knew then what I know now—but what about you and this Joszef?"

"My Joszef is mathematician, but he is not needing to leave Poland like myself. He has no politics. He lives on the inside, which makes him sometimes very difficult man. I wonder if he remembers to feed himself or my cat after I go." She looks up and smiles from where she's been stooping. Now she stands up and offers her arm for support.

"Not easy to love, huh?"

"Not really, I am afraid, but brilliant difficult man," Irena blushes.

"Would you like a cat?" Mr. Waters asks suddenly. "We could afford a cat for Irena."

"I am not certain, Mr. Waters, if American cat can replace—I do not know what."

"I know, Irena." Now that he's fully dressed, Irena observes his one vain ceremony. Daily in the mirror, smiling at both profiles, which defines his jawline and pulls his face into youthful tautness, Mr. Waters uses a new, streamlined shaver that he bought on their last shopping spree. Its optimistic hum makes this moment a soothing refrain after dressing.

"It is very nice of you to ask," Irena says when he has finished. "But I do not know what I need here, Mr. Waters. Perhaps later I can have cat. Unless, of course, you are wanting cat now."

"I never had a pet in my life. Gwen had a little dog for awhile. One of her many sisters left it with us, but the thing was always underfoot. Sometimes it nipped me too.

"Which reminds me of a funny sight, Irena. Once I saw a beautiful tall woman, probably a model, chasing her wig down the street. I tried to help, but when I caught the thing for her, she snarled, just like that little dog. I had insulted her by noticing. Wouldn't you have noticed a nearly bald, beautiful giantess chasing some hair down the street?"

"It is funny what you are always telling me. Maybe because you are musician, your stories are like jazz, which happens suddenly, I think, with surprise. This is also how I solve new mathematical problems. At one moment I do not see next step. Then suddenly next step is clear and beautiful. This is why I hesitate with my phone call. I am not certain that it is next step."

"Would you like to see this Joszef again?"

"Well, I think yes, but he is there, and I am here." Feeling overwhelmed by mixed emotions, Irena turns her face from Mr. Waters and polishes away a grease spot on the mirror with her sweater sleeve. Now she can hear him sighing and knows that when she looks back, the scene will have changed. Mr. Waters will look tired and sad, as if knowing Irena has taken too much from him. Old men inflate and deflate so easily, she thinks, following him to the kitchen where she has already laid out his fat-free sweet roll and juice and pills and numerous newspapers.

Maybe she shouldn't mention Joszef. Maybe it frightens him to hear about Irena's former life. She turns on the coffee-maker, grinds the almond-flavored decaffeinated beans, and jumps when the phone rings.

Mr. Waters listens too. A ringing phone is an unusual event for them both. "Yes," she says, and "maybe," and "I ask."

"Mr. Waters," she says, "this is Elizabeth O'Conner, friend of Jack Kaufman. She requests that I have lunch today."

"Please, Irena, feel free to go."

"Yes, then," Irena says. "Twelve-thirty so I can give Mr. Waters lunch first."

Now that she's off the phone, her heart clenches. What will she tell this woman during a long American lunch? Maybe she'll tell Elizabeth O'Conner about her Joszef, how his nails are bitten down to the quick with concentration. How he can go without a coat in deepest winter because he is insensitive to cold, and heat, too, and sometimes love, so pure is his intellect. But that is unattractive. How she had baked him bread the day before she left, and how they had eaten it silently with her mother's best plum preserves, then made giddy, nervous jokes about their sadness. After all, she had chosen to leave. She had left it behind. Because she needed to, she and Joszef understood, because she couldn't work in a place that hated her because she had once held views. Because so many of the new reformers were just old communists in better-fitting suits. Because they had broken her father's will and made her mother old and bereft. All of this would be too depressing for the American woman with the small dark eyes and large, capable shoulders.

But does Elizabeth O'Conner maybe understand the feeling Irena has been having lately that one's history is like Hannibal's trip over the Alps: extremely awkward, slightly absurd, requiring elephants, all too much of a bother? Maybe the clean American landscape exists to advise people to forget history. You are in a land without history, the lake stammers, and the gleaming buildings rising from the flat, unattractive land. Forget about the past. It isn't useful here. Yes, she will give Joszef up some day, like chocolate at Lent.

She sees Mr. Waters opening his wallet. He is about to hand money to her. "No, please. I have money in my room, and you are not my sugar daddy."

*   *   *

Does Irena know that Jack Kaufman once killed a man? Elizabeth O'Conner asks matter-of-factly as they navigate through heavy traffic toward Water Tower Place. That he bought houses for three women? That their husbands knew perfectly well why they were given the houses? That one day, while at Water Tower Place, a woman had plunged to her death just forty feet from where Elizabeth O'Conner stood? That killer bees from Africa are approaching Chicago in herds, or did she say hordes? That a new, deadly form of tuberculosis has appeared among the homeless—like that man right over there with all those newspapers—she points. Now, don't touch his hand if you give him money. That Irena would look better in lighter, less oppressing colors? That Irena should wear more makeup to look less pale?

Irena has heard a word called "banter." "I am learning to make banter," she has written Joszef. Now, between banter about the weather and the sights on Michigan Avenue, the new F.A.O. Schwarz with its giant animated bear and the old Water Tower, which withstood the famous Chicago fire, Elizabeth O'Conner takes Irena's elbow in its oppressive brown sleeve and speaks more softly but with concentrated enthusiasm into her pale face. That Jack Kaufman knew Jack Ruby and has a theory about Kennedy's assassination—who doesn't these days? That he once got a judge indicted over an insult at lunch. What she says amazes and sickens Irena, who is prepared for slow sentences about their employers' sluggish intestines and minor foibles, cliches about the sadness of good men growing old in a world where age is not valued. How can she keep up with this almanac of strangeness, somewhat like the tabloids that perplex her at the grocery with their stories of babies from Mars and Elvis sightings at the Vatican?

See the carriages, Elizabeth O'Conner asks, pointing to a group of horses arrayed in flowers and top hats, manes curled, outside the Chicago tourist center. Among them, a man in a baseball hat gathers steaming piles of excrement onto a large, dull shovel. Irena watches him, wondering what country he recently arrived from, perhaps Mexico. All of the carriage drivers are young and white. Some wear costumes to match their horses' decorations, Irena notices.

Well, one night Jack Kaufman dragged himself out of bed, and showered, shaved, put on a baggy suit ("You know he has cancer"), and took Elizabeth O'Conner on a carriage ride. He was very proper for once and only patted her knee a few times. He also paid the driver twice so they could see all of downtown, not just the Magnificent Mile. It was rather pitiful and charming, how he had caressed her knee with his speckled hand and shown her, everywhere, to the left and right, and in front of her eyes, the real estate that he owned. From their high-rise window, his sites littered the streets like toys. The extent of Jack's kingdom had taken on new eminence.

Did her old man ever make a pass at her, Elizabeth O'Conner asks, as they enter the Four Seasons Hotel and ride the huge pink elevator, big enough for a queen-sized bed, to the marble-decorated restaurant. No, she will not answer in front of the young elevator attendant, who, in his military uniform and foolish feathered hat, is pretending not to listen.

"What shall we eat? Oh, here is the wine list," Elizabeth O'Conner says brightly, holding a padded book thick as a bible.

Irena takes in the oversized floral arrangements, the plush carpeting with the seashell pattern, the rich walls of swirling marble and glass. She eyes the dessert cart, on which a swan of chocolate and a kiwi and strawberry pyramid stuffed with white cream, sit on silver doilies. She has never dined at such a restaurant. Answering Elizabeth O'Conner's question about what to order might take her the rest of the afternoon, the menu is so full of descriptions in difficult English smattered with French. "What do you recommend?" dizzy Irena finally asks.

"I'm having the wild greens salad with the raspberry vinaigrette and the duck breast. Would you like red or white wine?"

"I will have same as you," Irena says, and looks down at her unadorned hands and plain brown, oppressive dress, which she has decorated with an Italian scarf painted with a trellis of lilies. "This is very beautiful room," she says, but the waiter has arrived and is talking to Elizabeth O'Conner at length about wines.

"There," Elizabeth smiles. "Now we can relax. Sometimes I just have to get away from Jack. He goes on and on. It's different each time, but it's all the same."

"My Mr. Waters is very quiet man."

"Jack tells me he was a musician."

"He was jazz pianist. I take him to radio show, where Miss McPartland plays very old music that he recorded. He was excellent."

"What did he tell you about Jack?"

"That he is prominent citizen of Chicago."

Elizabeth O'Conner looks amused. "And what about you?" Elizabeth asks.

"I am new here. Since April. I am single woman with new home."

"Did you, I mean, were you—"

The waiter has delivered the wine. Elizabeth O'Conner waves off the opening ceremony with her hand. "I'm sure it'll be fine," she says and turns again to Irena. "I mean, were you attached to someone in Poland?"

"I have long and difficult relationship with fellow mathematician named Joszef, but we do not marry after all these years."

"Is that why you came here?"

"So many reasons," Irena says, and feels she can't say more without losing the composure for the words she needs. She swirls her wine and rearranges the many pieces of heavy silver on the three layers of tablecloth, white, salmon, and dark green. Touching her neck, which feels hot, she finally says, "I am at loss for words."

The salad of wild greens has arrived, an array of what appears to be different hues of weeds. The waiter produces a giant pepper mill and asks if he might offer Irena pepper.

"Please," Irena says, and watches him twist the bottom grinder in endless circles.

"Thank you," Elizabeth finally adds, which makes him stop.

After he has gone, Elizabeth points to Irena's salad with its small mound of ground pepper. "You have to tell him to stop," she admonishes, removing the excess pepper to her bread and butter dish with one of her many heavy silver spoons.

"This is new for me. Mr. Waters take me once to steak house with beautiful walls of wood and many famous sportsmen's photos. I do not know sports, however, and they did not offer pepper there."

"So you're happy here?" Elizabeth O'Conner asks, seeming bored, taking delicate bites of her salad and drinking her wine rather quickly.

"I am very happy in this beautiful restaurant, but in America I am not certain. And are you happy in Chicago?"

"Happy as possible, I'd guess." She finishes her second helping of wine, refills Irena's nearly full glass, and pours her third.

"Jack's right about one thing, Irena."

"What is that?" Irena asks, serious and sober.

"He says that eating, drinking, and fucking are about all there is." And she raises her glass to toast Irena.

The beautifully sliced small breast of duck arrives, pink slivers of meat with a darker crust, stippled with black olives and capers. A curling tower of food that Irena doesn't recognize has been erected in the center of her gilt-edged plate.

Irena hopes that no one has heard Elizabeth say this last simple truth, so crude that it embarrasses her to hear it spoken in this grand room with its seashell lamps listening like ears.

It is true for barnyard animals, she knows, for pigs and goats and for cows, but is it true for people? And even if it is so, even if natural desires determine most everything—banishing her beautiful interest in numbers to a fool's purgatory—one's conversation should suit the context. She directs them back to the mundane subject of herself.

"I also believe that one's meaning is important."

"I'm not sure I understand."

"Where one finds meaning, I believe," she says softly. Elizabeth O'Conner is eating very quickly. Irena takes several larger bites, samples the tower of what now appears to be cabbage, yes, her taste confirms, is cabbage, and waits for a reply.

"So what is it like in Poland?"

"What would you like to know?"

"Oh, I don't know. How people live."

"Women my age are very busy. Most work very hard. Children are natural part of life, of course, like other things you mention before. But in Poland people are careful to have small family now. Things are so few, so my friends who are married have one child."

"Like in China."

"Not really," Irena corrects. How can Elizabeth O'Conner compare her friend's admirable self-discipline with China's voucher system? "In China, the government decides how many children and gives license. And many people refuse to keep girls."

"Why?"

"Girls are not needed maybe."

"So what do they do with them?" Elizabeth asks nonchalantly.

"I have read that many girls are killed by parents or maybe sold to families with no children for very small sum."

Irena stares at Elizabeth O'Conner's small, averted eyes. She has stopped eating and is holding her fork in the air. When her silence continues, Irena feels pressed to talk.

"I have read that sometimes babies are drowned or with a

pillow—" and she motions with a napkin on her face for want of the word.

"Smothered," Elizabeth says so quietly that Irena must lean forward. She looks at Elizabeth O'Conner's blank expression, her skin, which seems suddenly paler, the pinkness of the skin around her eyes.

"But maybe this is poor topic for beautiful lunch," Irena adds, smiling nervously.

She sees that Elizabeth O'Conner has stopped listening and is motioning to the waiter.

After a long while, she catches his eye, and suddenly, when Irena has pictured her own silver pot of tea with its private steam and extremely wicked dessert from the lovely tray, Elizabeth O'Conner announces that she is paying their bill. Don't even try to argue. This is an order, she has stated in a commanding but slightly ironic voice. Irena is to leave a tip, ten dollars, yes, that would be right, on the table.

"Okay," Irena says hesitantly, holding the bill in her hand. Elizabeth takes it from her and puts it under a water glass, which magnifies its features. Irena worries that someone will snatch it before her waiter is able to put it in his pocket. Could that happen in such a tasteful room? But what is worse is that her first sinful dessert will have to wait. Irena stares longingly at the chocolate swan, whose breast looks like it's made of marzipan.

CHAPTER FOUR

"ONLY IRENA leaves Poland for political reasons after the communists have resigned," Joszef is telling himself. "Only Irena leaves me like this," he says, kicking a bedroom slipper aside, one of the pair she gave him last Christmas. It lands near a pile of old journals. Sentences about Irena have been his lament since her departure in March. "Only Irena leaves me these problems, this life, this damned cat."

How does the cat sense that Joszef is trying to capture him? "Kitty, Kitty," he croons, stooping to look under the bed, trying to lure Chopin out. "Come here, you fucking cat," he says in a seductive whisper. When he catches Chopin, he will place him in a pillowcase for the ride to Irena's mother's house near Lazienki Park. She has agreed, hesitantly, to take the cat, which Joszef constantly forgets to feed, which shits and pisses on his two good bath towels, which startles him at night with its iridescent eyes steady as paperweights. If it were larger, it would eat him, he has begun to imagine, as the cat wakes him with sudden movements and stares grudgingly at Joszef in the morning until he is fed. Sometimes, he is more stealthy. Chopin creeps onto sleepy Joszef's chest and massages him with its paws. "What can you be thinking? My teats are dry! I am not your mother!" he shouts intermittently, but do cats understand? Their brains, the size of walnuts, or acorns perhaps, comprehend very little.

Maybe Irena's mother will let him roam as cats should, hunting for birds, filling his mouth with blue and brown feathers and entrails and rodent ears, taking care of himself. Try to tame a cat! But on this busy residential street with its cafes and pastry stores, a cat can hardly survive. What was Irena thinking to bring a cat here? What would it eat, a Napoleon? Maybe he should send the animal to his brother in the country, but then he would have to phone his brother, the born-again peasant, to whom he rarely speaks, and "sell" him on the idea of this bothersome pet. No, he would not wish this cat even on his brother.

It seems that Irena should have to keep this nuisance by some Divine Law, but cats don't emigrate. It seems that she, who found Chopin as an infant crying in a rainy park, should have had to stuff him in her suitcase. Be that as it may, Irena's mother, Pani Profesora Bozinska, bearing proper responsibility for her reckless daughter, has agreed to inherit this dreadful, shedding, pissing, shitting legacy.

To lure the cat from under the bed, Joszef has placed some slivers of chicken directly onto the floor. This is how he feeds the cat whenever he remembers. Improvised islands of food spring up momentarily, but Chopin is ravenous. Joszef could be a food cartographer, designing vast maps twenty-four hours a day. And when he buys himself milk, which he does now and then for his putrid coffee, he leaves some for Chopin. But this ungrateful cat is not fond of milk. He probably misses the chicken livers that Irena lovingly cooked for him, in butter when it was available. Saucers of yellowing, solid milk decorate the maroon birds-of-paradise and graying flowers of the Oriental rug that Irena has left behind.

Staring at the cat, who, seated on the bed now, looks past him with foolish disinterest, Joszef's anger grows at Irena. She has left too much for him to tidy up. Like a child with a messy room, Irena has gone out in the world to play and left him with the debris. And who's to find the time for her cat and her pot of rotting ivy and her letters, this constant flow of sad and hopeful letters and postcards, which, he supposes, he's to answer cheerfully. How can he appreciate Irena's postcard of the tall, ugly, rusting Picasso statue resembling an Afghan hound when each day has been a slow, hellish dream since Lot Flight 422 took off and deposited Irena in Italy, then Chicago with an old black man? He has so much to do with her gone—shopping, laundry, haphazard cleaning. How to whiten his aging underwear or find the right coffee, the one with hazelnuts, that she made every morning they were together? How to complete the patternless crossword puzzle on Sunday? He can barely keep up with his academic journals and students and scholarly work. This cat nearly pushes him over the brink. No one ever suggested to him that losing a girlfriend is so much like losing the part of your mind which you can usually forget exists, the part that keeps phone numbers and bus routes in order, and makes shopping lists and holds infinitesimal instructions for useless, annoying objects he now must master. What good is a clock radio that doesn't wake him? He'd might as well throw it out the window.

He has now captured the mewling, foul cat and pushed it into the pillowcase. It's dug its nails into him twice and snagged yet another good sweater. He can feel its bones and muscles and claws working inside the bag to escape. Do cats have natural fears of pillowcases? Of drowning? He remembers hearing that baby apes are afraid of snakes from birth. Chopin is now pushing his hard little doorknob head toward the top of the bag. He is about to spill over like lava. Joszef tightens his grip and fights off the notion to peer inside and give the cat a spiteful, victorious look. "You are going to live with Irena's mother," he tells the straining, muscular lump. "With Grandma, who will feed you. . . . Maybe," he laughs. "You deserve this," he says, releasing his bottom hand that supports the bag and swinging it slightly recklessly by the top. And with his free hand reaching under the bed, where he has found many pieces of memorabilia since Irena departed, he locates yet another souvenir, a loose velvet hair ribbon, and ties the bag shut.

"Yes, you will go to Irena's mother," he tells the cat as he descends the stairs. Noticing the rather long line at the taxi stand, after all it is Saturday and many tourists have come to see the boring Curie museum nearby, he obtains his bus ticket at the Ruch newsstand and boards the bus for his ride to Irena's mother's house. Leaning his head against the bus window, he places the bag near his feet and closes his eyes. Since it is a rather long ride, he is not afraid to nap on the sweltering bus. Why is it so warm this long October with Irena gone? Why does he notice flowers he's never seen before, stands everywhere, and window boxes full of unnamed vines blooming profusely in October? Love is like a chronic infection, flowers the rash, he thinks, and begins to close his eyes. He feels with his foot that Chopin's activity in the bag has more or less subsided. There will be no antic scenes involving a bag moving by its own powers down the crowded aisle. The other bus passengers, laden with sacks and bottles and newpapers, had seemed oblivious to him when he boarded. Yes, he will sleep the duration of the trip and not think of Irena. Then he'll walk the distance to Irena's mother's little house, embrace the old woman—thank God Irena looks like her father—and hand over the dubious prize.

"Mister, Mister," a man is suddenly saying. Opening his eyes, Joszef sees that he's the only passenger remaining on the bus. Reaching for the bag, he sees nothing but his feet and the floor. He frantically looks under the seat, in front of him, behind him. How can it be that the bag with Chopin has disappeared? How could something invisible be stolen? How could it? What will he tell Irena's mother? How will he tell Irena? Maybe she was right to leave this country, where a man can't sleep without some thief, probably a foreigner, a Russian or German, to be sure, absconding with his property. How can people behave this way in a civilized modern country, he won-

ders, wiping his eyes again as if to confirm the theft, and curs-
ing under his breath.

"Sir, have you seen a bag?" he asks the plainclothes ticket
inspector standing in the aisle. Can the man hear his heart
pounding? Does the man know the foolish idiot Joszef has
become, the bumbling idiot, reduced by Irena to being the
owner of a stolen cat? Looking puzzled and cross, the man
furls his sweaty brow and shakes his head in the negative, then
turns his formidable back on Joszef.

CHAPTER FIVE

ELIZABETH O'CONNER has hooked the blue container of liquid to a special rod from which it dangles while the mixture enters Jack's shunted vein. He feels a slight, tingly burning as the liquid rinses him. Every Wednesday and Saturday is the same routine. Jack imagines the chemicals exterminating the bad cells, chasing them down like spies, but he always humanizes this image. The bad cells are often naked and pitiful, human in form. Sometimes when he feels especially sorry for himself, he pictures the bad cells as his son. Multiples of Roy are hunted by these powerful chemical agents with silencers on their guns. The image makes him feel guilty and foolish. He is an old man in a dark room playing vengeful, irrelevant games. But the chemicals don't make him that sick anymore. Besides, how can he tell which sick he is feeling? Is it the cause or the cure nauseating him? He can't tell anymore, and he's frankly stopped caring. It really doesn't matter, does it, when you're his age and Roy doesn't call?

"Who was it, Shakespeare, who talked about the Seven Ages of Man?" Jack asks Elizabeth O'Conner, who is hovering above him like a giantess.

"I don't know," Elizabeth says. "Probably Shakespeare. He said about everything."

"Well, I'd like to argue with this Mr. Shakespeare," Jack Kaufman tells Elizabeth, who has covered his dangling old man's legs with the stadium blanket he used to take to the Bears games, where he had a box at the forty-nine yard line. He never even owned a robe until he got sick. Now he lives in one. "I'd like to tell this Mr. Shakespeare to forget birth and death. What can you remember of either, for God's sake? Do you remember being born, Elizabeth?"

"Can't say that I do," she says, looking up from an old issue of *Vanity Fair* that she's retrieved from the floor. A naked, pregnant Demi Moore, peering from the cover, captures Jack's eye for a moment.

Jack seizes her hand. "Well, the same will be true of dying. So I say dismiss them as evidence. Now we have five if I'm counting correctly. But I want to further dispute this point with Shakespeare. Bill, right?"

"Yes," says Elizabeth, lips slightly parted, acquiescing to Jack's hold on her, which brings her face almost into kissing range. She's a beautiful girl with shiny hair, Jack Kaufman thinks, if only, once or twice a week, she would smile.

"Bill, I beg to differ," he says patting her smooth hand with his mottled shiny one. "I submit to the court that there are three ages of man. First you have this little wee wee that does nothing. Then it grows and you're a man. Then you have this little wee wee again that does nothing." He laughs heartily and releases her.

He observes Elizabeth O'Conner stoically watching his bag of chemicals sway with his movement. She has forgotten to laugh again, but if he laughs any harder for the both of them, the whole gizmo will tumble. Maybe men with cancer shouldn't laugh.

"Really, though, I was going to say something else before that thought occurred. These are the three ages of man. First, you have to do everything for yourself. You have to figure out how to make the money and stop the people who are trying to stop you from making it. That's Stage One. Then you do some things for yourself. You still make the money, but you're like a director. You have a whole play full of characters. There's one guy like that gravedigger in Hamlet who makes small talk and maybe buries a few things you don't need. There are people to drive you, people to carry your things, people to massage your back. People to call the right people. The right people. You just keep making the money, raking it in, and a cast of characters works for you. Need your shoes shined? No problem. Want a few cigars from Cuba? I have a man. Need a loan to make more money? Here's a million dollars. Shall I carry it to the car for you, Sir, or do you want it sent? Need a little love? I have a number right here. And on and on. That's Stage Two."

"Do you want to get back in bed?" Elizabeth is asking.

"Why should I do that?"

"I think you're more comfortable—"

"I'm fine here. Thank you, Elizabeth," he says softly. She looks so sad, and she's all he's got. This tall, often humorless woman with the shiny hair and the angular body that she used to give in silence before he got so sick, like a pioneer woman who'd been captured by Indians.

"So here I am, Elizabeth, Stage Three. Not quite dead yet, which, remember, doesn't count, but not quite alive either. Doing nothing for myself. You feed me, clothe me for what it's worth, give me shelter. I sit on this pile of money like an old rooster—cock-a-doodle-doo—and that is that. Oh, people visit but since I was never too big to begin with, it just makes me sad when they see me. Stage Three, I'd say, stinks. And I thought Stage One, with so much to do, was a headache!"

"We could go out more, Jack, like we used to."

"What?" he asks cautiously, almost incredulously. "You want to schlep around with an old man and his tubes?"

"You don't need tubes if we just go to a movie or something. We just need a cab," she smiles.

"Nuts," Jack Kaufman says. "If you want to go places, we'll

hire a driver. None of these cabbies know English. You say you want to go to the movies and you end up at Niagara Falls. I'll call Julius again. Or didn't you like him? Did he say something to you 'cause if he did . . ."

"Julius was fine, Jack. I didn't want to make it complicated."

"Where would you like to go?"

"Oh, I don't know. Maybe for a ride. Maybe to a movie. Whatever. It just gets so, I don't know . . ."

"Confining?"

"You could use the change, I think. You watch TV all day or sleep."

"Sometimes you read to me. I like that."

"I do too, but there's no reason—"

"You're right. I should enjoy before Stage Four, which won't count because I won't remember. Which makes me think, if I may be a little nosey, Elizabeth, what do you believe about the Hereafter?"

"Oh," she says quietly. That's what he likes about her, her seriousness. Nothing is ironic with Elizabeth. Maybe Jews invented irony in some little unlit shack near a potato field in the Old World. Maybe they had to. But his girl is sober as a judge. Even her little eeks of pleasure used to come out in official whispers. Who knows how reckless she acts in the rest of the world—she could be a flame-thrower for failing restaurants for all he cares—but she means business when she talks to him. "Well," she pauses again. "I'd like to think there's a place where you go if you're forgiven."

"Forgiven for what?"

"Well, for whatever."

"Why does a pretty young girl like you need to think about being forgiven? What could you have done?"

"I mean people in general. Not necessarily myself. I was taught that we're all guilty."

"At Catholic school?"

"Where else? But really, Jack, don't Jewish people worry about sin?"

"Sure they do. It's a sin to put ketchup on corned beef. It's a sin to put ice in a chocolate phosphate. Those kinds of sins."

Elizabeth O'Conner's laugh is small and throaty, but then she turns away and busies herself with his supplies for what seems like forever.

"Did I say something wrong?" Jack finally asks as she fumbles among his medicines and tubes and he hears a low, small sound like maybe she's crying or whispering to herself.

Turning back toward him, she manages a smile. "No, you're fine, Jack. You're very inspiring. It's just that I get a little depressed at times."

"I know. The . . ."

"No, not because of you. Because of me. It's just how I am."

"Do you want to talk?" Jack asks and thinks what Essie would say to make this pretty girl feel better, whatever it is that is hurting her. Essie's eyes could forgive Jack and the rest of the world and never get used up. They could have sent Essie anywhere to forgive, like Mother Teresa, only Jewish. "Do you need maybe a cup of tea?"

"That'll be nice. I'll fix us some. How about chamomile?"

"Lipton is fine with me but suit yourself. Whatever you want as long as you're with me, you take."

"Okay, I'll be back," Elizabeth says.

"Wait. My treatment is over. I'm full of deadly chemicals. So let me go with you to my own kitchen for once."

"Okay," she says, and begins to unhook the tubes and cap the i.v. shunt. "I'll get your slippers and your walker."

"Screw that," Jack says. "Just give me your arms. We'll pull me up and be on our way."

Grunting, he strains to get to his feet. What does he weigh now, ninety pounds soaking wet? Holding her elbow tightly, he pads toward the kitchen. "I used to play tennis," he tells her, ashamed of his slowness. "You should have seen my backhand. It had oomph."

"I know," she says, smiling kindly at him, almost beaming for once. For a man in Stage Three, full of cancer, with no relation in the world who cares, he feels pretty good. Elizabeth O'Conner believes him, likes him, has accepted his body in hers when he was able. And maybe, just a little, he loves her.

* * *

Maybe once in a movie Irena has seen such a car. It is the size of her former apartment but sleek and long, the color of an endless swath of pearly cloth. It has two antennae, this car, and a gold hood ornament, and a black cloth roof that shines like satin and what else? Certainly a bar and a color television and perhaps a swimming pool. Perhaps a runway for landing small airplanes and a department store with a counter displaying precious gems. The car also has tinted glass, so, as she stares into the black window in which she can see herself, pale, plainly dressed in her beige trenchcoat and flowered Italian scarf and laden with a sack of groceries, it is very possible that someone is staring back at her. Perhaps a bored driver is wondering why this woman is looking at him. Or, a young couple, locked in an embrace, observes this intrusive, drab, mousey servant of someone's staring quite boldly. She thinks of Madam Adamowoiska, the manager of her building in Warsaw, how she stiffly nodded, knowing and judgmental, whenever she met Irena and Joszef on the stairs. Sometimes she imagined Madam A. in the bedroom below theirs, straining to hear them make love. Now Irena is gaping with spinstress-like abandon. Maybe vision was genetically enhanced in humans to promote this fine-tuned envy. Maybe the communist world has collapsed due to deprivation of this one sense alone, which needs constant feeding. Has she lost her manners, her European reticence, her refined veneer, she wonders, as her eyes continue to fix on the car.

And she had thought herself better than so many people she meets in this amazing country of mile-long limousines, where education means nothing and being cultured even less. This car is culture, she thinks, this monument to envy, this yacht on wheels. *Move your eyes,* she tells herself. *Don't gape like a peasant,* she is saying softly when she sees Elizabeth O'Conner step out of the limousine, her old man following slowly and painfully.

"Irena!" Elizabeth says warmly. "I want you to meet Mr. Kaufman. Mr. Kaufman, Irena. Irena, Mr. Kaufman."

A tiny withered man in a shiny, expensive suit two sizes too large for him has taken Irena's hand and brushed it with his lips. Thankfully, he is saying nothing about her bad manners.

"Call me Jack," he smiles crookedly, as he clings with his other arm so tightly to Elizabeth O'Conner that she has been pulled uncomfortably close to Irena. It is like her hand has been kissed by them both. Now erect again, Elizabeth O'Conner towers above this small, shrunken, boy-sized man, wobbly on his legs, but finely dressed, and very gallant. So the car, which takes up the entire curb in front of their building on Elm, is his.

"And this is Julius," Jack Kaufman says, pointing out the equally elderly driver, who has stepped out of the car to assist them.

Julius, too, is splendidly dressed. He is wearing a uniform of sorts, though Irena thinks it hardly suits a chauffeur. It reminds her more of the uniform worn by the captain on the TV show *Love Boat,* which she sometimes watches while writing her letters to Joszef late at night. Sometimes she jokes in her letters that they need to take such a romantic cruise and drink fruit-garnished drinks dispensed by a waiter as wise as a judge.

"Where have you been?" Irena asks politely.

"Oh, just to a movie and for dessert."

"And please, what did you see?" Irena sees that the group is glowing with pleasure. After all, they have done something out of the ordinary and deserve to be asked. She recognizes the bittersweet feeling, that sharing the story of an evening's adventure lengthens and glorifies the event, instant nostalgia accomplished. Many times she would call her mother to redeem her modest experience from oblivion in just such a manner.

"Some depressing tale," Jack Kaufman sighs. "Clint Eastwood has turned philosopher on me."

"We saw a wonderful movie, Irena. I'll have to tell you about it when Jack's not around," she teases.

Jack winks in appreciation at Elizabeth's taunting. "She's some kidder," he tells Irena, who can see his endurance flagging. Now Jack Kaufman motions with his hand for them to move inside the building. Before Irena can follow, Julius has taken her small bag of groceries from her.

They seat themselves in the beautiful, high-backed, sea green chairs that Irena has never seen occupied. She is surprised the building hasn't roped them off, like the museum-display furniture they've always appeared to be. Julius removes his captain's hat and places it on the low black marble table.

"Elizabeth tells me that you live with a musician."

"I am working for Mr. Harrison Waters, a very fine man."

"I've heard him play. He was terrific. He could make the piano sing. Couldn't he, Julius?"

"He was among the best. Right up there with Art Hodes, only he played sweeter. Like a black angel."

"Well, maybe we could all get together some time. That stretch has lots of room, you know. Would you ask your Mr. Waters if dinner on—let's see, this is Sunday, how about Tuesday before they poison me next—would be fine? How would that be, Elizabeth?"

She nods her approval.

"I will ask him tonight," Irena says. "I am sure he would love to ride in your beautiful car and to meet all of you."

"*Whose* beautiful car?" Jack Kaufman asks Julius with feigned surprise. Irena thinks of a movie she watched the other night about a vaudeville routine with a similar pattern of deliberate prodding.

"*My* beautiful car. A present from Mr. Kaufman. I put six grandchildren through college driving that vehicle."

"So Tuesday night at, shall we say, six? Early enough for us old men, right, Julius?"

"That would be fine."

"In the lobby then."

"Thank you, Mr. Kaufman," Irena says as she rises to leave. "I must be getting back now." She reclaims her bags and offers her farewells. Tonight she will write Joszef about Jack Kaufman.

This car alone, she thinks in the elevator, is too much to describe in one letter. Where does one begin? Perhaps with its captain, Julius, who had a diamond stud in one ear and a glossy scar shaped like a scythe under his chin. Or Mr. Jack Kaufman, a dying man, who took her hand, and dared to kiss it. Or Elizabeth O'Conner, who is sporting new sapphires in her ears. But first, certainly, she'll describe the amazing car with its long pearly side, where door handles and yes, even doors, are invisible, where she will ride to dinner with a gangster and his private captain.

CHAPTER SIX

IT IS BEAUTIFUL by the bland lake. It is like closing your eyes, and seeing nothing, being nowhere. Elizabeth O'Conner can look out past the water filtration plant, where water and sky no longer separate, and see a seamless, colorless world. She can observe her eye viewing Lake Michigan, tiny floaters in her vision, like the delicate signatures on Japanese brush paintings, marring the perfectly gray, unevocative water. She can be calm here at Olive Park watching the repetitive waves, which the world ignores in autumn. There are no lovers walking on the beach or children playing in the sand or reporters with their mini-cams to cover the ongoing scandal. Lone joggers sometimes stream past, but they're irrelevant as the time of day.

Behind her is her favorite building, somber Lake Point Tower, curved black glass shooting up into the sky like a monument to grief. Anyone who thinks the Viet Nam war memorial impressive should come and observe this solemnity. Though the weather is bracing and her legs, even in jeans and a long coat, feel bare—why didn't she bring Jack's blanket?—she can regain her balance here.

Day to day with Jack is another story. He must think her mad, the way she turns away from him, shattering like brittle glass, at the least little thing. Would it matter, she wonders, if suddenly, in the middle of fixing him dinner or unwrapping a syringe, she couldn't stop crying? What would he do with her then? Would he keep her around?

Of course, she reassures herself, since they'd been lovers, exchanging their separate identities for moments of a shared belief in something smaller than either one of them—for a gasp of pleasure, the mechanical release, the ohs and aahs of the darkened room, the soothing connection of flesh, hair, nipples, fingertips. In those times when Jack was newly ill and so afraid to die, he'd wrap himself around her like a wrestler and Elizabeth would reciprocate fully, muscles tightening everywhere, grappling until they were soaked in sweat, dizzy from the effort. No kisses were exchanged—Elizabeth's rules did not allow kisses—but Jack had a way of rubbing his face into the curve of her neck that had assigned to the moment its needed tenderness. What of the rules she'd made against kissing of any kind anywhere? She wanted him to understand that this was part of her work. He shouldn't have the wrong idea, though she had liked it more than some of her other duties. She was kind, she involved herself, she earned her keep. But no, she didn't love Jack, wouldn't love him—or Jack her. But her affection did grow for him. Often on Sunday nights, after *Sixty Minutes* and *Murder, She Wrote*, he would summon her, and quietly, reverently, she'd join him for the nearly silent ritual. Did they ever speak? Only now and then. Only in reference to the act. "Like this?" Jack would ask, as he traced a path to her nipple. "Yes," she'd sigh as he followed the curve of her back to her buttocks, then under, then in with his fingers. "Yes" was all she said. And "yes," he'd groan, as he came, and sometimes said her name. Then they'd lie quietly together, and the talking would start. He'd whisper stories to her until they fell asleep. Now that he was too ill for this part of the routine, she'd have to say she missed its comfort, that the body gets lonely remembering.

But under the weight of her daily concerns, thoughts of her body disappeared. It was a crumb under her cargo, which she'll have to unload soon. She'll have to tell someone. But she knows that she's kidding herself when she imagines confessing to Jack, not even when he gave her an opportunity as he did the other day. It was really so touching how he offered her tea, but what can Jack understand, the sentimental old man? His eyes well over whenever he sees a parade on TV or photos of immigrants at Ellis Island in airline commercials. He'd probably weep at a discount store ribbon-cutting or when some corrupt candidate gives his stumbling concession speech. He can't talk of Essie or Roy without a catch in his throat. Why should he cry for a son who hates him? Once he told her he felt sorry for Hitler. Why? Because someone has to, he said. His conscience is so guilty that he can forgive anyone—blanket amnesty—to save himself and keep his memory of Essie pure: good Essie, who never knew about his endless swindles and deals and lies and affairs.

Elizabeth hears several cars glide past—they never stop this time of year—and looks out toward the filtration plant, where, despite human corruption, Chicago's water is chemically purified. Some day a cure will be found for everything, she thinks, even guilt, and she will drink it, and Jack will, and millions of others: Whole guilty nations will line up. A fountain of youth isn't needed but some magic water, bottled instant forgiveness.

It excites her to think that maybe she will tell someone soon. She watches a locust tree shake off a few small orange leaves and thinks about fall when she was little, how she knew things before they happened. She was walking to school— God, how she hated that building and the people in it—and suddenly she wished that her teacher would be gone. It was innocent enough that she wanted Mrs. Colon to disappear. She made Elizabeth so nervous with her timed tests in math. It made her stomach hurt.

But when she got to school that day, it was as if she had hidden powers. Instead of Mrs. Colon, a pretty woman was smiling at her. Mrs. Colon had broken her elbow, the woman announced. She had fallen down the stairs at home after trip-ping over her dog. "Could you run an errand?" she was asking Elizabeth, who was never good enough for special privileges. Not in her life would Mrs. Colon have chosen her. She thought Elizabeth didn't listen, but the truth was that she heard every word. She just didn't care.

Now there are things she could tell Jack, whom she trusts, because he's so guilty, but it doesn't seem right to tell a man certain things. How could he understand what it's like to be a woman and have a baby kicking inside you, and its foot pro-truding through the skin of your belly? How, when it pushes out, you feel like your whole body will tear open, and it would still be beautiful. Would Jack understand that, sticking your hand between your legs, you can touch your own blood?

No, she'll have to wait and tell someone else. Maybe that nervous little Polish woman, the one with the terrible eye-brows, whom she met in the laundry the room. The one so ill at ease at lunch. The one afraid to speak. Maybe she'll hear the full story.

"You are needing to tell me something?" the girl will ask, eyes pooled in uncertainty.

"There is something that I need someone to know."

"Yes?"

"I need to tell someone so I don't feel guilty all the time. So I don't have to keep taking long walks and pills to fall asleep and turning away from Jack."

"Perhaps you should go to church."

"I don't want to talk to a priest," Elizabeth will tell her sud-denly pious friend.

"I had to leave Albany."

"Like me, perhaps, leaving Poland, where I could not live."

"No, different."

"Everybody is different but maybe also the same," Irena will commiserate.

And then she will speak the words that will make Irena understand. Now, in place of Elizabeth O'Conner's view of the familiar lake, she sees water in front of the water, a flow of tears so thick that she can't suppress them. "I had a baby who died," she will say. "I put her to sleep and never saw her alive again."

The glistening, drab lake knows her intention and solemn Lake Point Tower and the bare trees and her bench, her broken, private bench. The wind that chafes her neck and musses her hair knows and a few still green leaves that have landed in the sand across from the sidewalk. Jack thinks she can't tell stories because the only story she could tell is unspeakable. What are words, she thinks, brushing away a filament of leaves from her lap?

What will she do with her tears? Keep them as souvenirs until they evaporate? Remind herself that they were cried for her?

CHAPTER SEVEN

JACK KAUFMAN is sitting on his leather couch sipping hot tea out of a tall glass with three lemon wedges and six sugar cubes, which are in various states of decomposition. Elizabeth wonders why they don't melt uniformly. Jack swishes the tea around in his cheeks like mouthwash. He sticks his finger in his hairy ear and digs into the ear canal and rotates it. Rubbing the bottom of his face hard with his palm, he thinks of something, whistles under his breath, and mutters. Then, pulling a small tortoiseshell comb through his thin silver hair, he notices that Elizabeth is observing him and motions with his half-empty glass for more tea.

"I wish Roy knew what we were doing tonight," he says shaking his head in regret. "I wish he could see me all gussied up like this," he says as he plugs in a flesh-colored hearing aid that Elizabeth has never seen before. Like a boutonniere, he'll wear it tonight with his pin-striped suit, and light blue shirt, and maroon tie. "I'm still pretty cute, aren't I, Elizabeth, and tonight, with this in," he says pointing to his ear, "I won't miss a beat."

"You look great," Elizabeth agrees. She has put on a red knit dress that hugs her thin waist and behind, and new black flats with tiny silver bows, and silver bow earrings. She is wearing a diamond watch that Jack tossed her earlier in the day when she went to straighten his bed. When she refused it, he had sworn. "Take the goddamn thing. Take it, for Heaven's sake," and she had.

"Maybe you could call Roy," Elizabeth says softly.

"Elizabeth, I'm surprised," Jack says, "frankly surprised. Every day I lie here and listen in the hallway. I hear the elevator going up and down. Occasionally the door opens, and each time what do I think? That Roy has come back to me. He's home, I think.

"I remember how I used to sit in Ma's god-awful chair with legs like lion claws and huge flowers, begonias or something, that looked like they could eat me. I'd watch over the tops of the elms out of the window on Hirsch Street for Ma to return. I'd sit still in that chair as a statue of a saint and wait for her. Just like this," he says, pointing to himself composed on the couch. "Over seventy years ago, now mind you.

"She'd take Joey along because he was a handful, but me, she'd leave at home.

"'Stay in that chair, Jackele,' she'd say. 'Just sit and be a good boy.'

"And all the time she was away—how long does it take to go to a little nothing store?—I'd be on pins and needles. What if she gets hit by a street car or a horse cart? What if some gonifs take her purse and knock her down, and she hits her head and forgets me?

"I'd make up superstitions, funny ones like when the third car comes around the corner, Ma will be home. When I hear three sounds in the flat downstairs by the Karnikovskys, whose place smells like a pickle factory, Ma will open the door. Silly things like that.

"Finally, she did come every time, but I never told her how happy I was. Sometimes, Elizabeth, it made me cry.

"And it's funny, as much as I loved Essie, I dream of Ma more and more. And I'm little Jack Nobody with the big ears and rickety legs and feet like gunboats. And Ma is cooking or coming for me at school or waving a little flag on the curb at a Labor Day parade.

"So how can I call Roy when he makes me crazy as a kid again? At seventy-eight years old. Waiting and waiting for nothing. When that elevator comes up again, it'll be Roy, I still think. But it's the cleaners or the deliveryman or you."

"I don't have a son, Elizabeth. Roy is dead," he says and stares defiantly at the opposite wall with its heavy gilt frames and still lifes of dark, wrinkly fruit and shiny dead fish.

He is expecting her to speak now, but what can she say? How to fill the moment, she wonders. I know this, Jack, she thinks to herself, Jack with your stories and oaths, that you never, never, say things like that about your living, breathing child, son-of-a-bitch that he is.

"Okay, then, we have about half an hour before we go," she finally says. "Do you want your medicine now or when we get home?"

"A little now, a little later," Jack says, "but tell me, Elizabeth. I'm pretty good at this, at guessing. I can tell by your face that you don't agree, that something's not right. Now I don't want to spoil our special evening with the 20-ounce steaks and the whole Maine lobsters and the champagne. I don't want discord. So tell me, what is it?"

"I was just thinking that people should be kinder."

"How much kinder should I be? Should I throw myself in the river because the boy hates me? Should I drown? Should I have you take this pillow and smother me like this"—and he holds an embroidered gold pillow over his face—"so that Roy can say, 'The crooked bastard is dead?'

"Do you understand what it's like to have a child who you carry around and take to ballgames and give all the best say you're not good enough?"

Elizabeth can see him breathing harder, his cheeks puffing like gills with exertion, his face red and overwrought.

"I'm sorry, Jack. I should mind my own business."

"He's not my son," Jack says breathlessly. "You're more my

daughter than he is my son," he smiles weakly, regaining his composure. "You care for me."

"I do, Jack."

"You know everything about me. More than Roy. More than Essie. I've told you things that nobody knows, Elizabeth. I trust you. And do you know why?"

"Why, Jack?"

"Because in another life I'd marry you. Essie would understand all right. All these years I've been alone. Get this. Since the day Essie died, I've been faithful. I've taken care of my needs, of course, but I've never thought of love. Never before this. Redheads, blondes, society ladies with their hospital auxiliaries and fancy-schmancy parties, bimbos, judge's wives, showgirls, waitresses, cousin-in-laws: never, Elizabeth, have I cared for one the way I care for you now. I want to help you out."

"Thanks."

"Only don't mention Roy."

"Okay, Jack," she says calmly, watching his breathing take on regularity, watching the usual jaundiced tan return to his face, watching the vein in his temple under his sheer, translucent old man's skin grow small and spidery again.

"So fuck Roy. We'll paint the town and Roy can drop dead for all I care. I won't listen for elevators anymore. On the memory of my Ma, I swear I won't."

*   *   *

"How can it be?" Mrs. Bozinska is asking her daughter's friend. "How can you lose a cat? On a bus?"

Tousled, red-faced, poor Joszef is standing at her door with his hands in his pockets like a child. He is two days late and has arrived with nothing to say, no excuses to offer.

"And then you didn't call!" she says with a sneer distorting her plump cheeks. "I wait and wait that day. I am worried sick about you."

"But I called that night."

"And you didn't have the heart to tell me."

"It was too foolish. I felt humiliated that it happened."

"And what shall we tell Irena?"

"I don't know, Mrs. Bozinska."

She makes an angry face. Why does it seem to annoy her so that he calls her Mrs. Bozinska? After all, that is her name, Lina Bozinska, wife of the late Professor Bozinski, mother of Irena, future owner of the lost cat.

"And why, Joszef, why didn't you watch?" she asks, wringing her hands dramatically.

He is not a child. Is he supposed to wait in her chilly doorway with the yellowed photographs all day and take this abuse? Soon he will fall asleep on his feet, lulled by the chiding rhythms of her voice. This whole situation is so ridiculous. He, who understands the cosmological constant, having to stand here endlessly, being harangued.

"Who would think that a pillowcase would get stolen? Who would know that one must watch pillowcases like a hawk?"

"Well, come in," she nods abjectly, and turns her squat frame away from him. He sees the uneven hem of her old flowered housedress and her floppy, worn-out slippers. Her ankles are swollen, and her hair is in a tight gray bun. He proceeds to her old gold sofa, which probably predates Irena, and sits erectly at one edge, keeping his distance from the decorative pillows and doilies, and embroidery that is tossed haphazardly over the edge and spills onto the dark, carpeted floor. No wonder Irena is so untidy. Look at the example her mother has set.

"Mrs. Bozinska—"

"Call me Lina," she says.

"Lina—"

"Here are some pastries." She points to a rose-covered china plate already on the table. "Please eat."

"Lina," he repeats, filling his mouth with a buttery, raspberry cookie, "I do not know what we should tell Irena."

"We?" she asks, eyes large with contempt. "We did not lose the little thing. You have a problem, Joszef, not we."

"I was thinking," Joszef continues in the way of philosophers, linguists, semioticians—people who ignore the evidence of the world for the evidence of their own minds—"that we could simply keep the myth alive."

"'How is little Chopin?' Irena will ask. And we, I, erhem," he clears his throat nervously, "will offer various reports.

"'Chopin is well. He is happy at his new home. He chases birds regularly. He eats heartily. He sleeps bundled at your mother's feet at night. I think he is content.'

"Then several months from now I can report that Chopin is gone. 'He went out at night and didn't return in the morning. Perhaps he chased a female cat—I saw a little tabby near your mother's house—to the other side of the park and got lost. It is very tragic.'"

"Then we must find him," Lina responds. Her voice is assured, lacking irony. "We must find Irena's beloved cat."

Joszef is puzzled. Is Irena's mother not understanding? "How can we do that when this is a story?" he asks.

"How can we make Irena worry so?" she asks raising her voice. "Don't you see, Joszef, this all leads to the same conclusion: poor Irena, no cat."

"Then we can say," Joszef suggests, stuffing another apricot morsel into his mouth and slurring his speech with tea, "that the cat is still fine. It is spring now. It sits in the sun and looks happy as a king. It chases a bird now and then and sometimes succeeds. We hate to see the results—so many feathers!—but what a full, round stomach he has, and, after all, he is only a cat."

"Then you must bring me Chopin."

He regards her broad forehead for a moment, her small blue eyes, her hard little mouth buttoned in defiance or stupidity. "But how can I . . ."

"You can, Joszef. You can bring me a new Chopin."

"An imposter?"

"A replica."

"But Irena will know."

"How will she know? Will we tell her?"

They exchange cautious smiles. Joszef snorts a thin laugh out of his nose and Lina actually giggles. Should they shake hands, he wonders, sign contracts, mingle blood to seal their treachery?

"I need a real cat, Joszef. I am not a fiction writer. I must know what this cat does day to day. I must be able to tell Irena. He eats so delicately. He sleeps on the green pillow near the window bench in the afternoon sun. He seems to like the painting of Father in the hallway. The pink rug in the lavoratory is accumulating his fur. I must wash it."

"But what if Irena says, 'This is not what my Chopin does.'"

"How will she know? Has the cat ever stayed here? Can she predict all of its actions? Really, Joszef, for a mathematician, I am sorry to say that you lack imagination."

"And where shall I procure such a cat?"

"Where did you procure Chopin?"

"Irena found him in the park. He was a little wet thing."

"Then I would suggest that you wait for a heavy rain," Lina laughs. "Or that you look at a shop or ask friends at the university. But remember, it must resemble Chopin. Black and white, correct?"

"But why is that necessary?"

"Can I say to my only daughter, my dear only child, 'Your cat's lovely gray fur heats up in the sun? Your cat's round blue eyes—'"

"Green," Joszef mutters.

"Your cat's round green eyes grow small with pleasure when I stroke his black belly."

"White."

"White belly, if I can't see the cat? I must have the cat in front of my eyes. Remember, Joszef, you didn't want the cat, the cat that our Irena left you. You brought it to me, and what happened?" She serves up a spiteful look.

"Now you must find me a cat just like him!" and her voice explodes in indignation. "And you bring him to me. You are an intelligent man, Joszef, and the world's full of cats. On the streets I see yellow cats, gray cats, cats with one ear and no tail.

Cats with kittens. Squashed cats on the boulevard. You find me this Chopin. You bring him here by next week.

"And you don't breathe a word to Irena about what's happened. If you dare tell her, Joszef, if you write and say, 'Irena, my lovely Irena, I have misplaced little Chopin, who I was trying to dump at your mother's, who was too much trouble for an important man like myself,' I will never forgive you." And she looks thoughtful, wipes some crumbs from her bodice, and continues.

"Irena will tell me, Joszef. Don't think that she won't. And if you do this, if you confess, I will come to the university every day, I have so little to do these days, a lonely widow, and I will remind you of how you were so careless. I will remind you in front of your colleagues.

"Thank God my Irena never had children with you! I'd be missing several grandchildren by now. Oh, I left one on the bus, Nanny Lina. I just fell asleep for an hour, and she was gone. Oh, I just had one at the zoo near the lion cage, but somehow he disappeared. A whole generation lost! How can it be, Joszef?"

And for a minute he doesn't know if she is about to laugh or cry, but instead she takes the best pastry left, a large slab of white powdery substance, and pops it into her mouth. A frenzy of dainty chewing follows, then silence.

"So by next Sunday, a cat," he promises.

"Chopin."

"A replica of Chopin, delivered here."

"No excuses."

"Well, I must be going," he is saying.

"Wait!" Lina heads toward the kitchen. After what seems like many minutes, she returns. She is carrying a variety of objects in an old, military green cardboard box with funny stiff handles. Joszef sees his favorite hazelnut coffee—where do they find it?—a small ham, a box of imported British cookies, some fruit preserves—yes, he is delirious with pleasure—and a mottled red rubber hot water bottle.

"Fill this at night," she says, demonstrating with her hands. "Put it next to you."

"Why?" Joszef asks as he stands holding the treasures.

"So you won't miss Irena. I have used one since the professor's death six years ago. It is really a comfort."

"All right," Joszef says tentatively, slipping it under the other provisions. Maybe he'll find a taxi back home. Maybe that's the one lesson of this whole ordeal: no matter the chaos at the taxi stand, always queue up.

"All right," he says again, and takes Lina's hand and kisses her on either cheek.

"By next Sunday!" she says in parting.

And now Joszef is back on the street in the suddenly frigid late October evening. The swirling sky looks full of trouble, and he wonders if he'll ever locate his muffler and winter cap, which have disappeared since Irena departed.

It would be too convenient if that thing he sees in the shadows of the bushes adjacent to Lina's house were a cat, a cat resembling Chopin. "Some kind of rodent," he says, and without observing it further, begins his long, cold trek to the taxi stand on the other side of the park.

*   *   *

Dear Joszef,

I am sorry that I have become an inefficient correspondent lately. You probably are thinking me rude or unfaithful, but it is not that I am forgetting you or the beloved language that we share. So many things have happened. They accumulate like laundry that I have no time to wash. Finally, before it is morning, dear Joszef, I am trying to write you a letter. If Mr. Waters needs me, I will have to go, of course, but let me begin now, sitting in my bed, propped on three fat pillows, using my lap as a desk. I must say that morning is a luxury with ample heat and a view of the lake, where the sun will rise at 7:12 A.M., just forty minutes from now.

*I have met several new people, who have changed the daily
flow of my quiet life here. First, there is a woman, Elizabeth
O'Conner, a tall, pretty American woman, who works for another
man in this building. I have come to believe that this building has
one of everything: I have the black musician. Maybe another
woman has the retired opera diva or the circus aerialist or the
archbishop. Elizabeth has the underworld figure. Elizabeth's Mr.
Kaufman is not world famous, like Al Capone or John Dillinger.
He is only locally famous like some of our own priests or commis-
sioners of parades. He is a businessman who knows how to make
deals. In his seventy-eight years of life, he has managed to buy up
a vast amount of Chicago. He is like a character on a video game
that I've seen advertised on American television. The crescent-
shaped face with legs opens its wide mouth, and the landscape
vanishes bit by bit. It is insatiable, Joszef, like our Mr. Jack
Kaufman.*

*He is the owner of many buildings and restaurants and night-
clubs and groceries and bridges. Do Americans own bridges?
Maybe I am wrong about this. And Elizabeth, who works for
him, she was his lover before he became so ill. She is not a very
discreet woman. She tells me everything, that he is ruthless, that
he has ordered one man killed and maybe more. I believe her
about this. But such a man is not typical in America. I think that
my Mr. Waters, so very kind and well behaved, is more what one
finds here. So please do not think I am in any danger, Joszef, from
knowing such a man. Mr. Kaufman is very old and sick, and
besides, I have nothing to give him, so I am safe. And Elizabeth,
I think, is safe too, because when he looks at her as he did last
night, I can see that he is in love. Does Elizabeth understand
this? I do not know.*

*But let me explain more slowly, Joszef, how last night we
"painted the town red," meaning that we celebrated. What did we
celebrate? I am not sure, but I am sure that it is typical in America to celebrate nothing with great fanfare. I only know that a
man named Julius, an elderly black man with a handsome, shiny
suit, drove us in a very large limousine—like heads of state use in*

Europe—to dinner and a club. Right within the car, we had a drink with ice. I had vodka, but it was American and tasted rather bitter. When we arrived at the Ambassador East Hotel, we dined at a beautiful place called the Pump Room. So many shiny plates and such crystal! Julius dined right with us—Americans are very democratic—so there were five: Mr. Waters, Elizabeth, Mr. Kaufman, Julius, and, of course, myself. We had some lovely food including Alaskan crab legs, which I dipped in sweet sweet butter and sucked ferociously. Such food, Joszef! I thought of Chopin then, how much he would have loved our feast, and how I was eating as he would but perhaps less delicately.

Tell me, Joszef, how is Chopin? Do you think he misses me? I hope that he is not too much trouble for you, busy as you are. I hope that he is eating easily prepared food and not making a fuss because I am gone. After all, he is only a cat, but sometimes I think that I have turned him into more with my pampering.

Well, after dinner we got back into Julius' limousine and drove very far, it seemed. I think I fell asleep for a short while, and after I had awakened, we were west of Chicago in a place called Joliet. It was so dark outside that I saw my first American stars, a sky like our own, Joszef, full of bright and not-so-bright distant objects we could name. Remember, Joszef, what Urszula reported about Australia? How it was the sky that had discomfited her most, being so different than our own? Well, here I was looking at our familiar sky and wondering where we had been taken in this fantastic white coach.

And suddenly my new friends are pointing to a boat on a river, a shiny new white boat covered in small lights. How white everything in America is, like a dental office or blank paper or a snowfall. I come to understand slowly with much explanation that this is a gambling boat. I am at a small Las Vegas on a river. I can put my money on a roulette table and watch a wheel spin or pull the lever and have enough coins to make domestic phone calls forever.

Mr. Waters, who is too kind, wants to give me money to gamble, but I tell him no, that gambling is not something which interests me. Elizabeth, who is sometimes rude, rolls her eyes at me, but I am not ashamed to save my money. Maybe, I tell her, before we leave, I will play one slot machine. Yes, I will, I assure them all, so then they can ignore me.

Mr. Kaufman, Mr. Waters, and Julius go to the tables of card games. I do not know what they are playing, Joszef, but I know their probability for victory is small. I could easily calculate it for them, but I am not asked to perform this service.

Elizabeth takes my arm and nearly pulls me toward the slot machines, which occupy another room, mostly full of older women. "Here," she says, and gives me a roll of quarters, Joszef, a package of plastic-wrapped tokens. "Compliments of Mr. Kaufman," she says, and nods her head toward the machines.

"But I can't," I begin to protest, and she looks very bored and slightly angry as if I am a stupid child not listening to an adult.

"Just play," she commands, and so, sheepishly, looking at no one, I make my way toward an empty spot on the wall. The quarter is in, the lever is pulled, and I watch the three images, which do not match. Maybe grapes, and two sour lemons, but I do not remember anymore so many times did I pull that lever with nothing coming of it.

"The well is dry," I joke with Elizabeth, for she is having no luck with this amusement either. Meanwhile, down the row from us, a woman, perhaps a grandmother in green slacks and matching sweater and very short hair like a man's, is shouting for her husband. "Frank!" she calls. "Frank!" She is maybe going to faint, I think, as quarters spill out of her machine, more and more quarters tumbling, a flood of silver. And she is opening her shiny patent purse and shouting for Frank-Frank, and giving free advice to us poor unlucky gamblers, our features sagging like old luggage.

"Just keep working the machines!" she encourages before she goes off happily into the American night.

Well, I am not encouraged. I decide that I am tired and go sit in the bar, noisy with old tunes, which I do not recognize. A waitress takes my order—I am only drinking orange juice—and I sit alone at a low table, and think. Joszef, how can this be? How far have I come to feel such alienation, to act so unlike myself that I wonder how I will ever locate my core again? And this is a serious matter, Joszef, not how I felt as a young girl wondering what I would study in college or whom I might someday marry. There is an active principle in America, Joszef, of mindless activity. Everyone and everything demands that I enlist in the gaiety. It mocks me when I say I don't know who I am becoming. It soothes me with rolls of coins and promises of more. It whispers in my ear to forget that I can no longer hear myself thinking. I believed when I arrived knowing so little English that working for an old man would be the perfect way to avoid this American intoxication, this army of happy souls, but Mr. Waters too is subject to fits of amusement.

I see our old friends, Witold and Katarina, who have become Americans, Joszef. Their yard has a small pool in it for their dear American child Alexandra, and their house is filled with televisions. Katarina watches a TV the size of my hand as she prepares a salad for us, an American-style salad with only lettuce and orange-colored dressing. I can sense that something has happened right in that kitchen. We will not talk familiarly and seriously ever again. Soon our old language of pain will be officially forbidden. "Speak English," she will demand, and laugh at my protests in our bitter old tongue.

I go to find my Mr. Waters, perhaps he needs help, and I see him with Mr. Kaufman and Julius, three old fools, trying to forget sickness and age and sadness and death. And I understand then, Joszef, what is strong about America. It is so amusing here that the fright can leave them. Three eighty-year-old boys playing, I think, and I must smile. I recall the boyish faces of Mr. Reagan and Mr. Bush, never unhappy because they refuse to be. In the American rendition, even the Four Horsemen of the Apocalypse are smiling!

Is it wrong to be happy, Joszef? I have always thought so. I have always been proud of denying myself. That is how I've become brave. But perhaps I have only been a fool. Purity will not help me when I am old as these men and need comfort. It will not help me even now, when I attend the celebrations of others. I cannot leave the party to which I was not invited.

My life is provisional at best, Joszef. As if making a real life might have offended someone: you or my parents or perhaps the government. But Communism is over. Poland is over for me, and still I carry it as a disease. I am afraid to buy objects I see and can afford. I am afraid that I do not deserve a new watch or the opportunity to meet people more like myself, or the chance to pull the foolish lever of the slot machine and win.

So this is the story of my rather self-conscious trip to the gambling casino. I am afraid that I have not made it very interesting for you, Joszef. You probably want to know more about Mr. Kaufman, his manner of dress, his life of corruption. You probably want me to tell you about the inside of the car, its gray crushed-velvet upholstery, and the piped-in Sinatra music with sweeping orchestration that sounds like the ocean. You probably think I have cheated you out of a good story. "How much did they win?" you are asking.

The truth is that I don't know, Joszef. I am not interested in knowing. I can only tell you about myself, about whom you already know too much, and how I darken things with my gaze. I thought of you many times, Joszef, of our Warsaw cocoon, with its usually cold water, lack of heat, and limited comforts. We were happy as stoics there. As I looked at the insular sky, our car glided past factories and railroad yards and the ugly industrial suburbs and the West Side of the city back to our gleaming building, my temporary home.

And when I laid my head on the temporary pillow that night, Joszef, I didn't dream of you, and what I would be unable to let you know. I didn't feel guilty that I had let you down with my poor story. I thought of Mr. Waters' happiness, his temporary joy at forgetting himself, how it made him suddenly so young that he played a few notes for me on the abandoned piano when he got home. And though I recognized the beautiful song, its title made no sense to me in English. Listening to the music, I understood. I am in America learning to accept the blankness of the sky over Chicago, how, when the wind blows and the clouds roll over the lake like smoke, I won't even try to make it all seem melancholy by thinking of you.

Love,

Irena

She looks in on Mr. Waters, who is moaning in his sleep—the old sleep as noisily as broken engines—and shuffles to the kitchen to make coffee. Later she will stamp and post her letter, which will travel in a sleek jet to Joszef. Burdened with immigrant fears and anxieties, her letter should wear a babushka and travel uncomfortably, by sea mail at best.

Now, she takes the skillet, two eggs, and some artificial butter from a tub. Turning on the discrete electric power that makes fire obsolete, she watches the coils heat up. She measures off a small dip of the yellow substance and listens to it sizzle. Breaking the eggs, she stirs them until they nearly reach solidity. Then she quickly adds some slivers of raw onion and what remains of a tomato. When Mr. Waters wakens, she will repeat the same process, taking his eggs, however, from a little carton that pours a facsimile of eggs, minus the damaging ingredients.

To think of eggs as unhealthy seems a contradiction in terms. Are they not the purest food on earth? She remembers the photos of eggs in whimsical wire baskets that Urszula had shown to Irena after a stay in Greece. The baskets, from which one egg dangled at the bottom like a forgotten punctuation mark, were connected to pulleys the egg vendor raised and lowered for customers. The whole display was a form of food bravura. In other countries, people perform dangerous feats for the benefit of tourists. She thinks of young men in Mexico, who dive from cliffs for pesos. In Greece, however, the inventors of *pi* and geometry have created Platonic daring by suspending perilous eggs in space. Each purchase becomes a philosophical circus performance of skill and nerve. Had Urszula bought eggs there? Had anyone actually seen the eggs change hands? Perhaps, then, it was only a visual illusion meant to hoodwink tourists?

Spooning breakfast onto her plate and pouring herself some coffee, she remembers the silent taxi ride with Joszef to the same clinic that Urszula, Alicia, Eva, and hundreds of thousands of women before them had visited repeatedly. The surgical masks and gloves. The unremarkable, unceremonious procedure, the white sheets worn smooth with use. The pinch of pain that didn't seem sufficient to memorialize the act. The silence that surrounded its completion. The lack of sacramental words or incense or candles. How she had sealed the absence of meaning with a promise to Joszef that it would never be discussed. Joszef, whom she hadn't married, who hadn't become a father or husband. Nor would she become a mother. Not that it concerned her immediately or concretely. What would she have done with a small child now—impossible luggage—and her need to leave Poland?

The decision not to be parents had been inviolable between them. Like the American constitution, it had created a system of governance and belief. The possibility of a child had been a serious infraction, an invasion, a permanent, unspoken strain. Perhaps now that she reconsidered it, it provided her a motive for her departure among all the others they had paid lip service in odd ceremonies of talking it through: career, government, opportunities, commitment. Their litany of platitudes, their phrasebook of dissolution.

So many women she knew were childless. And the ones who entered motherhood displayed their one precious offspring with great pride, the culmination of scientific planning and serendipity. They acted as if they'd chosen to grow a perilous crop in hostile soil or host an important dinner on the one day that the stores in Warsaw had affordable food on their shelves. How clever of them, how brave to produce this miracle! Their infants were the most gorgeous, most intelligent in the world. None were old enough yet to disappoint with slow progress in school, or a nasty temperament, or poor eyesight.

One afternoon shortly before Irena's procedure, she had been walking alone on the austere grounds of the university when a swell of noise that first resembled geese cackling had interrupted her mood. A group of schoolgirls being led around the campus hadn't surrendered their exuberance at the gates. Their teachers, trying their best to reinstate silence, were powerless. Yes, life makes its demands, Irena had thought, observing their animated faces. Life squawks noisily as geese. Then several complaints about the unruliness of children entered her head, creating the delicate defense she required. She thought of her own mother then, never too busy to beam at her. During the awkward time she was sprouting breasts and blemishes, her mother had called her beautiful. My lovely Irena, she had named her awkward, gangly, perpetually flustered daughter. That's what Irena would withhold from life, her unmitigated approval.

"Good morning," Mr. Waters says quietly, pleasantly. "Are you a casualty of last night too?"

"I did not participate to that extent, Mr. Waters, so I am myself today."

"I'm afraid the rest of us got a little carried away, Irena. We should have your good sense."

"Maybe no. Maybe my good sense is a little dull."

"Well, my head feels swollen and very fragile. No breakfast today. Just toast and maybe tea?"

"Sometimes in Poland people drink brandy to cure headache like this."

"Sometimes here too, Irena, but I think I'll opt for sobriety. Plain toast, some tea with sugar, and lots of quiet. Maybe I'll lay me down and rest a good deal. Jack has invited me to lunch, but I need a day off first. I wonder if he's any worse for the wear."

"I would imagine that he too exceeded himself last night."

"So we'll have a quiet day? We'll keep the shades pulled? We'll hear a little soft music, but don't even bring me my newspapers."

"Would you like to go back to bed?"

"No, there's plenty of time for that. I'll just sit here and balance my poor head on my shoulders. When I finish my toast, I'll hobble back, Irena, and you'll be free as a bird."

"I do not wish to go anywhere, Mr. Waters, so I will spend the day cleaning and reading. Maybe I will make some soup for dinner."

"Soup is nice and quiet to eat." He smiles.

"I remember first time I have headache like this from champagne. It was a wedding for my friend. I sit in the washroom all night in my beautiful gown, and in the morning my mother asks me, 'Irena, why is your bed not slept in?' and I tell her a little lie, but I think she knows."

She serves him his tea and toast, and they sit silently. Ten in the morning, the day is already finished.

*   *   *

"Jack, it's that man again. He's downstairs."

Jack can see that last night has had its toll on Elizabeth too. She's too weary to register the amusement that she usually reserves for illegal proceedings conducted in Jack's bedroom. Lifting his head tentatively from the pillow, the room swirls and Jack groans. "Don't people know about phones anymore? About appointments?"

"Should I send him away?" she whispers, door partially closed, as if he were waiting on the threshold rather than twenty-nine floors below.

"Send him up." His throat feels dry and sandy. "And get me something sweet to drink to wash down these damn pills." He sits up for the first time that morning and measures his general health. He gathers up his dressing gown, which he reserves for business guests, and runs his palm over his sparse silver hair.

The night before has lifted his spirits, but there are conse-
quences for every action. A dull ache in his liver has joined the
other, more acute pain in a wrenching duet. Between the usual
painkiller-modulated stabs, he feels a bloated aching. It can't be
good that pain can be so various. Who invented this array of
suffering? What kind of sadist would devise such torture? He
tries to focus his watery eyes enough to find his glasses and a
notepad. He's better able to concentrate through the pain with
a pen in his hands. It focuses him to doodle or scribble as someone talks away. He blinks to clear his watery vision. Outside in
the hall he can hear Elizabeth's voice rise and fall in conversation with Eddie Floekorn, who walks like he's stiff, who whispers like he's embarrassed when he talks, who's making his third
visit in a week, and who, by now, will be desperate.

In walks Eddie, the son of Ziggy from the neighborhood,
Ziggy who could cheat at cards like nobody's business but
smile with such aplomb that people pardoned him—usually.
In walks Eddie Flokoern, who used to ride a two-wheeler, up
to his neck in a scheme he should have tossed in the trash like
some bad news. Elizabeth has taken his coat and led him up
to the door. Little Eddie Floekorn in his Brooks Brothers suit
and Gucci attaché case and slicked-back hair is going to jail,
no matter what he's bringing Jack.

"Sit down," he tells Eddie as a manicured hand is extended
toward him. "How's it going?"

"You know how it's going, Jack. It's still in the papers." And
Eddie Floekorn drops his face into his hands like a strange
weighty parcel and closes his hooded sullen eyes. "They're
about to arrest me. I haven't been home in two days," he whispers through the mesh of his fingers.

"That must be hard."

"It wasn't supposed to be this way."

"What's supposed to be what, Eddie? How old are you?"

"Fifty-two."

"Then you should know better. Didn't your dad, who could
cheat an executioner out of his ax, teach you?"

"What do you mean?"

"Kids are impetuous, Eddie. Kids do things without thinking. But here you are sitting before me, a man in a nice suit with a box full of money on your lap, and there's nothing I can do for you because you didn't think.

"You behaved like a child. Maybe one night lying in bed, you couldn't sleep. You looked at your wife and said, 'I'm going to make us rich, honey.' Or, maybe with a sinking feeling you looked around and said quietly so the wife couldn't hear, 'God, I need some fast money to get away from this place.'"

Eddie is smiling like Jack's dart has landed close to the truth. Smiling and speechless, Eddie is waiting for Jack to reveal more.

"But then you made your mistake. You didn't hook up with someone. You acted like some schmuck in his basement inventing the light bulb a century late, thinking you're real smart. This can't fail, you're telling yourself. Soon you'll be rich. But everything can fail. Everything does fail. You have to plan so it doesn't fail.

"You're like a kid with a head full of dreams. Why didn't you come here first? I could have directed you to some people with more promising business ideas. Your dad and me were like this, the gonif," Jack says, crossing two thin fingers. "I could have made a few calls."

"Can't you make a few calls now?"

"Eddie, I'm an old man. I have—what?—maybe a year, six months? You need something big, Eddie, and I haven't the energy for that. I'm not fucking Superman. Already you're making me tired. I'm doing all the talking and you're sitting here like a girl waiting to be rescued. There's no one who can rescue you.

"Go home. See the wife and kids. Have your papers served. Get out on bail. You have money for bail, right? Get a good lawyer and wait. Nothing's open and shut. Maybe the police will fuck up, they do that a lot, and you'll get off. Meanwhile, I'll put in a few good words, but I can't save you up front. Not after you were so stupid."

"I can't go to jail, Jack."

"Believe me, better men than you have. I could name you men who should be in the Hall of Fame, princes, who went to jail."

"Jack, I have lots of money here."

"You went babbling into a microphone. I can't erase what they have on you. Wait. See what judge you get."

"But what if you're not around then, Jack?"

"If I'm dead, that's another story. That's a story I won't care much about."

"I expected more."

"This is what you're getting, Eddie. Now move your ass off my chair, or I'll have my girl call security."

"Jack—"

"You needed to be thinking all the time, not just that one night. You should have planned like you were starting a new life, like the world's future depended on it, not like you were poking some whore you met."

"Thanks, Jack. I'll tell my father . . ."

"I thought your father was sick."

"He's had a few strokes, but he listens when I talk. I'll tell him that Jack Kaufman can't help me."

"Tell him," Jack shrugs, "that Eddie Floekorn needed some brains with his balls. I'll have my girl show you out."

*　　*　　*

"Here, kitty," Lina is saying. "Here little Chopin." Joszef can see that Lina is dubious as he watches her observe the cat make its cautious round of the unfamiliar corners of the parlor, where motes of dust float like phantoms.

"Is he not too small, Joszef?"

"Chopin was once small. This cat will grow."

"And his gender?"

"He used to be a boy like Chopin. We can tell Irena that he was spotting your carpet. The odor was unpleasant. She'll understand getting him fixed."

Surprisingly, Lina nods in agreement to this idea. Now Joszef smiles with relief. He has delivered her cat after much difficulty and anxiety. Now Lina will have to stop her daily calls of prodding and reproach. After all, she is not his mother-in-law. He does not have to continue to know this woman.

"So, then Joszef, I will tell Irena by letter, of course, that Chopin has become more of a gentleman," she smiles, offering a platter of powdery sweets resembling small igloos to Joszef.

He removes a sugary construction from the tray and takes a satisfied bite.

"I wonder where the real Chopin is," Lina says, pouring some tea from a foreign-looking, ornate teapot with small, thick legs. "Will you have sugar?"

"Please."

"One hears terrible stories about missing pets," Lina continues, shaking her small round head. "Some end up in laboratories in brain experiments." She makes a dreadful face that sends her eyeballs up toward her hairline. "And Mr. Grubnz tells me that some get eaten," she whispers, leaning toward Joszef, as if Chopin might be alarmed by the news.

"I would hate to speculate about what some restaurants serve," he agrees.

Joszef and Lina share a glance of commiseration suitable to the moment—guarded but ironic nonetheless. Joszef basks in satisfaction. He has pulled off a coup by getting Lina to accept this shorter-haired, neutered, skinny feline, half the size of the original. Virginia, the Fulbright woman from New Jersey, had known a man who had a friend who had a cat—and constant fits of sneezing. Luckily, it too was black and white. Joszef supposes the cat is used to its old name, which he has forgotten, just as he was going to tell it to Lina.

"Well, then, what do you hear from Irena?" Lina asks as she brushes sugar and crumbs from her bodice to her generous lap.

"Your daughter is having adventures. America turns out to be a land of vast entertainment for Irena."

"My Irena is enjoying herself?"

What does Lina imagine? That such a state is impossible for Irena, or that life without Joszef would indeed be an improvement?

"Her old man knows another old man who is rich. Irena has dined in the best restaurants and gone gambling."

"Joszef," she says, shaking her head, "I am surprised by what you are saying for several reasons. First, because she merely tells me about her duties. She cares, does she not, for an old black man whose heart is impaired? They lead a tranquil life. Nor can I believe that Irena would gamble. In Warsaw she wouldn't even put her small faith in religion. Why should she arrive in America and suddenly believe in anything? What kind of gambling is this, Joszef?" Lina asks with trepidation.

"There are boats on rivers, Lina, where one can wager money, but Irena, in truth, only observes."

"Irena could perhaps tell me more," Lina suddenly says. She purses her lips with regret. "Thirty-four years we have known each other, and my daughter doesn't yet confide in me."

"Perhaps she wants to spare you worry."

"Why, then," Lina asks, brushing crumbs from her lap onto her broad feet, "did she leave Warsaw?" She shakes her head and regards the carpet. "I am thinking, Joszef, that this will not do."

"What, Lina?" Joszef asks, regarding the crumbs at her feet.

"I lie awake worrying about my grown daughter. When she lived with you, I did not worry daily. My fears then," she continues with assurance, "were more general. How would my daughter become a woman when her head was full of numbers and when you, pardon me, Joszef, offered no inducement?"

"I am not understanding."

"Joszef, we are not children. Humans are capable of reproduction. As a species we cannot survive without it. The human race . . ."

"Pardon me, Lina, but the cat is perhaps needing a place to void himself. I have brought some materials."

She drops her large hand onto his wrist and holds it there. "What I am saying, Joszef, is that I am maybe a selfish woman. Soon you will stop calling. You will have a new life. And Irena, too, will go on living. I cannot understand why it is that she has left us, Joszef. What did you do?"

"Me?" he asks indignantly. "I did nothing. As you know, we were together for six years. We shared our work, our meals, everything."

She is silent. Then a potent idea lights up her small, troubled eyes. "That was the problem, Joszef. My Irena needed something different from you. What is that foul cat doing now?"

They watch as it tries to dig a hole in the magazines.

"Here, kitty," Joszef says. "Here Chopin," he repeats, as he moves towards the hallway. Lining a box with newspaper and sand, he gathers up the animal, and peremptorily drops him in. "This is where you shit and piss," he whispers.

"Is it all right?" Lina calls from the parlor down the hall. She is planted firmly on the couch. Joszef wonders about her former threats of retaliation if she had remained catless. Could a person of her bulk actually waddle to the university and locate him? It is out of kindness, really, that he has brought this excuse of a Chopin.

"Cats understand what is important in life," Lina continues as Joszef seats himself again opposite her. "They do not waste their time learning cello or studying mathematics. They hunt and eat and reproduce."

"Well, Lina, the hour grows late, and I have many things to do." Joszef hesitates, hoping that Lina will offer another basket of rewards. His supply of delicious hazelnut coffee has already dissipated.

Looking at him regretfully in the dimming light of the parlor, Lina pours another cup of tea and sighs deeply. "Do you know how old I was when Irena was born? I was exactly her age. The Professor was a bit older and worried about a baby in his life, but never, Joszef, was he more happy than when he wheeled Irena in the sunny park or talked to her softly as she drifted to sleep. It was like watching the ocean for him to have a child.

"People like you and Irena don't understand this. You think that life is hard enough already. But remember. Life has always been difficult. People had babies during the war, in internment camps, in Siberia.

"In the desert today women have babies. They just walk into the bushes and push. I've seen it on television. They may eat termites for dinner, Joszef, but that's no excuse to live like a recluse. Why has my Irena chosen such a life?"

"I do not know, Lina," he says softly, looking longingly at the door. "It's getting late."

"You two are not young. Soon you will have no memories."

"I will call you, Lina," Joszef says, rising. "I will see how you and Chopin are faring. You can depend on that."

Is the old woman crying? Yes, she is sobbing quietly and rocking forward so that her belly precariously brushes the edge of the table, where numerous small china plates are stacked. "Please, Lina, what is it?"

"We must get Irena to return. She cannot be replaced like a cat."

"Have you told her, Lina?"

"How can I, Joszef?"

"Then how will she know?"

"You must tell her, Joszef, that life is impossible. You must say that I am not doing well. She must at least visit us, Joszef. She left so abruptly. Nothing was said. We were all walking in a dream."

"I will tell her that you are unhappy, Lina. We will see what she says."

"I must see Irena again. There are things, Joszef, that her father left us. I must be able to give them to her."

"Perhaps they can be mailed."

"They are of some value. I must give them to her personally."

"Why didn't you tell Irena before she left?"

"I didn't know then that she must be given them. I thought perhaps I would live forever, Joszef," she states, dabbing at her puffy eyes. "It was enough to wake up and say to myself, 'My Irena is leaving.' A terrible trance I was in, unable to think things through. Don't you agree we must have her back?"

He begins to wonder how he would answer this perilous question, but he can see that the woman is not listening. She is busy baiting her Irena trap with hope.

PART TWO

CHAPTER EIGHT

WHAT WILL ADAM DO when he sees the old man, whose voice on the phone bore his prognosis like a B movie? What will he say for himself if the old man asks him probing questions in his raspy voice thick with pain? How can he explain his project, conceived out of vague interest and maybe perversity, if his grandfather says instead, "Where have you been for twelve years? Where in the hell were you? Adam, who used to call me Goopa, where the fuck have you been?"

"Sorry, Grandpa," he will say shyly, in the voice that becomes boyishly thin, childish really, when challenged by authority. And then he'll turn his back and set up the necessary equipment decorously and slowly, as if he were already making a strained condolence call. He'll run wires around the old man's bed or chair and tell him what a nice view he has of the lake. And then he'll take some shots to judge the best angles. Seeing his grandfather, small and concrete as a religious icon in the frame of the lens, he'll begin to ask questions.

No, he won't do that first. They'll probably talk casually. Maybe his grandfather will have a few insights on the recent news—his dad says he knows every crook in town. What's his take on the scandal? Are politicians involved at a high level?

What's it like to be a crook, Adam will ask. No, he's not rude like that, not an investigative reporter, not here to exploit the man but to know him. Adam's ashamed that he thought even for a moment like his father, who's so bitter on the subject of Jack that his usual bland restraint cracks to hear his name spoken.

No, they'll be businesslike and discuss what they hope to accomplish. Maybe his grandpa will ask him questions similar to those posed by his graduate thesis advisor with the graying ponytail and workshirt opened to reveal a few black chest hairs and a scarab from Nepal worn on a leather choker. Will Adam's grandfather be a willing subject? Will he tell the truth? Will Adam have what's needed to coax it from him? Has he read Oriana Fallaci, seen *Best Boy* and *Roger and Me,* learned the editing techniques taught in Video 402, taken Ethnography 347, seen *JFK,* all of Ophuls, and read the latest feminist, Marxist, and deconstructionist critics, who view the camera as a phallus, a fascist, a false angel of order in a universe laid bare by chaos theory?

He smiles to think how far these questions will be from his subject's mind. What does his grandfather know of Jameson or Barthes, or phalluses, except his own? His grandfather is more likely to make a joke about getting laid! Or maybe he'll offer reassurance to his small, blond, stranger of a grandson in his tastefully hip black clothing, who appears to be dressed, prematurely, for mourning. "If you can't trust your own family, who can you trust?" his grandfather will ask. "Want some meat? Bread? Tea?" Monosyllables spoken without ambiguity, which was invented later than Jack Kaufman learned to speak. He's always been forthright with Adam. But Adam isn't like him; he can't imagine telling his father where he is going with his fancy camcorder and list of questions. Imagine his father seeing the proposal for the project Dr. Sherry has somewhere on his massive shrine of a desk with its computer and herbal candles and New Age crystals and photos of his too-young wife.

And even if it doesn't go well, Adam's half-cocked scheme to document this man he's never been allowed to know, its disastrous possibilities will create a marvelous tension. Carla, his latest girlfriend, had already given it her seal of approval, the withering "Oh-sure!" of her beautiful, playfully contemptuous gaze. It's not like writing a paper requiring huge and rigorous preparation, a thesis, and an outline. It's more like taking a cruise and seeing sights as they happen into view. Whatever is revealed will suffice. In fact, its fallibility is what his advisor finally most appreciated, the fantastic disaster it could turn out to be, how Adam would have to redeem the project by letting it fragment into moments of poignant disconnection. "Family biography is so old," Dr. Sherry had sighed. "Family deconstruction would be terrific. Take him apart. Challenge his coherence. Look for openings, Adam, where the story falls apart and pursue them like . . ."

"Like a cross between a pit bull and a French philosopher," Adam had thought.

"Don't let him get away with where he met your grand-mother and what he thinks of old age. Gather by dispersal. Slice him apart. Short of killing the man, don't give him an easy way out. Remember *Hearts of Darkness*, Adam, coercive documentary. You're not his guest but his Grand Inquisitor."

It might have been his father talking, if his father had filmic pretensions to meld to his contempt, his father, whose futur-istic desk at Graystone, Inc., laden with brochures and pro-posals and letterheads of Chicago's most prestigious clubs, conveyed how far he had moved away from Jack. His father, whose Rauschenbergs, Warhols, and Oldenbergs—messy political collages, a checkerboard of Mao's head, human-sized paintbrushes—provided further evidence that the Kaufmans had legitimized their business concerns in one generation.

"People talk in straight lines, Adam. They think their lives are linear," Dr. Sherry had explained. "'Tell the truth but tell it slant.' Emily Dickinson said that."

"But in a different context," Adam offered.

"But in a different context," Professor Sherry agreed.

"You'll have to meet my father some day," Adam had told Professor ("Call me Hugh") Sherry, but he hadn't explained why.

Now Adam was off of the subway and onto Elm Street, where the air was so cold and full of car fumes that it felt like a different substance. He took long nervous gulps of the concoction, trying to slow himself down, but his heart was racing, and the smell of Carla's hair kept intruding on his walk, on his assignment to reveal November 28th, the 79th autumn of his grandfather's life on earth. Philosophical reconstructions aside, his grandfather was dying, and the large black square case Adam wore slung over his shoulder would capture something about it. Not in the large way that his father's paintings spoke to viewers; more like the miniature realistic portraits that Roy kept in another hallway, paintings of a lesser-known artist's bohemian friends, which hung opposite the washroom, reminding Adam of the minor station that intimacy holds in the world. He still wondered what had happened to the talented man who'd made these beautiful, small paintings when he was only Adam's age. He had probably fallen off the art world cliff like a coin. Still worshipping their light and privacy, Adam was drawn to his project as a small gesture of kindness, a decent thing, a quiet statement of loyalty, a small detail in the collage of Kaufman family love and rancor.

The project gave Adam a curious power, a new focus which Carla had probably felt when he had said good-bye to her last night. He was absorbed in what the next day would produce, abstract and rather distant, like a body of water before a storm or a soldier about to go off to war.

"Don't leave so soon," she had pleaded, dangling her splendid hair in Adam's face. "Make a movie about me instead."

They had laughed at the idea. "We've known each other three weeks," Adam smiled. "I suppose a movie would be a new kind of progress."

"C'mon," she had teased, beginning a narrative about her British father and Colombian mother meeting in Mexico City during student riots. Her performance lasted until Adam's head fell on his chest and Carla hit him, lightly, with an old ballet slipper.

Walking to the el that morning, he had felt surprise at everything. His life had been short of amazement, but now everything seemed new: his own visible breath, how whiteness creased his hands as they reached their winter level of dryness, how brown and swollen the ground looked with its cover of moldering leaves, Carla's beautiful fragrance as her hair had grazed him and her small breasts hovered near his mouth. Would he ask his grandfather about sex? They, were, after all, adults, who shared knowledge of many subjects. Would they talk, say, of positions the body finds itself assuming in the beds of women? Do these positions change with age, level of accomplishment, economic considerations? Does one's own flesh surprise one as it ages, or does it happen without cognition? Adam could remember standing on a small suburban hill many years before and noticing how large his hands suddenly seemed. Had they grown overnight, or did something that morning stun him into self-awareness? Did the same process occur as a man's sickness whittled him down? Could Adam stop this terrible knowing from occurring? What would his grandfather want, help in stopping it, or help in explaining it?

The whole world appeared to be softly decaying, worthy of sympathy and repair. The sky was a uniform gray, transected by delicate rips of jet engine exhaust, and somewhere, invisible over that, a great hole was expanding in the ozone. What a strange word—o-zone. The concrete neighborhood was soft and fuzzy with tentative edges. Steam burst from grates in wavy, noiseless torrents. Pitiful, fledgling trees, which had taken root in sidewalk cracks, bent and broke. Gray ice massed in small dirty islands near the curb. Masonry crumbled and was carelessly patched. He felt like telling the stubbly clerk at Sonny's, where he bought his coffee with double cream, that he was about to redeem his grandfather from his own indifference, his father's hatred, and the lack of consolation of philosophy. He remembered as he watched his coffee steam from the spout of its pug-nosed lid, how he'd discovered at five years, in a museum paleontology exhibit, of all places, that he would die some day. And every day since then, in some form of language or feeling, he had admitted the light of that knowledge, bathed in it, washed the terrible secret words around in his mouth ("Don't tell your friends. Their parents might disapprove," his mother had admonished), rubbed his wounds with it, and defied it in typical fashion—by driving too fast, by drinking too much, by stepping close to the edge of the train platform, by not brushing his teeth properly, by sharing a needle once, by fucking, by feeling huge anger and huge love, both of which made his heart pound like a perilous engine.

Since he was thirteen, twelve years ago, he hadn't seen his grandfather. Though Jack did his best with the two grandchildren while their parents toured Tuscany, there were moments of discomfort that Adam still remembered. Driving them to a movie in the sweltering air of Miami, air so thick and humid that it waved its long sweaty fingers in front of the windshield, Jack had come dangerously close to a head-on collision by going around a car parallel parking. The incident had passed unacknowledged. Maybe Katy, many years later, had told their mother how they had almost lost their lives that day, but the moment stood like bookends with nothing between them. Every morning of their stay, Jack had made them what he called French toast, a concoction on which the egg congealed, yolk unbroken in the middle of the bread, which was fried in a pan with butter and served without syrup. "Maybe it's Moroccan or Spanish toast," Adam had whispered to cheer Katy, who, at ten, was far more passionate about her food preferences. Even with Adam's prodding, Katy had trouble pretending that it tasted good. These were small things, Adam knew, petty things, really. After all, what is an egg on toast or bad driving, but it, along with Jack's cigars and rough language and unexpected moments of paralyzing grief over Essie, dead four years, made the children uncomfortable enough to evoke their stay with Jack as an absurd, recurring motif of their childhoods.

Shortly after their visit, Grandpa Jack inexplicably became a forbidden topic, though the trust funds he'd created for their schooling bore his name and a check came on birthdays. More bookends, more space. No explanations offered. What was the source of the fracture, Adam had always wondered. Like a subliminal message, his video might reveal that and more. Like a seismometer. Like an EKG. Like a plumb line. Like a bullet traced to its source.

How many times had he seen his grandfather's high-rise when he went to the Esquire Theater or shopped on Michigan Avenue? How often had he remembered the old man? Every other time? Four times a year, perhaps, counting the birthday check? How can people become so useless to each other, he wondered, as he thought of Carla's very useful hair, coarse as a horse's tail, smelling of gardenias, and walked through the revolving door of his grandfather's lobby.

*   *   *

"Sit right down," Jack says, pointing to a barrel-shaped green velvet chair with cane backing. His large, semi-dark bedroom is set up like a hospital with tubes and clamps and vials of liquid and bags of medical supplies and shiny IV poles. The shades are drawn and the only light Adam sees is from a small, white plastic gooseneck lamp near Jack's bed. Among the other dark, rich furniture, it seems improvised. In the dim bedroom light, Adam can see the small man, tanned or jaundiced a brownish yellow. Face pulled taut by disease, he is so thin that he appears younger than the last time they were together. His clear blue eyes are large and alert. His grandfather has beautiful eyes, Paul Newman blue, like Adam's own. "Make yourself at home," his grandfather says, as Adam, seated in the corner, feels dizzy and wounded with knowledge. His grandfather will die soon, Adam can see that clearly. Maybe today, Adam suddenly realizes, his heart pounding absurdly. "Oh," Jack rasps, "let me introduce you. Adam ('who hasn't visited me forever,' Adam imagines him saying) this is Elizabeth O'Conner, my special assistant."

"Nice to meet you," pale Adam says, shakily extending a

hand, really, an excuse of a hand to her. She towers over him, and in her grasp, her hand obliterates his. She'd be another species next to his shriveled grandfather.

"Can I get you a sandwich and some tea or coffee?" Elizabeth asks.

"What do you want, Grandpa?" The last word probably floats towards Jack's ears as strange and uninhabited. His concentration on Adam is heightened, as if he's searching for the ventriloquist behind his grandson-dummy.

"I'll have the same," Jack says. "A sandwich and tea."

"Shall I bring in a tray, or do you want to eat at the table?"

"We have work to do," Jack insists, regarding Adam for confirmation of the import of their meeting. His eyes are pitifully hopeful and sincere. "We'll eat in here so we can talk."

When she leaves the room, there is absolute silence. Adam wonders if Jack can hear his stomach turning or the noise of blood, pulsing in his ears like hoofbeats. What does his grandfather resemble? A starving man stranded on a mountain who, to his own surprise, has been found alive.

"So how've you been?" he asks casually.

"I've been fine," Adam says self-consciously. "You know. I went to college, and now I'm ready to do this last project, and the thought came to me that I'd like to know more about you." He pauses, then smiles tentatively. "So here I am." He throws his hands up in a vague gesture of surrender.

"How old were you last time?"

"Thirteen."

"That's a long time, Adam, almost half your life. Remember how your sister was so worried all week like she'd never see your parents again?"

"Katy's always worried about something."

"Where is she now?"

"She's in Athens living with a family for a year."

"That's nice," Jack says distractedly. Adam can feel him withdrawing and wonders what he's really thinking. His chest must feel tight with a blend of sadness and happiness so rich it might choke him. Two weeks ago when Adam called, Jack had said, "I never thought I'd see a soul on earth again."

"So what do you want me to do?" Jack finally asks. "Just talk myself silly and you'll listen?"

"Well, I've prepared some questions, but it's very free-form. You can begin or I can, whatever seems right."

"Adam, tell me," Jack says quietly, holding up his hand for time out, "does your dad know you're here? Not that he has to know. I mean, here you are, a man. You probably have plenty of secrets from him, but does he know about this?"

"I didn't tell him," Adam smiles bravely. He can feel his face straining to maintain this stupid, reassuring grin.

"We're both men," Jack shrugs. "What goes on between us is our business, right?"

"Whatever you want to keep confidential, you don't have to tell me. It's up to you, Grandpa, what happens in the video."

Jack's voice rises a little in annoyance. "I mean your father doesn't have to know you're here, does he? Not that he could stop us from talking like this, man to man. I'm just not sure it would be worthwhile for him to know."

"I haven't told him," Adam reassures. He won't talk about the project again until his grandfather resolves his main issue, Roy.

"All right, then," Jack says more relaxed now. "Elizabeth will bring the sandwiches, and we'll get down to business. I've been thinking a lot, Adam. What kind of grandfather do you want to remember? Because I can concentrate on lots of different aspects. I've lived a long time, almost eighty years."

"I was hoping that you'd decide, Grandpa. I don't have a particular agenda. We'll eat our sandwiches, start talking, and at some point I'll record. I can set it up so that we can talk and it'll record us. It's more intimate that way."

Jack is shaking his head. "I keep thinking of your grandma, Adam. All the gizmos she missed. Believe me, it's like science fiction. I remember getting our first radio, shaped like a fat brown toaster. And a used Victrola. And when planes in the air were so new, we'd run out on the lawn and follow them with our eyes. Joey and me would fight about who could trace them the farthest. And family movies with projectors that weighed a ton and a half and snapped the film like that." Jack snaps air between his fingers. "I have films of your dad here. Want to see them sometime?"

"Sure. I can convert them to videos for you if you'd like. Then we can watch them together on a VCR."

"But you wouldn't tell your dad you had them, would you?"

"Not unless you wanted me to, Grandpa."

Jack stares at Adam as if he's an idiot, then falls silent. Adam had better learn the rules, he thinks, waiting for Jack to speak again. He won't fill the silence with his stupid voice this time.

After what seems like an hour, Jack says, "Roy looked like you but darker. You have Susan's complexion." He pauses and takes a deep breath. "But pardon me for saying this, Adam, about your father. There was always something missing. I keep thinking of it this way. If we all lived in caves, and I'd invented fire, Roy would have said 'So what?'"

Elizabeth, who appears to be wearing his grandmother's old wristwatch, the one with jagged diamonds scattered like rock salt around the clockface, arrives with a large bamboo tray. It is stacked with thin sandwiches, a teapot, a lemon on a Thanksgiving napkin, a sugar bowl, two cups and two tea-spoons. She props it on the dresser. "Shall I give it to you, or will you just help yourselves?"

"We'll take care of it," Jack assures.

"She's a good kid," Jack says when Elizabeth leaves the room. "I think she's pretty for a big girl too," he smiles. Adam watches his grandfather pick at a sandwich, then close his eyes and fall into a light sleep. Watching his breathing, Adam wonders if the camera has already missed the most important moment of this project, the negotiations.

"Adam!" his grandfather rasps suddenly. His eyes are large and frightened.

"I'm here," Adam says from a corner. "We both nodded off. I fall asleep sometimes when I'm tense."

"You gotta stop me before I do that. Shake me. I won't break. And why would you be tense? I bet you're just tired. I bet it's a girl."

"I do have a girlfriend. Her name is Carla."

"I bet she's real nice," Jack says and then moves the program forward with a broad, impatient smile. "So let's talk."

"Do you want me to record this?"

"Isn't that why you're here, Adam? Do I look like I have time to lose on warming up? I say 'Roll the cameras,' or 'Turn on the damn switch.' Whatever."

"Okay, Grandpa. I'll set it up and we'll begin."

Adam races through the preliminaries. The camcorder, which is already trained on Jack's face, is given its directions. All the time Jack is watching him impatiently, like a man waiting for a stalled train he can see at a distance.

"We're ready," Adam smiles, and is about to give instructions when he's interrupted. Adam stares as Jack begins speaking, as if he's prepared a script.

"So I'd like to begin with myself, if I may, Jack Kaufman. Believe me, I never thought I'd live this long, but here I am, almost seventy-nine, a whole life behind me. It's packed full of events like a big suitcase, and I'm wondering if I should show you all the things I've packed or what I couldn't fit inside. By the way, I'm talking to Adam Kaufman, my only grandson, who wants to know about me because he's a hell of a lot smarter than his father and understands I have important things to tell him. How's that?" he asks, chin perched cockily in his palm.

"It sounds fine to me. You needn't talk about me at all though, Grandpa. Unless you want to."

"I just thought there should be a little introduction. Who has aimed this machine at me is something the audience should know. By the way, who is the audience?"

"Just me and my thesis advisor and the panel who will grant me my degree if I do this right."

"So this won't show at movie houses?"

Adam laughs.

"What's so funny?"

"I'm just trying to get down your story, Grandpa. I never considered movie houses."

"So what are you going to do for the rest of your life?"

"Probably make more videos, paint, I was thinking of teaching. Carla thinks we might find jobs in Prague or somewhere in Latin America . . ."

"But this particular film that I'm in, it's more personal? Between us?"

"My advisor and a few others will see it."

"But you don't care, Adam." Jack hits his forehead and makes his eyes small in concentration. "What is it I'm trying to say? You don't care what they think about me? It's you, right, who wants to know. You want to know me?"

"That's right, Grandpa."

"The rest of your life will take care of itself? You and this Carla have plans, so I don't have to worry that we're making a box office hit here? Your future doesn't depend on this because if it does, I have money. We can get actors and make a real movie."

"No," Adam chuckles. "I just want to know you better."

"So forget the actors?"

"Videos are more private. All I'm making is a video."

"Is this on the film too?"

"Whatever we say is being recorded. Whatever we do."

"You mean you're never going to turn the damn thing off?"

"I'll edit it later. I'll remove what we don't need."

"How will you decide that?"

"We can watch it, and decide together, or I can decide on my own."

Jack grunts. "It's your movie, Adam. I can't imagine why you'd want me poking around in your business."

"Well, let's continue, Grandpa. Probably we can talk for another fifty minutes before I'll need to change the cartridge."

"How many rolls do you have?"

"The supply is endless. We can talk for days or weeks."

"You don't have a job?"

"This is my job."

Jack chuckles. Then Adam watches as he turns his face toward the camera. "Okay then," Jack says with a reassured sigh, "as I was saying, my grandson asked me to make this video for him. I checked my schedule." Jack winks broadly at the camera. "Then I said okay. There won't be much action, except maybe, if I need a shot or some medicine, or if I drop dead. Mainly it'll be me, Jack Kaufman, just lying in bed talking to this boy.

"I say 'boy,' but he's already a man. He's the age I was when I served in the navy in World War ii. Back when things made sense and the world was simple. There was no trouble like now everywhere you look. And the trouble we had was big and important, so people got involved. Nobody said, 'I'm too good for trouble,' like people do today. 'Trouble's for somebody else.'

"Anyway, I've been on earth for seventy-nine years, and a lot of times the names on the marquee have changed. I remember before Adam was alive, that everything looked different in Chicago. The Prudential Building was the tallest—I had a real nice office there—some crook was mayor (that never changes), and I was a young real estate executive with a lovely wife Essie. She had big curls, and a son named Roy, who wasn't a good-for-nothing, cold-hearted bastard yet. I needed a zoning change for Lake Park Point, my first big project, and the big guys said no. I leaned a little heavier on them, and then they said yes, and the skyline changed into the postcard it is today. There's much more to that story, but I thought I'd tell the major points first and then get back to the details.

"How was it that a little boy like me with bow legs and big ears became so important? One day I'm a punk with no future and ten years later, by the time Roy is born, I own lots of things. The answer is brains, which you must have in this world. I don't care if your father is Daddy Warbucks. Without brains, you're kaput. But you also need sense. What I mean by sense is the ability to know the truth. You have to know who's leveling with you and who isn't. Then what you need is guts cause when they're lying and you know it, you have to act fast.

"Now, one day a very close friend of mine, a man I trusted, though we were different in every way, lied to me. It wasn't a little harmless, 'I-think-your-turdy-green-suit-looks-nice' kind of thing. It was big and messy and could have landed me in plenty of hot water. I found out that the fat lying bastard had tricked me, and I took care of the problem. More on that later.

"Another thing I'd like to discuss, of course, is women. My favorites have been my mother and Essie. I want to do them justice here. My little mother, who looked like a sparrow, came from Poland before they got rid of all their Jews. She landed on Hirsch Street and learned English. She was a wonderful woman because she was happy. Whatever was wrong, she never let me know. I grew up thinking she had no trouble, but now as an old man, I know she was just being kind. It's an obligation of love to hide trouble from your kids. If not, they'll resent you. One day Ma came home from the doctor real quiet. I didn't know 'til three years later when she died what was wrong. Whatever I am that's good, I owe to her. She helped me understand how important it is not to be a prick.

"How do I know that? Because when my father was a prick, which he sometimes was, she took it kindly. When I criticized Pa for going after her like he did, berating her in front of us for nothing but thin soup, she just said, 'Jackie, forget.' Just like that.

"So when I looked for a wife and found Essie, I thanked my lucky stars that I had learned not to be a prick from my father and mother in different ways. I treated Essie good. Anyone will tell you. I never raised my voice to her except about one thing. She was willing to forgive a little too much, where Roy was concerned. She'd say, 'Jack, understand,' but later, how could I?"

"What did he do?" Adam interrupts. It's hard to imagine his father doing much of anything, his father who's committed to keeping his voice low, who gives discreet economic advice to not-for-profits, his father who could be president of a small neutral nation, maybe Costa Rica.

"He did what you never do, Adam. Let me tell it this way. One day when me and Joey were little, there was a problem at home, some petty jealousy, that spilled over into school. I shouldn't have done this, but I gave Joey such a punch, the punch of his life, but only on his arm. Joey cries and tells the school on me, and I get suspended. Ma cries and Pa beats me, but no one tells Joey the lesson of the day: *Never tell stories outside the family.*

"Well, one day someone from a magazine approached your dad for a story about me. Roy's a smart man, so he knew just what he was doing. He talked way too much just to hurt me. Maybe he bore a grudge that I wasn't a model father, that I was always so busy with my work, but your dad should have known better."

"Do you have the story?"

"Do I what?" Jack asks, as if coaxed out of sleep.

"The story about you that my dad . . ."

"Of course I do. Do you think you throw away these things? It's locked in my closet with some other souvenirs. I can show you later, but Adam, it's not the story that's interesting. The story is harmless," and Jack turns back to the camera.

"Now what Roy said was harmless because I kept what was harmful from them both. Essie and Roy I kept pure. They didn't know the first thing about trouble, I was so smart about what they should know. But when your father thought he could get me, when your father did that to me, it was all over as far as I was concerned.

"My first impulse was to say nothing. What was there to say to my lousy son? But for Essie I swallowed my pride and went to see him. I told him how to act properly. I sat him down at a nice restaurant, and we—should I say I—talked for hours. I even admitted some blame for his unhappiness with me. 'Start,' I said, 'with your grandfather, my father, who humbly unpacked crates of potatoes and cabbage. His hands were crusted with dirt, but they couldn't solve the problems of the 1930s. Then there's me, a Jack-of-all-trades ('Pardon the pun,' I said, but your father didn't laugh). I was too good at things, Roy. I brought you to this state of comfort. I've ruined you by solving all your problems. I've made things so cushy that you have too much leisure. You don't use it wisely. You go talking like this two-bit journalist is Edward R. Murrow, and you have history to share.'"

"So what did Dad say?"

"He said zip. Instead of learning the lesson from me, your father took offense. He became defiant. He said he knew all along what I was, that Essie knew too. He said they protected *me* by pretending not to know. He said that Essie cried herself to sleep about me all the time. He said he didn't know how many times she was broken by me.

"'So you're not ashamed?' I finally interrupted. He stood up like a gunfighter, knocked over his drink, and stomped out. Go explain how someone who won't take blame can take offense.

"One day after many months of silence over this issue, I find Essie crying and I know it's about Roy. We don't see Roy and Susan anymore. We're not seeing our grandkids, you and Katy, who we're crazy for. So for the sake of the family, I call Roy and tell him, let's forgive and forget. I'm not a religious man, but I know that the Bible says we can forgive each other. Not even God can do that for us. We have to do it ourselves, without rabbis or Jesus or Pope Shmendrake or anyone else. I give Roy credit. I ask him to try and forgive whatever it was I did to him. I say I'll try to forgive him for squawking like a parrot.

"And Roy refuses. It's that simple, Adam, how he made the Kaufmans a broken family."

Jack takes his small face in his large bony hands, squints his eyes, and rubs his knuckles over his puffy eyelids. Adam goes behind the camcorder and watches through its lens, a guilty voyeur, as his grandfather quietly weeps.

CHAPTER NINE

"W E'RE INVITED TO JACK'S for lunch," Mr. Waters tells
Irena. When he is happy, his eyes grow squinty and
indirect and gaze lovingly beyond her shoulder. With
his contentment vague and as remote as heaven, he reminds her
not of a philosopher, but of her beloved Chopin, presented with
a plate of chicken livers fried in butter. Irena herself is not
pleased by the news. She has just placed their usual baked potatoes into the oven. It is against her nature to waste food. She
wishes that Americans were more formal about arrangements,
more like their British ancestors, who might send a calligraph-
ic announcement on creamy stationery: "Please come to tea
tomorrow at four." But a telephone summons is the favorite
social device, abrupt as the weather in the city whose skyline
lurches toward the lake. There is no sense of careful planning
anywhere. Everything—invitations, buildings, trees, conversations—are scattered like urgent news flashes. Where is the
order of it? Where are the palaces and boulevards, the stately
homes with rosebushes older than Napoleon? There was much
beauty in Warsaw, though the communists did their best to de-
emphasize it. Still, it was noticed peripherally. More than beauty, it was nostalgia. In America, where such strictures were
never attached to life, a forward gaze is warranted. Each

moment has the audacity to shout at you. Whenever time the phone rings, it commands Irena to alter her life. Be that as it may, Mr. Waters' wish is her command. They are to abandon their humble potatoes for Jack's feast. "He called while you were out, Irena," Harrison Waters adds apologetically. "He wants us to meet his grandson."

"Elizabeth tells me this grandson is making a video about Jack. He comes every day and listens forever to him. Elizabeth has nothing to do now that this boy has arrived."

"And Jack's happy as a clam. You should hear him make over this boy."

Irena imagines a clam being pleased. Is it pleased because its shell protects it from the world? How does its happiness compare to that of the lark's, she wonders. "I hear that this boy is very handsome. Perhaps, I think, that Elizabeth is finding him pleasing. She says he is small, however, like his grandfather."

What shall she wear to this luncheon with the moviemaker? Of course, her usual brown dress with the new woven belt that Elizabeth bought her last week. Perhaps her new fat gold hoop earrings and the specially-brewed lipstick from Henri Bendel, which cost $32, another gift from her American design expert, whose abrupt manners must be related to frequent use of the telephone. "You could look better," she tells Irena daily. "We have to improve you," she adds sternly, as Irena tries to look duly jaunty in her shiny accessories.

She can hear Mr. Waters' impatience. He is sitting in the front room shuffling papers because this invitation has delayed his lunch. In that one respect, Mr. Waters acts his age: he likes things to be predictable. Perhaps she should have made him a demi-meal, so his mood wouldn't darken. Her Mr. Waters will turn on the strangest music and play it as he eats his eggless eggs and his butterless buttered toast, but the preordained eggs and toast command more attention than the improvised music or the stories he occasionally tells of playing in small night clubs not far from where they now live. "But they're no longer in existence," each story ends. Eating is a retreat from the disappearing past. This would be a kinder country if buildings endured, if old men could walk down a street and find their memories intact. Maybe senility is architecturally induced.

Irena throws her skirt and sweater onto the bed, slips the familiar dress over her head, latches the finely woven belt with the beautiful buckle shaped like a conch shell, puts on her earrings, which feel smooth and cold, and grabs the lipstick, which she gently applies to her thin lips. The light orange shade, more of a melon really, is very flattering, she admits to herself, as she takes Mr. Waters' arm and leaves the apartment with him.

"But the potatoes," she suddenly frowns after he's closed the door.

"I turned them off already, Irena. You can mash them later."

She smiles at the joke he makes at the expense of his routine of baked at lunch and mashed for dinner. Perhaps a jazz legend should be more experimental with his food, she thinks, as the musical elevator ascends to Jack's apartment.

The grandson is young and frightfully thin. He looks as if he needs feeding. When he stands in profile, he hardly possesses a body. The way his bony, black-clad back arches reminds her of a cat's. His face, however, is very good, with an intelligent brow, high cheekbones and deep blue, sunken eyes, like his grandfather's. His mouth is pretty and full, and his fine blond hair is worn long on one side, as is the fashion with the young men she sees on the street. Men are very showy, particularly young intellectuals, who strut like peacocks, exhibiting their disdain for conventional dress.

"Adam," Jack says from his outpost on the couch, "I want you to meet Harrison Waters, a fine musician, and his assistant, Irena."

"Pleased to meet you." Adam smiles shyly in their direction. He is not of the generation that casually extends a hand in greeting. Nor is he a kisser or hugger, a trait Irena associates pleasantly with Europeans and unpleasantly with movie directors. In fact, he appears so shy that Irena is reminded of a child made uncomfortable by adult attention. In that way, he is like her Joszef, who always found casual mixing as painful as surgery. In a roomful of strangers, Joszef would find a wall. Will this Adam pander to the crowd or make a Joszefian retreat? Choosing neither option, he stands among them silently as he is discussed.

"He's been here two days now," Jack nods. "He'll take off on my chemo days, but picture this. Adam's idea is to put that in the film too. Then the world can see the amazing chemical man."

"But where's Elizabeth?" Irena asks, imagining the gory details she would add to this intimate discussion of Jack's blood chemistry. Jack wouldn't believe what Elizabeth reveals when she dines with Irena and discusses Jack's organs like specimens in a horrific museum.

"She ran out for a few last-minute details. You know how she is. Very casual. She'll be back soon." When silence becomes the dominant theme, Jack turns to Irena, and as intimately as one can talk in public, asks her to reveal a secret: "Maybe you can tell me," Jack says quietly, "if Elizabeth needs anything. I'd like to give her what she needs."

"I think she is happy and satisfied with you," Irena says so as not to embarrass Mr. Waters, who, after all, can't provide whatever Irena might foolishly have on her mind or imagine Elizabeth to want. Furs, jewelry, vacations, endless fancy lunches, no bitter season of winter, someone handsome to love, Irena thinks to herself on Elizabeth's behalf. For herself, peace and quiet and a chance to work with her beloved numbers in a beautiful dark university library with oak tables and marble floors. Quiet so pristine that her breathing would be an interruption.

The conversation remains open to this page while Jack prods for more. "I mean, what does she tell you? Is she happy?" The question brings an embarrassingly lurid smile to Irena's face, but before she can utter a single censored word, there is Elizabeth, tall and ruddy from the wind, holding two shopping bags loaded with what will be their lunch.

She says a peremptory hello and commands Irena to come into the kitchen.

"Please excuse me." Irena follows her friend.

"Give me a hand," Elizabeth says as she removes her coat. "He tells me half an hour ago that we're having a party." She tosses it over a chair, and pulls some trays out of a low kitchen drawer. Old men's kitchens are so pathetic by European standards. Where are the cherished antique bowls imported from France in better times, the polished samovar, the dainty dessert plates of creamy porcelain smeared with flowers, which, on closer inspection, are a fretwork of cracks? Neither man has bought a pot or dish since he lost his wife. The avocado and orange stripes, the full ceramic moons and smiling, voluptuous suns testify to time stopping somewhere in the 1970s. Elizabeth covers the rather terrible plates with large leaves of romaine. Then she curls turkey and rare roast beef onto the greenery, erects a fence of palm hearts topped with olives, and fills two large mixing bowls with colorful salads. "We're celebrating today," she says, eyeing the festive plates.

"What is the reason?" Irena asks.

"Jack has nothing to say, but he doesn't want Adam to leave," she whispers. Then she smiles. "It's a holiday when Jack has nothing to say."

"I have always known him to be full of ideas. A very lively man. I hope he is not ill."

"Ill?" Elizabeth says puzzled. "He's dying."

"I am aware, but I hope he is not feeling poorly."

"I think he's gathering strength. He told me he's about to tell all the exciting stuff and needs some energy. Like an athlete before a big meet. This is his power lunch."

"I can understand. But is the grandson working him too hard?"

"Too hard? The grandson is putty in his hands, Irena. He's not half the man his grandfather is. I haven't described Jack very well if you can ask me that. Before you came, before Jack was terribly sick, he could go half the night. Sometimes he wore me out. Like a fireman. Always ready," she laughs.

"Now Adam? Whatever Jack tells him, he runs like a rabbit." She makes a clucking noise in her throat and adds, "I'm hardly needed anymore."

"You are feeling lonely?" Irena asks.

"Silly, isn't it?"

They have laid the bread in a silver woven basket, placed mayonnaise and horseradish on small holiday dishes overwhelmed by poinsettia leaves, and arranged a plate of bakery cookies, each sinfully coated with hazelnuts and dark chocolate, onto a wooden tray. Irena carries out the beverages, cans of soda in different primary colors, and they all take their places before the colorful array. Irena watches Adam support his grandfather as he makes his way to his seat with huge effort, disguised by brave banter. His constant patter is a diversion from the pain every movement must cause him.

"Can I get anything else?" Elizabeth asks.

"What more could we want?" Harrison Waters asks, and then they all dig in. When each diner has made his choice, conversation may resume. The importance of eating can't be overemphasized, however. Perhaps food asylum should be a new category on immigration forms. People kill for land, for money, out of jealousy. Why not consider the proper role of food in people's discontented wanderings on earth? For isn't the earth a giant buffet table and history a series of ever more splendid banquets? Man the gatherer gave way to man the hunter and cultivator of soil. Man the consumer of specialty shop delicacies demands that his plate be filled and has very little to say to his fellow man until it is. She watches Harrison Waters slice his turkey into a patchwork of bite-sized pieces. She observes Jack taking heaping servings and wonders where he possibly stores them.

"So," Jack says, exhaling when his plate is duly crammed, "Irena here is from Poland, Adam."

Adam smiles at her. "I have a friend at the Art Institute who taught film in Poland. Maybe you know him."

"I do not know many filmmakers, but, yes, many of us have left the country for many reasons."

"His name is Tadeusz."

"That is good Polish name."

"His wife is Syrenka."

"She is beautiful legendary mermaid, founder of Warsaw, who is a statue. She is very famous in Poland. Do people here know her?"

"Sy—who?" Jacks asks, and everyone laughs.

"Irena was a mathematician, Adam, before she became my bodyguard," Harrison Waters smiles. "I bet the night we went gambling Irena could have helped us in that respect."

"This is true," Irena says, "but you did not ask about probability, which shows how easily you would be defeated. You didn't want to know exactly."

Both men laugh heartily.

"What is this about gambling?" Adam asks.

"Your grandfather took us out on the town," Elizabeth explains. "We ate lobster at the Pump Room and then drove out to Joliet to a gambling boat."

"We got creamed," Jack smiles sweetly. "Remember Julius?"

"Your chauffeur?"

"We got him to take us, and we had the time of our life."

"We painted town," Irena smiles.

"I remember when Julius was a youthful seventy-five. How old is he now?"

"About ninety. A long life runs in his family. Julius was visiting his mother well into her nineties, and when he was running numbers not so long ago, she was one of his best customers. She knew how to enjoy herself. I wish my mother could have lived long like that."

"How do you like Irena today?" Elizabeth asks, glowing in her friend's direction.

"I like Irena every day," Jack smiles.

"No, I mean her hair. It's different. Look. And her earrings and her lipstick. I took her Monday to Vidal Sassoon and Henri Bendel."

"She looks terrific," Adam says, "but I've never seen her before."

"Like a Polish mermaid," Jack adds.

"Thank you, everyone," Irena says shyly. "I did not know that I was chief exhibit at lunch, but thank you still."

From the bedroom comes a large, ruddy-faced man carrying the supply of chemicals that must be administered to Jack each week.

"You must sign," he tells Elizabeth. His manner is direct but his speech is slow and labored. Irena recognizes kinship in his high cheekbones and pale eyes, in his embarrassment as he waits for his signature, in his tortured English. Discomfort is a ready bond, a lasso. Irena tightens the rope in her hand.

What is your name, she asks him in Polish. Her cheeks take on color; she is feeling intensely embarrassed and exhilarated at the same time.

He smiles shyly and tells her that his name is *lummox,* carrier of goods to foolish Americans. Catching her eye as her lasso spins deftly over his broad chest and snares him, he adds that he's Cristof from Krakow.

While the others wait for an explanation, the linguistic co-conspirators share amusement as delicious as anything on the table. Both have probably hoped each day for such a moment to arise as spontaneously as a well-contained fire, though Irena hasn't recognized this as her hope until now.

We must talk, Cristof says softly before he smiles at Irena and carries the finished bottles of supplies out of the apartment.

For a long time after lunch, Irena wonders about the meaning of their shared look. She didn't know until that moment that a glance could interest her in America. Usually she can cause pain real as a toothache by recalling Joszef's mottled flesh against her own and then imagining him at present, cavalierly eyeing his classroom of bright math students, young women with good brains and very nice legs. But now, in the midst of a meaningless conversation, she has shared such a look with a delivery man, Cristof, and words that connected them even as clouds are connected in the air. Human beings are amazing, so full of mixed motives and feelings, as messy as a full plate of American lunch. She thinks of two warm bodies in bed, the long and short story of human passion. The amazing variations on the two particular bodies: Jack clinging to Elizabeth for life. Her body and Joszef's under their familiar comforter, the careful knowledge of thigh and breast and neck and armpit, the algebra of coupling. Fingernails, collarbones, waists, the mound of flesh under the mound of fur.

Is it simply that Cristof is a fellow tourist in her usual country of old men? Or is there something about his eyes that indicate sympathy and generosity? Surely his kind gaze, hesitating on Irena for only a second, is the first gift that has really mattered in Chicago.

*   *   *

They decide to meet at the Lincoln Park Zoo, which neither has visited. But Cristof has connections. There is a Hungarian, Laszlo, who is a zookeeper, and can get them behind the scenes. Has Irena ever seen big cats up close?

It thrills Irena that the jaguar, the tiger, the indolent angular lion, which they view in turn, are versions of Chopin from the undomesticated past. It saddens her that the black leopard ("That's what panthers are," Cristof's stocky, owl-eyed friend explains) was once the loved housepet of a rich woman from New Orleans, who tired of her toy. Now the poor animal is confused. Unlike the others, who offer occasional meaning-filled snarls like rumors of war, the leopard reaches her paw out towards them and requests to be touched. Stretching out on her back, she makes her eyes into small cajoling slits.

"But she is wanting affection," Irena tells the two.

"We are not allowed to touch her," Laszlo sadly confirms. "She must grow used to us in this way. It would be cruel to confuse her further."

"Let's go," Irena suggests softly. Cristof, a diffident companion thus far, bids a rousing farewell to Laszlo. They exchange information in a language Irena doesn't understand—Hungarian—which sounds coarsely improvised and full of perhaps unintended sarcasm.

Outside, sulking over the fate of the leopard, Irena takes in deep gulps of chilly air. The season has changed in a day. Even the sky has been washed a menacing gray that prophesies winter. "That animal has made me so sad," she confesses, pressing her body towards Cristof's vast shoulder.

Locking his arm in hers and patting the bare skin of her chilly hand, Cristof laughs nervously. "It is dangerous to care too much," he admits with a concerned smile. "We mustn't do that."

At tea in the Brauer Cafe, they ignore Cristof's good advice regarding indifference by composing endless lists of grievances. Cristof's complaints concern his jobs, thus far menial, and his lack of dreams. "I never dream in America," he laments. "In Poland, my dreams were like operas: full of scenery, language, and beautiful strangers."

"You do not sleep well?"

"I sleep like a bear," he laughs. "I am a laborer. Laborers don't have the leisure to sleep otherwise. In Krakow when I was a draftsman, my dreams were as vivid as your face."

"Perhaps laborers do not dream," Irena replies. "But my dreams are solid and very satisfying. Better than my life here—and often in Polish."

"No doubt my dreams, if I were to dream, would be in Polish too. Toilet paper," Cristof smiles, "is very fine here. Like cloth. And the phones too are dependable, if there should be someone to call."

"And why did you leave?" Irena ventures, stirring her tea absently and regarding the door, where a raucous family has entered. Families are lucky, so full of life that they can dispense with silence.

"I wanted more."

"And what did you want?"

"I wanted to see if I was right in thinking I hadn't enough."

"And were you?"

"Irena, you strike at the heart. Who can answer such a question? Who can know until too long from now to remember I'd been asked?"

"I sometimes think, Cristof, that I will open my eyes and be in Warsaw again."

"And would you be pleased at such a sight?"

"Amazed, of course, but not pleased. Who wishes to return to the past? What do they say? *We have burned our bridges.*"

He lights a cigarette, offers one to Irena, which she accepts, and they smoke heartily.

"Only immigrants smoke," he smiles.

"And teenagers."

"And spies."

"And which are you?" Irena asks brightly.

"I was sent as a spy to learn your attitudes on large cats, on captive animals, on dreams, and on cigarettes. And now that I know these things, would you like to see my apartment, Irena?"

"I must get back, Cristof. My Harrison expects his meals on time. That is one requirement. Perhaps another time."

"Perhaps is an unfortunate word. It reminds me of my dreams."

"But soon you will dream, Cristof, and I will see your apartment."

"Would you consent to setting a date for our next amusement?"

"Next Saturday? I can give Mr. Waters his dinner and see you then. He has no requirements beyond that."

"And would you like to dine prior to that visit?"

"I would certainly love to," Irena smiles into Cristof's broad, happy face.

CHAPTER TEN

RAYSTONE, INC., had always reminded Adam of a futuristic back lot, with its black reflective surfaces and affectless exterior. An unearthly wind could have blown through the halls, moon dust appeared on the bathroom fixtures, or Antonioni appeared to direct the scenes of his childhood without surprising Adam. Visiting his father at work, Adam would sit behind the empty marble console in the entrance hall, pressing intercom buttons and pretending he was in command. Riding the elevator to three, he'd spin the plot for his adventure, then race down the corridor toward his father's inner sanctum. As associates met with Roy (named after Roy Rogers, the nice American cowboy who Essie liked so much) to discuss fund-raising, Adam would pretend that space aliens were chasing him with guns that had the capacity to destroy all life on the planet. Did anyone mind that he was enacting his fantasies outside the meeting rooms where not-for-profits brought their million-dollar challenges? Did the Heart and Lung Association representative notice a little boy lurking in the hallway making laser gun sounds?

In the halls of Graystone, while his mother ran "important errands" and a constant flow of summer helpers flew back to Europe, Adam had simply raised himself. He thought of an account he'd read once of art critic John Ruskin's childhood spent staring at floor tiles. Through trial and error and good instincts, Adam had become a man, as distant from his father as Roy was from Jack. Maybe this was instinctual too, the tendency of the Kaufman men to pull away from each other, the opposite of magnets. From Jack's father, who had left his own father in Poland—to Jack, caring for his father in a generous but impersonal manner—Adam saw no place a branch for intimacy had sprouted on the family tree.

Before he'd reach his father's suite at the end of the corridor, he'd always check his mother's "office" to see if she was in. Usually, she was seeing her psychiatrist or hunting for the perfect African mask to add to her growing collection. Sometimes Adam stopped to play with Katy on the floor, where she sat like a little Buddha amidst her recorded story tapes, coloring pads, and rainbow markers.

If Roy's business had been less abstract, Adam and Katy might have been trained to comprehend it. But what was it Roy actually did? Add up columns of numbers, identify donors and patrons, think of ways to make the 49th annual cruise better than the 48th? Consulting didn't seem like a business in the way Alex's father had a paint and wallpaper store or Jason's father a musical instrument warehouse.

What was it that Roy produced, Jack demanded of Adam, waving a tasteful Graystone brochure in his face. A comment worthy of Karl Marx, Adam thought, of Jack's attempt to disqualify Roy from capitalism's rough scheme. "People listen to Roy about money?" he snorted. "Who set him up for life?"

"You, Grandpa?" Adam asked meekly.

"Damn straight," Jack winked, before signalling for Adam to turn on what he called "the machine." Smoothing his robe, slicking back his hair with a deft wave of the palm, Jack, never weary of revelation, began another day of talking.

"So I'm about to tell the truth, Adam, the whole truth and nothing but the truth. So help me whoever. Fasten your seatbelts. Check the exits. Look out, everyone. Get the children out of the room. Some of this may not be proper viewing for kids under fifty, but it's my life, the life of Jack Kaufman.

"I was born during World War 1, but it wasn't World War 1 in my house or for anyone I knew. In Europe, which Ma and Pa had left in 1914, it was World War 1, and for some American GIs. But for us at home, it was the everyday business of good people, unimportant people, living a life. It went on like that day after day. Breakfast, lunch, dinner. Soup with chicken feet and tough dark heels of bread. An orange now and then and baths on Sundays in water Ma heated on the stove in an iron pot. A postcard photo from a studio to send to the relatives at home. I'm wearing a little dress and sitting on a furry rug next to a potted palm. Songs sung in a language I didn't really know because at home Ma and Pa spoke Yiddish, a sweet and heavy language almost extinct today. I learned English in school, Adam, like the Mexican kids do. I can remember singing Christmas carols in my class and feeling relieved that I was like everyone else now.

"At home there was me, Pa, Ma, and Joey. God, Pa was a homely guy. A small man with big hands and feet, hands the size of clubs, squared-off fingernails as big as the top of my whole thumb. But how he worked. In the morning he'd leave before four to go to the produce market with Mr. Bruno. He was Mr. Bruno's beast of burden. The old man would point, and Pa would lift sacks of potatoes that weighed a ton and apples and cabbages onto the wagon. Imagine that. In Chicago, a wagon with a horse. And when me and Joey were good, Pa would take us to work and let us sit on the horse's big brown back like real Americans did in the Western serials I watched for a nickel. We just sat there. Maybe we said 'Giddy up!' now and then and gave a kick, but the horse knew the plan was to go nowhere. He was the best thing about Pa's job. The worst was everything else. Pa was tired all the time, a worn out man by fifty when he got into bed and barely moved again for twenty years. Maybe it was because Ma died, but I don't really know. People didn't talk things over like we do now, Adam. People didn't ask the experts. There wasn't even Ann Landers or her sister what's-her-name to write, for Heaven's sake. 'Pa's in bed,' Joey would say to me. 'Still?' I'd answer. 'Yeah,' and that was that.

"Ma, of course, stayed home. She cooked and sewed, and it was important work. She made us clothes from scratch from lousy ragman's cloth, but by the time she finished we could be proud of how smart she was. Sometimes I'd sit and watch the treadle on her sewing machine and listen to it hum. She used her teeth to cut the thread, and there was always a pile of work waiting on the floor. She was the official seamstress for the entire block. One summer everyone was getting married. Ugly girls and pretty girls, even some pregnant girls blooming in plain sight. Mothers of brides were lined up in our little dining room the size of a shoebox. And did Ma make dresses, all colors of the rainbow out of shiny cloth that people got at the big stores downtown. Cloth and lace and ribbons everywhere. Joey liked to touch everything, so Ma was always saying, 'Joey, wash your hands.' It was a joke between them that 'Joey-wash-your-hands,' was his full name, like an Indian name.

"Sometimes our clothes looked so nice that other kids called us Jew sissies. That's how good Ma was at it. And that's also a lesson for you, Adam. When people insult you, never mind. When they call you names, forget it. They're jealous, that's all. They want you to lie in the dirt with them. They want you to be ashamed like they are. Well, fuck 'em. I understood that real early. Whether it was a kid or a teacher or a cop, they had nothing to say to me unless I wanted to hear it. I guess you can call me arrogant, but I see it differently. A man is what he is. If someone else doesn't like it, so be it. Amen.

"So I grew up in a good house. Not that we had lots of things, but there was a sidewalk in front and kids around all the time. I had a ball and a stick, and there was Humboldt Park with plenty of places I could wander. There were hills I could climb in this flat city and places I could stand, where I saw nothing taller than a tree. And standing on a green hill, I was as tall as anything around me. There were hardly any big buildings yet. Nothing taller than three-floor walkups around for the most part. And there was no skyline in the sense we say today, so the skyline was the sky. Period. I'd sing and shout and no one could stop me. I think we felt freer than kids today. I could go anywhere, Adam. I'd ride a trolley car down to the beach, which was clean as anything, and jump into the lake off the rocks, in places I shouldn't have been. I'd try to swim to Michigan, and no one batted an eye. I could sleep all night in the park or just lie in the sand without a damn interruption until the fat sun sat on the water at 6:00 A.M. I bet you can't imagine Chicago like that, but it was a big open place full of parks and sun. People didn't bother you, and summer lasted forever. Nobody went to camp. What was camp, we'd have asked. We found our own fun wherever.

"Joey and me played all day. Sometimes when the weather got nice early, you know, those few beautiful days in April that feel like June already, we took off from school. We rode trolley cars all over the place or just spent a day skipping stones. We'd watch them send out circles as they sunk into the lake, which was shimmery and full of winter cold. I'd stand in Joey's shadow or he'd stand in mine, big as a giant. And we were full of it too.

"Sometimes when we were too much for Ma and Pa, Pa took a hand to us, more of a club than a hand. He'd whack us good, and no one cried foul. Then he'd hug us and kiss us and pull on our ears. We all understood what this meant. And if he wanted to, he'd take off his belt and teach us a thing, but that only happened a few times. Once Joey took a kid's school bag and sailed it into a tree, where it stuck. Pa came home from work and heard about it, and we both had hell to pay. It wasn't any good telling Pa I wasn't around when it happened because Pa always thought I was responsible for Joey, and after awhile I started agreeing. I didn't behave so hot, but I made Joey toe the line. I made him into a citizen and the man he is. And Joey's smart. He appreciates what he owes me in that regard. So in a sense, I was already a dad to Joey before Roy.

"With Ma it was another story. I was her first boy. She almost died on the boat in crummy steerage without any light on her face for weeks. She had me about the minute they landed in America. I had rolled in her belly in the belly of the ship, and this had made me special to her. She used to tell me how she had talked and sang to me all the way from Poland and kept me alive inside her that way, the skinny little thing she was. There were no books on how to do this then. She just knew. She loved Pa and she loved Joey, but Jack was the one for her. Sometimes I think Ma wouldn't have minded if the other two disappeared forever. Pa was always schrying about something being too hot or too cold. And Joey could be a whiner. When they were out of the house, I was happy with Ma, and she was happy with me. We could do no wrong with each other. It's like we were in love as long as she was alive. She'd slip me extra pennies and little gifts, and I'd always run home to see her. Sometimes I'd pretend that I'd forgotten something, and dash up all the stairs to our apartment just to take another look. By age ten I was a big as she was. I'd pick her up for fun. And boy did I miss her when she passed. I stopped being a good boy then.

"I could describe the funeral, but I hardly remember it. I could tell you everything up till then about Ma getting sick and just fading away, but that part has become a blank. I have it in my head like a movie but without the proper words. There are no proper words for this. One minute she was happy sewing. Later we lost her. They didn't have tubes and radioactive chemicals then. You got sick and you died. Like in those paintings by Goya, right, Adam? I bet you didn't know I know about art, but I do. Someday we'll discuss that, but right now I want to tell you how Ma's death affected me, how I became a man.

"For one thing, I was lucky when Ma died that I already had Essie. I cried on her shoulder, and she let me. I told her stuff I couldn't tell anyone. Men aren't different now, more sensitive. People have always talked to each other in this private way I can't describe. When you describe it, it sounds so dead. 'Essie,

I love you. Essie this. Essie that.' 'I know, Jack. Come here. I know.' Good luck making that sound lively. Essie knew I was sad, so she made me happy in many ways. It's not proper for me to tell you certain things about your own grandmother, but I'll just say we loved each other like crazy. A good way to feel better after Ma passed and the apartment was empty and cold was to let Essie in. She came over all the time, a girl of sixteen, to help three sad sacks fumbling around like we're blind. She brought hot food her mother had cooked to the three homely orphans. And she loved me. She'd do anything for me, and I was the same for her.

"So after Ma died, there was a season of love. All my grief poured into Essie. It was the Depression and kids found their own fun that way. There wasn't this and that dance for teenagers like Roy had and cars available all the time, so we screwed everywhere. All the places I told you about with me and Joey? I bet we screwed in every one of them, including the water at the lake and the place our shadows stood on the beach. Our favorite location was the Humboldt Park Boathouse. It was like screwing on vacation in Spain or some-where fancy to look up through the leaves of the elm trees into the sky, which was bluer then. I'm not kidding you. Before all the poisons, it was blue as heaven up there. It was better than a bed with mirrors to see that blue. And how the clouds moved then, like nobody's business. Like they were rushing somewhere important.

"But people were careful. We never had to get rid of any-thing. If we had needed to, there would have been ways. The lady downstairs knew a lady on the next block who knew a lady. It was like that back then. One of Essie's sisters once needed to see this woman, an old Bubbi from Poland with no teeth and no English and capable hands, and we helped her out, but that's another story.

"The story I want to tell you is how I got started in business around the time that Ma died. Because of the Depression, the smart boys like me weren't going to college. Oh, some of us went to the junior college at Crane for awhile, but there was money to be made, and I figured things out fast. Pa wasn't going to change our life. He wasn't even going to get out of bed to change his smelly sheets. You could say it was a priority of his not to lift a finger after Ma passed. 'So what,' he thought, 'do me something for closing my eyes for twenty years of rest,' and with Ma gone, I didn't blame him. So first I thought this: Who is the worst guy I know? Who could I maybe trust to strangle me if I had something he needed real bad? Who would do something mean, not for a stupid but for a good reason?

"The answer was Arny Sloan. A big galoot. Strong as an ox. Summers he worked as a lifeguard at North Avenue Beach. You should have seen the girls circle around him like he was giving away money. And he'd pose like a pinup for them and make a serious muscle and show them his sweet dimpled face. But when it came to business, he was dedicated as he was on the wrestling team at school. He wasn't a palooka. You could talk to Arny about things, and he understood just fine. His face might have been kind of doughy, but you could see in his eyes that he had a good head.

"So I start hanging around Arny Sloan when I'm not with Essie. I heard that he knew a few people. How did I know that? I knew that like I knew the abortion lady's location. I knew that like I knew where to get laid for a dollar. I knew that like I knew my own name. I was born knowing everything I needed to know. In the dark inside my mother, I knew to wait 'til we got to America, land of opportunity, to come out. I knew not to be born early and maybe die in steerage somewhere near Greenland. There wasn't a thing I needed to learn from anyone because my instincts are good, Adam. They're first class. I'm like a force of nature when it comes to knowing what I need. Pa was lying in bed, Joey was still a kid, and we needed to change our lives. If we relied on Pa, we wouldn't have enough to eat by the end of the month. If we relied on me, we might wind up with a nice apartment on Logan Boulevard, which looked like Paris then.

"So I stopped going to high school before the end of my junior year, I stopped goofing around with my friends, I stopped being a clown, but I have to indulge a youthful laugh for a minute. One of my last memories of school is of James Norcutt, a big pimply Irish kid, hanging a teacher out of a window by his heels. Hell, we were men at sixteen, seventeen; and this little shit history teacher a hundred years old is calling us names. I don't know what he expected when he called Norcutt, who wasn't afraid of his own mother, a Mick. It's a warm day in late April, and Norcutt walks nonchalantly toward this mean little guy with too many yellow teeth, and drags him to the window by his collar. We're all speechless. I can still remember the sound of his heels grazing the wooden floor.

"Then Norcutt, whose arms are like heavy machinery, picks him up and throws him over a shoulder like a fireman carries a lady out of a smoky building. Maybe Mr. Douglas has fainted. Anyway, he's silent, and he's shedding too. His glasses fall off. Pencils and chalk and change roll out of his pockets. *Plink plink plink.* He's like a sawdust dummy all of a sudden. And Norcutt has a plan. That's what distinguishes people like Norcutt and me. Once we have a plan, no matter how stupid it appears, nothing can stop us. And guess what? It usually isn't stupid after you see its results. It was one of the smartest things ever for morale at that school that Mr. Douglas, who called us Micks and Jews and Wops and Krauts all day, got to enjoy the weather that morning. We all went over to the window and watched as his carcass swung slowly. A few of us, me included, wondered if Norcutt would be crazy enough to just let him go from three floors up. Good-bye, you mean horse's ass. But the fun ended somehow, and Douglas was improved by getting aired out. In fact, he retired that summer. I'm very fond of that moment, Adam. I remember it when I need courage. It was the right thing to do, that was for sure.

"So I stopped going to school around then, and Arny began taking me around, introducing me to people. Now let me tell you, there were all sorts of people just waiting to be met. Many, because of the Depression, had nothing to do. Today we'd call them underemployed. Just a few streets away, there lived some-one who'd have been a CEO today, a powerful man, but in the Depression Abe Bushwitz had to do all he could to stay afloat, though he was like someone who'd come over on the fucking Mayflower to the rest of us. His father made it here a good twenty years before our families had the sense to get out of Europe, where everyone and his brother hated Jews. He worked for the city in some minor way and then sent for Abe and his ma and sister a little later. Abe had things, a car and patent shoes and women, not girls but women, around all the time. He was maybe three, four years older, but already Abe was a man of the world. Word was out that he was recruiting smart Jewish boys like me and Arny to help him in business. He had his own enterprise zone near the school, where he ran what would now be called a conglomerate. Today maybe he'd be in food supplies and theater concessions and waste disposal and casinos, but then it was a bookie joint and numbers and liquor and protection. He needed some reliable kids to fran-chise his services, and that's how I started my career.

"I can still remember my interview. He looked me over head to toe, asked me a few questions to test my command of the language, and sent me on my first assignment. A guy comes out of Abe's dining room with a pretty dead-looking wreath and tells me to deliver it to the funeral home on Milwaukee Avenue. Who'd pay for this thing, I wonder. And like Abe's reading my mind he says, 'And be sure to collect,' before I go out the door. They're not going to be happy with this piece of work, I think, as I march down Milwaukee Avenue on a sunny day in May, my arms loaded with wilted flowers. I try to fluff up the bow and hold the flowers away from the sun to avoid further damage.

"When I get there, I have my first lesson. I've prepared an apology about the flowers, if necessary. I'm making speeches in my head about the quality of this product when a big Italian lets me in. He shows me into a room off to the side, like a storage room with chairs, where I sit with the flowers on my lap, thinking about who's died and will be dishonored by this display. Maybe a woman like Ma, who's left a family without a center. Maybe some kids are crying their eyes out just a few blocks away, and now they're going to get this crummy wreath. But when another man enters the room, he doesn't take the flowers from me. Instead, he gives me a big cloth envelope. He says nothing and offers no explanation. I sit there puzzled for a few minutes wondering when he's going to return for the wreath. What does this wreath cost? I have no bill to present and not a fucking idea in my head. 'Dummy,' I call myself. 'I'm going to fuck this up yet.'

"I wander outside into a hall that, believe me, no mourner ever sees. It's stuffed with furniture and dusty boxes and looks like it existed before the dawn of civilization. I find another door and knock. Someone mutters something, and I open it. I enter a narrow room packed with men of all kinds. I see old men and young ones and cigars and smoke and phones phones phones. The place is stuffed with phones ringing off the hook so loud it could drive you crazy. And all the men are talking at once and shouting to each other and writing things down. Have you ever seen pictures of the commodities exchange, Adam? Well, it resembles that mayhem in this bookie joint in the funeral home. Maybe outside there's a funeral going on with real solemnity. Maybe there'll be a wake tonight for Norcutt's poor mother or someone like her, but back here, where nobody would ever think to look, there's a major fucking enterprise.

"'Get the hell out of here,' one of them says as I stand there slackjawed. 'Take that to Abe,' he says, pointing to the envelope.

"'What about this?' I ask of the wreath, and no one replies.

"'He told me to get paid,' I say to no one in particular, in my voice small as spit.

"Finally, two older guys exchange glances. One with a moustache breaks into a big smile, and says, 'Okay, kid, bring me the wreath.' When I hand it to him, he tosses it like a hat across the room and it lands in a heap. Then he throws me a quarter, which was about two dollars then.

"'Here's your tip,' he says. 'Now get lost.'

"All the way back to Abe's I'm puzzled. I don't know if I've been to a funeral home or not. I don't know if I've been paid in the way Abe meant. I don't know what's inside the envelope, but I guess it's something having to do with bets. I don't dare look, I think. Or do I? Or do I? Or do I? I keep asking myself like a taunt. I dash into an alley behind a store, a kind of dead end alley that no one would notice. I stand between two big garbage cans like I'm taking a leak and don't want anyone to notice, I take a deep breath, unbuckle the envelope, and look inside. I see now what I'm carrying, lots of money. Tens and twenties all wadded separately. Maybe a few thousand dollars. More money than Pa ever saw in his life or Ma ever imagined. I feel hot, Adam. It's May, but I feel like it's August 15th. I lean against the cold metal garbage can and think, Shit, wait a minute. I'm a sitting duck. I open my vest and unbutton my shirt and stuff the envelope inside me and button everything back up again real fast.

"When I get to Abe's, it's like he's waiting for me at the door. Pretty casual, but you can tell that he's checking me out. Was I curious? Am I smart? He isn't angry that I realized what I was carrying. When I remove it from my shirt and give it to him, he takes my cheek and pinches it hard. 'Good,' he says. 'But where are the flowers?'

"'I left them there,' I say, realizing the problem.

"'When you come tomorrow at six, bring a new wreath,' he says and hands me ten dollars.

"I'm standing there with the ten and wondering again what wreaths cost. And I'm kicking myself for screwing up. Like Bushwitz can see me thinking, he says 'The wreath will cost you two or three, depending on how you want it to look. The rest is yours.' So I'm smiling and thinking about the quarter in my pocket, how I thought this was a good job when that smart-ass at the bookie joint threw me the quarter, that's how low my standards were.

"'Thank you,' I tell Bushwitz, who isn't much for emotion.

"He tosses me this 'Get lost already' look, and I'm out the door. Whistling.

"Now mind you. I'm tempted to stop and buy something real good to eat or get Joey a little something since he was so lost after Ma passed. But I don't. I walk into my bedroom and put all but the quarter into a sock, and I put the sock in a drawer behind lots of messy things I own. I lie on my bed and that August 15th feeling comes over me again. I'm sweating like crazy because I'm going to be a rich man.

"And for the first time since Ma passed, I close my eyes and feel peaceful because I have some good news to report to her. This makes me realize what's been wrong all these months. Since Ma died, I've been sleeping real rotten. Up every ten minutes shot through with adrenaline because I've been afraid to sleep, my heart pounding like nobody's business. I've been ashamed to see Ma and tell her how things are going, so I've been avoiding her. But you know what? From then on I dreamed of her almost every night.

"My life with Bushwitz continued this way. I got a little smarter, and he trusted me more. I was promoted from messenger boy to driver. That's how you learned to drive in those days. Somebody said 'Drive!' and you did. No licenses and tests. Nobody checking your eyesight or medications. Because of my size, Abe kept me away from the seamier side of things, which was lucky because I learned to work with my head, not my hands. So for awhile I was Abe's chauffeur, like Julius was for me later. Abe could trust me to be there when he needed me and to see nothing but the road. I would take Abe around town doing this or that. We'd stop and drink phosphates and bring whitefish wrapped in paper to his dumpy little mother on Fridays, and we'd go shopping for clothes at the big fancy stores downtown, where there were hundreds of suits all hanging together like a beautiful army regiment. I couldn't believe my eyes seeing all those suits, Adam. Every guy in Chicago could have walked in there and chosen one. Abe was a real dresser, and he wanted his chauffeur to look a little more spiffy. I started bringing home clothes that would have made Ma's eyes bug out. I can remember my first pants with a zipper, a real hazard for the uninitiated, and a shiny vest made out of satin with a pocket for a watch. Years later after Pa died, I finally started using his from Europe, but that vest was a little snug by then. How big was I at seventeen? Big as a minute. Meanwhile, where was I going to wear that gaudy thing? Driving Abe's car, if he wanted me to, and that's about it.

"Sometimes, when Abe was going to see clients, I would sit outside for maybe two or three hours, and a few times we had to drive pretty fast leaving a place. Pretty often he got rid of cars, so I never grew too fond of any particular one, though Packards were beautiful and big as yachts with the runners and chrome that reflected the whole world. Everything, I figured, was temporary anyway, so why get attached? Abe kept a vehicle for no more than a few months for safety reasons. Now and then he'd hand me a new set of keys and without a question, we'd be off. I can remember a lemon he once bought, though. I think I drove it for five or six days max. It made funny clinking noises and belched and grunted like a pig. Who could rely on the piece of shit? Boy, did that greasy little bastard who sold it to Abe hear about that mistake. One man like Abe could put you out of business in a week, maybe two.

"If you can believe it, Adam, I owned my own six-flat before I owned a car. Pa was still in bed when the bank foreclosed on our building. We could pay rent to the bank temporarily, or we could move out. The bank didn't give a shit what we did, but by then I had collected lots of money in my same brown sock. Who believed in banks then? So I went down there, and for a song, I bought the very building that we were living in. Where Ma and Pa brought me as a skinny baby. Where Joey was born and Ma died. Where Pa slept his life away without ever knowing we owned it.

"And I didn't let on to Pa, of course. I kept busy with Abe. We went everywhere. Sometimes to ballgames, where the betting was heavier than almost anywhere. Baseball moves so slow so people like Abe can take bets on the spot. But it was more like a hobby than a profession. I sit and watch Abe rake in a few hundred because some great thinker makes a bet that Yablonski's ball will fall short of the outfield. "Thank you," Abe says, and we go. It was his special talent, believing in the right people and not letting himself be persuaded by others. I can sit here and smile still when I think of Abe: how he walked with his chest out to make himself bigger, how he smelled like lemons, how he'd look at me sometimes without a word and tell me I was doing fine. It meant something that Abe felt you were okay. So I'm Abe's companion, his driver, his boy Friday. I don't talk a lot because what I can hear is better than what I can say.

"Meanwhile, Arny Sloan was moving up fast. Because of his size, they saw his value in the protection business. He was the kind of guy whose muscles bulge through a suit, who can walk like a schlump but you still know he's big. He's a mountain. But I tell you, it's no advantage. It's like a red cape to a bull being so damn strong. People challenge you at every turn. So Arny is involved in some of the uglier transactions. Just his physique is a temptation to every thug and moron on the street. During this time we weren't seeing much of each other anymore. And this is common, Adam, as in any company. The salespeople see the salespeople, the office help the office help, et cetera. But I still felt fond of Arny, so when he got cut up real bad on his face and neck, I visited him all the time. Some monster with a razor, mad at Abe over nothing special, came and surprised Arny in bed. Arny didn't stand a chance. He was bandaged like a mummy for weeks. Arny never was a big talker, but now he was silent as stone. Don't think that only women care about their looks, Adam. To someone like Arny Sloan, looks were vital. If he'd lost a leg, I don't think he would have taken it as hard as losing that handsome face of his.

"After this incident, his spunk was gone. Nothing was fun for him. I'd try to get him to come to clubs or at least to a show and a Green River with Essie and me and Joey on a Sunday, but it was over for Arny. He became sullen. I guess he was in a depression for years. Today they'd have given him pills, but then everyone just drank when they felt like shit. Arny drank so much that he couldn't be much help to Bushwitz anymore, so Bushwitz deployed him to another front. Remember the back room at the funeral home? Arny became its gatekeeper. He was out of the way there. For seven years or so, that was his beat, and I think he liked it all dark and private like hell on a slow day. And a once handsome guy like that never married, never even socialized. I practically had to drag him. He lived with his ma and big sister and got punchy from drinking and collapsed and died on some stairs, where Abe himself happened to discover him.

"What do people think when a guy like Arny dies? Nothing much, because to the world he appeared to be a loser. Even among Abe's men, he didn't get the time of day towards the end. But I can still remember Arny in the sun at the beach with his dimples and wavy hair, all the girls around him like he's a prize racehorse. I can remember him swimming way out past the floating buoys and back. I can remember his kindness too, believe it or not. A guy who breaks legs also walks his ma to schul and brings his meiskeit of a sister chocolate cherries every week. That was Arny. And how the Sloans carried on when Arny passed, like they had lost Moses. Abe gave him a beautiful funeral with the music and the flowers and everything, though flowers were frowned on by some of the more pious relatives. That's one thing you could say for Abe. When one of his boys passed, he showed he cared.

"Now as for Arny's conditions of employment, I feel like this, Adam. If you borrow money, you pay up. If the government had Arny Sloan to break legs, no one would have robbed the s & ls blind. The Boeskys and Milkens and sons-of-bitch sons of presidents would be floating in rivers. If courts used

Arny Sloan, nobody would cheat their own kids out of child support. These are grown men we're talking about who fuck around and cry when they get into trouble. Arny was there to remind them they had responsibilities. What is more important work?

"Meanwhile, though, I'm on easy street. I take Abe here and there. I watch him undress girls in the back seat. I can't say I'm impressed with this maneuvers, but who asks me? On Sundays I can use the car if I like. Sometimes I take Essie to the movies, and usually I take along Joey too. Essie was a real movie buff, especially when Cary Grant arrived on the scene, handsome and suave as hell. And Joey's almost ready for college by then, my smart little all-American brother.

"Sometimes I'd get calls late at night that I'm needed, and believe me, I went like to a fire. Abe was doing business at a bunch of South Side speakeasies by then. Before my time, there used to be these big clubs on the South Side, the Dreamland Cafe and Panama Cafe—nice names—fancier than in New York City. And there you could hear the world's best music. I don't know who invented it, but music is sublime. How one man can tap some keys and it's like you're off in a dream. And while people dream away, they like to drink and have a good time. But then there's Prohibition. Everything moves to smaller houses. Smart, huh, for the government to ban liquor? Abe never did better than in those years. Everyone needed him, and believe me, Abe knew how to please people. Black or white, he didn't care. You pay him the proper amount, and he gets you what you want when you want it. No games. No bullshit. That's what I liked about Abe. He was on the up and up with people.

"During that time, I met Harrison Waters. He was about my same age and playing on the South Side. These South Side speakeasies didn't have names. If you knew about them, you went. If you didn't, chances were there was a reason for you not to know, so it was safer for everyone that way. The one that Harrison played at was in the basement of a dress shop. It looked like nothing on the outside, which was the point. Once you stepped inside, though, you wouldn't believe your eyes. There were all kinds of people: beautiful women in furs, men dressed like sultans, a few strange guys dressed as women, and, Adam, they could have fooled me. Transvestites, flappers, Southern belles, businessmen, cigars, booze, a little love in a back room with funny lights, pink tongues and smooth black breasts with long pointy nipples. Long curving necks that could stop your heart with their perfume. A world down there you wouldn't believe.

"It's funny, isn't it, how people come back in your life? I can remember this young pianist with a strong left hand and an elegant shiny suit playing in a trio on 35th Street behind a regular wooden door. I don't think he probably noticed me because what was I then? But I remember him. He played so sweet, and there wasn't much sweetness in my line of work. What was sweet? Getting paid and getting laid. And songs. I have a good memory for words, so I always liked it when a band had a singer, especially a pretty girl usually up from the South, but Waters' band was the exception. With him, I could close my eyes and listen. Once Abe asked me to give Waters a hundred. I wonder if he remembers that. Probably North Side guys came all the time and threw money his way. He got rich off of guys like Abe because in that dark smoky room, Harrison played like God himself had come down for a solo. Sure, there were good guys on the North Side, playing their hearts out every night. But going with Abe down Michigan Avenue south was like going on vacation, only there were no snapshots.

"Then twenty years later when I'm someone in my own right, I run into Harrison Waters again in a nightclub on Lake Street. Black guys played on the North Side by then. Still the sweet music—Harrison hasn't changed—but by now I'm somebody. I once gave him a little token, a diamond stickpin I picked up here or there, for playing 'My Funny Valentine,' an all-time favorite of Essie's. I never had much use for jewelry, but I figure that someone who can make me cry with his music deserves the best. He's a wonderful man, Adam, and sometimes I think that it isn't fair that wonderful men get old too. But back to Arny, which is a tragic story, and to me, which isn't.

"Did you ever see a man die, Adam? I mean fast, like you wouldn't believe? Well, I'm happy to say that the first guy I saw was the fucker who cut up Arny Sloan. It's not a pretty story, but it changed me to see this. That's why it's important that you should know. Not because I want my grandson to think I'm some sort of big shot. No one's a big shot when it comes to dying: Dust to dust, we all go. But sometimes, when it's sudden and takes some doing, it's remarkable, like a moon launch. You'd never expect someone full of life to be done so fast, but the first death I witnessed happened just that way.

"I can remember it was a Sunday because I was usually off on Sundays, as I said before. I was just married to Essie. We were so young, twenty, so it was 1934. I got a call from Abe to pick him up right away. I leave our bed, which is where we spent the first few months we were married—like slaves to love. You should have seen your grandmother then. She was a flower. I shave in haste and cut myself all over. When I get to Abe's, he and another guy I've never seen, a small bald beaky guy who might have been an accountant, get into the car. Abe doesn't introduce us formally. 'This is Flaherty,' Abe says matter-of-factly, and I remain nameless. Then Abe tells me an address, and we take off.

"I can remember it was one of those hot days in September when your feet swell and feel stiff in your shoes and the sweat just pours off you. I try to make some small talk about the weather, but nobody's biting. I figure it's the heat, so I drive down Racine all quiet and watch as people come out of church and stand on the steps in big pastel hats and sheer veils. I think about Essie waiting at home with her reddish hair spread out all over the pillow, and I think about lunch. Essie and me are planning to go out to this funny little place near

Humboldt Park, a vegetarian place owned by a Lithuanian, who served these pancakes. I'm thinking about these thin pancakes and applesauce when Abe tells me to pull over and park. Then he says something unusual. 'Come with us.'

"I expect that we're here because someone is seriously behind on some payments, that this is a Sunday wake-up call to some dumb fuck trying to cheat Abe. I'm still not sure why Abe wants me along, but I'm not one to ask. I can sense moods, and the mood is Sunday quiet, quiet so heavy it covers the street like a fog.

"'C'mon,' Abe nods, and we enter a small building, an apartment on Loomis and something. We walk down a hallway, and the building is utterly silent. There are no kids in the hallway or women shouting. There's no water running from taps or food sizzling for lunch. It's like we're in a deserted place you might imagine from a dream. There's red carpet on the floors and funny little lamps along the hallway with miniature lampshades. I don't know why I remember them, maybe because there were so many, like a field of lamps, instead of flowers. So I follow Abe and the accountant down a hall, and we get to a door. Abe knocks on the door, and slowly we hear someone stir. A man finally opens it a wedge, and Abe sticks his shoulder inside. Now Abe's a big man, not a tall one but barrel-chested and thick as a tree. To knock Abe down would have been a trick, so when his shoulder's inside the door, we're as good as inside too.

"Flaherty follows, and I follow him. The man inside has realized he's made a mistake letting Abe in, but I'm not sure yet what the mistake is. He's a small man too, maybe Irish, with balding red hair and these small blue eyes, which remind me of pig eyes because they're set too close. He's been hanging around on a lazy Sunday morning in his undershirt and pajamas and bare feet, and now we've surprised him something awful. And he looks all exposed as he stands there wringing his skinny hands and pleading. 'Abe,' he's saying but not much else that makes sense. It's like his voice is working but the words have no meaning to my ears. And Abe is just shrugging like there's nothing to say.

"'This is the man,' Abe says turning to me, 'who cut up Arny. He's saying he had to.' Abe says this quietly, like he's the defense attorney, arguing the man's case in court. 'He says he had to,' Abe repeats to our sidekick Flaherty, who's said nothing. They exchange a glance, and then Flaherty pulls a big gun with a silencer, just like you've seen in the movies, Adam, out of his suit. Don't ask me the model. I was never into ammunition. As the pig-eyed guy is about to say something more, Flaherty shoots him once in the middle of his forehead. That takes care of it. The guy falls forward, and we watch his body lie still on the floor. We watch him in this quiet.

"Then one by one we step over the blood. Abe turns him over, so now we're staring at his dumb face. And the bullet hole isn't much in and of itself. It's smaller than my fingertip but what's leaked out of it will never get cleaned. I'm feeling full of adrenaline, like I could run through the closed door. But I force myself to stand stock still next to these two men. My heart is falling out of my chest, and I'm thinking of Essie's white neck, whiter than a lily, beating with its little human pulse, when suddenly, Flaherty takes aim. What the fuck's he doing, I wonder, as in quick order, he shoots the guy, *bam* in the hand, *bam* in the other hand, and *bam* near the crotch. What the fuck, I think, in the seconds before it's over.

"Then I understand that our hit guy is making a statement. He's shot him in the pattern of a cross because it's a Sunday, and he's a Catholic, and so is our deceased.

"Now all this time the room has been completely silent except for this little *pop pop* sound like nothing, which is Flaherty's sound, and also this one odd detail. This dead guy has a canary in a cage that's singing its lungs out. All that's been said in the room since the shooting started is 'Stand back!' 'cause when someone's shot, blood gets everywhere. You wouldn't believe how much blood is in this one pale guy. Abe stands for a minute and seems to be listening to the canary going on and on like an opera singer. I'm hoping that he isn't thinking of shooting the thing for its ruckus, but Abe isn't crazy like that. It's a myth, Adam, that gangsters are all hot headed. Most are sensible, quiet guys. So why shoot a bird?

"We turn on our heels and leave. Everyone's at church and we've done this, I think, as I pull the car out of its space and drive away at a leisurely pace. All the time I'm questioning why Abe made me see this. I don't have much time to contemplate, though, because once we're a few blocks away, Abe says a funny thing. 'Pull into that alley,' he tells me. So I steer the big car into the alley, and I see there's another car waiting, driven by Manny somebody, one of Abe's occasional employees, a big guy with a forehead that sloped backward into his hairline like a ramp. Abe hands me a license plate. 'Put that on,' he tells me, and I take off our old one and replace it with the new. It takes me a while because first I don't have the proper tools, and second, my hands are shaking like crazy, which is why, I decided, Abe brought me along.

"Death gives you humility, Adam. Here I am a cocky kid of twenty sitting on top of the world. I have a beautiful wife with skin like milk. I have a pocket full of money. My clothes are nice. People are polishing apples they can't sell, and I own a fucking building. Abe wanted to inject a little dose of reality. 'This is life, kid. This is part of what we do. You don't just drive a car for me. Your hands are dirty too.' It made me think, Adam, to see this man die. At twenty you're so philosophical—correct me if I'm wrong: it's like a disease how many opinions you have and judgments you make like you're throwing salt into a pot without tasting the soup. Maybe Abe thought I'd been cultivating an attitude as I sat there most of the time in silence. Maybe he imagined I was somehow judging myself different, maybe better. Whatever, he wanted to improve me. And believe me, I felt the change instantly down to my fingertips as I disguised the getaway car, as the sun glared on my back and neck, as I stood up and took my place beside my companions, for better or worse.

"When I'd finished, Abe tossed our car keys to Manny, and Manny gave Flaherty his. I watched as Abe waved good-bye to them both, like an uncle seeing off his nephews on a trip. I stood in the alley waving too, shaking and wondering how we were going to get home as Manny went off with our car and the killer with his. It turned out he had come down from Youngstown for the day and was going back home. That was how it was done, if you wanted to be safe. There was plenty of good local talent to choose, but you'd have to cover your tracks all the time. And people could be petty. It could come back to haunt you when you didn't hire So-and-So's half-wit brother if you used local talent. So Abe always hired out, like having it catered instead of cooking yourself. Leave it to the experts. Maybe it cost more that way, but it worked. And that's what counts, Adam, that it works.

"'C'mon,' Abe says to me, and we take off on foot, grabbing a street car back to the neighborhood. The streetcar is almost empty, and we don't sit together or pretend that we know each other. We sit in our separate places staring out the windows. I see the world all quiet and pure and know that this is something I'll never discuss. I won't even tell Arny Sloan. I wouldn't want the world to know what I've just witnessed. I watch the trees shake their leaves, which are still ripply green, but soon, I think, winter will come. I point my chin up toward the sky and close my eyes in the warm sun, which is guilty of nothing. Maybe I doze a little, but I can't say. Though Abe and I live so close, we get off at different stops, which is what we planned. I ride six blocks past home.

"But by 1:30 at the latest, I'm at the apartment, downstairs from where Pa and Joey are living. Essie, pure as cream, is dressed and ready for lunch. She's straightened up the place and put the combs in her hair, and she's smelling like a rose garden. We can't keep away from each other—we're like two magnets—but we try as we walk down the street holding hands after I tell her we don't have Abe's car anymore.

"'It's more romantic that way,' she smiles, and of course I'm

relieved that I don't have to lie to explain. And I'm feeling a
little distant and removed from things, like my shoes are walking without me. And the sun is hitting the sidewalk so hard, it
looks like I'm walking through shiny waves of silvery swelling
heat, like the world is slowly smoldering. I don't know if Essie
notices my distraction as we get our table and order the food.
But all the time while we're eating those pancakes and drinking the best tea on earth, I'm thinking that it's the damnedest
thing how close we are to being gone. What holds us together, Adam, is nothing at all. A man can pass while the world's
at church, and a canary is singing its lungs out, and no one will
miss him.

"'I love you,' I tell Essie at lunch, and then I'm speechless,
ready to bawl, because I know that I really mean, 'Thank you
for someday missing me.' The guy who did that to Arny
deserved it, the bastard, but I kept picturing him on the
bloody floor, pig eyes staring, canary singing, time standing
still, and I have to shudder like a big cloud is sitting over my
shoulder. At the same moment in church, his mother or sister—believe me, by the looks of that apartment this man had
no wife—is asking forgiveness for something about him. 'He's
sorry,' she's telling the priest, about some petty little sin. Her
lips are trembling with emotion. And the priest is listening
through his little earhole to her innocent confession. She
doesn't know the first solid fucking piece of truth about the
man who was her brother, the same man who held a razor to
another man's face and cut mercilessly. Meanwhile, back at
that apartment, someone is going to hell, if anywhere, and his
blood, his constant companion, is making no more sound in
the world.

"I could go on and on like this, Adam. But your movie
would last for weeks, maybe years.

"I stopped working for Abe soon after that incident. You
could say that Sunday permanently turned my stomach, and
besides, at my age, almost twenty-one, a man wants to test his
wings. There were opportunities for small businessmen every-

where. First, there were apartments to buy—nobody could pay his mortgage—so once every few months I'd take the money in my same brown sock and visit the bank. Soon I owned a quarter of the neighborhood. When I became a big-time landlord, I hired my own flunkies to manage things. Someday I'll tell you about these sorry guys, who tried to rob me blind. Now that's a comedy because I was way too smart for their tricks. I had my instincts, and I'd been trained by Abe, one of the best.

"Meanwhile time marched on. While I was taking over the neighborhood building by building, Hitler and the Japanese were taking over the world. When I was about to get drafted, I enlisted in the Navy. The Navy was better for Jewish boys, someone told me. I became a sailor and fought in the Pacific. In truth, I worked on a supply ship, where no one fought at all. I did a lot of bean-counting and some trading now and then. That's what few civilians understand about the service, Adam. They treat veterans like heroes and victims, for what? For conducting business? Meanwhile, where's the Purple Heart for the landlord who loses his building or goes bankrupt on a bad hunch? Believe me, wars are incidental to most people involved in them. You could get rich as a king on a navy supply ship, and that's what the smart guys did. There were cigarettes and food and even liquor, and electronics equipment galore. And there were sailors bored out of their minds and eager for something to do.

"There wasn't a single man on that ship, not a one, who didn't profit from those of us with business sense offering our services. There's no need to be wanting because you're in the middle of the ocean and every few months a crazy Japanese tries to land his burning plane on your deck. You can smoke and drink and play cards and even invent things. We had scientific geniuses on that ship. I remember a guy named Nuxel from the Bronx and a big Texan named Blankenship. I supplied them with parts galore. All the products that came on the market in the late forties were invented by sailors like these two. All the phones and TVs and fancy transistors and rockets were made in the minds of smart men at sea.

"Now, I'll tell you, I'd never want to be in the Army. There you're face to face with the war, and there's no time to think about anything but saving your ass. But a big supply ship in the middle of an ocean is like a floating M.I.T. You have your duties now and then, just like you'd have classes, but there's plenty of time to think, and all the materials you need, and tons of smart able guys ready to use what's available. It was easy enough to doctor the books. That's what books are for. Accountants do this everywhere, Adam, in big companies and small alike. The Pentagon does it in aces. They're the champs. But believe me, I never charged seven hundred dollars for a lousy toilet seat. I charged the fair price. And because I was fair, my customers always came back.

"While I was out in the Pacific, Essie was home with Roy, a new pink schrying infant. I got to see him a few times over the first year, but the truth is that when I returned, Roy was already walking and saying a few words. Oh, Essie had told Roy all about me, but what can a baby understand? He needs things in front of his eyes. He doesn't have the ability to trust in something that isn't there. So when I think about it, I'd say that we got off on the wrong foot. For how long, fifty years now, we've been doing the same song and dance: me trying to impress Roy with my presence, and Roy wailing, just like he did when I was first discharged, that I'm not his daddy. 'Who is your daddy?' I asked the little guy rubbing his eyes and hanging on to Essie for dear life, sucking on her collar. And you know what the little punk answered, Adam, like he could already read minds and break hearts? He's less than two, mind you. 'Mama is daddy,' he says, and shuts his eyes tight against me. And that about sums it up.

"Can a relationship between a father and son be over in a minute like that? I have the answer to that one. But shut off that camera because I don't want to share it with your damned movie."

CHAPTER ELEVEN

EAR IRENA

Probably, you think, we have learned to live without you. Poland has survived, this is true. Lech Walesa grows stouter and has finer suits, and his poor tired wife, for once, is not pregnant. The small leaves have fallen off the trees and clog our gutters. Tourists have deserted the Old Town market, and we have donned our drab winter coats; you know the gray one, of which I speak. Along the river the sun sets earlier, and Syrenka's sword is covered with a fine powder of snow. Yes, we are abiding your absence. But can we adjust when we have become childless?

You do not need to be lectured, knowing so well from your poor father's death, that one never loses so deep a connection, a well of echoes. I am not daughterless. You are not fatherless. He is always with you, as he is me. I remember the times we would talk of him, Irena, as if he were still in the next room working on his charts or squinting up to answer a question, when his presence was so strong we imagined he would return to us after dinner. We would dream, the both of us, separate in our beds, that he was laughing, that he was buying a newspaper, that he was dozing on the couch in his usual position, feet outstretched and crossed at the ankles.

Time is a mere breath, Irena. Breathe in, breathe out, and life *is lived, but memory is a monument, a piece of stone so hard that special tools must refashion it. I am afraid I have no such tools. All the time you are away, I've felt as if I'm holding my breath, waiting for your return. I am making myself into an instrument to convert time into a monument to memory. Just as we used to wait in the kitchen for father's return on cold nights in January when you were small. You'd press yourself to the dark glass and say, "I think I see him now." So I imagine seeing you in the street or hearing you at my door. My heart flutters when I think I see you in the market or on a bus crowded with strangers.*

Probably Joszef has told you that I own your little Chopin now. He is indeed a whimsical fellow. I enjoy feeding him and watching him lie in the sun, but a cat is hardly a companion for a woman of my age and disposition. How I long to see you again and have a conversation, a long, rich discussion, even an argument with you! I can see the teapot on its fat little legs, its sail of steam furled. I have tried to talk in earnest to your dear friend Joszef. Pardon me for saying this, my dear Irena, but my words fail to reach him, or his to offer comfort. We talk softly, we shake hands, we politely broach the only subject that we share. We speak your name reverently, but like a thin soup, it doesn't nourish us. Sometimes I think, and again you must forgive me, Irena, that if Joszef's words were more adequate, his skills in this regard more finely tuned, you'd still be here with us, consoled, wanting very little. You'd be reclining on my sofa, content as your little cat when he watches a shadow of a bird on my bedroom window shade.

As accustomed as I am to being alone as a widow, I am not accustomed to loneliness. When your father was alive, especially when he took up his political cause, there was every reason to feel alone. But I was never lonely. There was always the knowledge of his return. The times he sat silently in his baggy sweater and fell asleep, his glasses slipping from his hand to the rug. And the memory of your frequent visits, of course, always lighten my mood. Remember the endless walks we'd take? The roses we'd stop to inhale? Our sense of smell is so strong, Irena. It's our best one, I think, more enduring than sight and hearing, which are failing me as I age. But apples still make me recall my childhood in my mother's sunny garden. I can smell you and me together preparing dinner in the sausage I fry at night, and after all these years, there is a still a fragrance in the bedsheets that must belong to your father.

I would imagine that your old man delights in your company. Of course, I could not pay you large sums for the privilege of walking in the sunshine as he does, but certainly it makes more sense to walk with your own mother than this foreign stranger. Isn't it odd, Irena, how like a puzzle—in pieces—we all are? Some fool has put us together wrong. Where are your old man's own people? Where is the only person still connecting me to earth? My life is a dream of strangers, shadows of movement; nothing in the present is of interest, and though I eat well and try to care for myself as best I can, every night when I close my eyes I am ready for a better place.

I know you have scorn for religion, but I am certain, Irena, that even in a communist country, which, to be sure, was no fault of our own, a lucky few were allowed into heaven. Surely Our Saviour understands history as well as human weakness. No doubt your kind, good father is there with his whimsical smile and brave ideas. No doubt Uncle Krysto, with his dirty mechanic hands and big heart and fast eyes for women. No doubt Cousin Ruta, you remember her photo, who died of polio before we knew it existed. I would like to go there, too, though I don't wish for you to think me melancholy. I can live my life, drink my tea, dust my house, feed your cat, or I can go. Whatever the Lord wishes.

Meanwhile, Irena, before this inevitability (I will be sixty-nine in January, you should remember), I must give you something. I didn't tell you in the haste of your departure that your father had accomplished important work before he died. I've had it here all the time along with a few other valuable items that would interest you. You would need to see them to understand their worth, and since I do not trust the Polish postal system or the American one, for that matter, I hesitate to tell you more by letter.

Telephones are no better. Satellites in space carry our voices everywhere, helter-skelter. Sometimes I am calling Aunti Beata and suddenly I hear loud men's voices babbling in an unknown tongue. I am intercepting two rug merchants in Istanbul or maybe Chinamen! How can I trust this medium to express what it is that Father left behind, what I know he would want you to have should I be taken in my sleep.

Wouldn't your kindly old stranger understand if you took a one-month's leave and travelled here? I am certain you would be allowed back into Poland. Certain, because Ranziowska's awful son returned just two weeks ago with his homely American bride and skinny baby. We had a feast at her dusty little house. As I drank plum brandy, I watched the little monkey attach himself to the American girl's meager breast and fall asleep. I thought of my Irena, how round your breasts, how full of milk they would be, how much nourishment from this source, how much opportunity in this regard. But that is another matter, and I digress from my point.

Please, Irena, consider a visit soon. If not in harsh winter, wait until the fields outside the city fill with wild flowers. We will pack a lunch and take a ride on the Vistula. I'll make a torte for you, and we'll sip tea. Then I'll open the unassuming little drawer in my bedroom and show you things you never knew about your father. Of course, you could see your cherished Chopin, who is growing very fat, and Joszef, if you wish. All of these things, Irena, we could do together.

Perhaps your old man has not described all of his relatives to you. Perhaps there is a niece or nephew in one of America's fifty states. I hear many black people have families in the South. I also know from television that America is full of retirement villages, where foolish old people dance in Western costumes and play checkers all day. Perhaps your old man can do that while you stay here with me. All I need is ten days of your time. I will call you in two weeks to see when you might come. The prospect of hearing your voice delights me. Joszef tells me that you two have spoken, but he is a poor storyteller, vague at description, and I get no sense of your well-being from his reports.

I can remember times, Irena, when you were like my moon, rotating around my kitchen orbit, always there, reliable as the heavens. Irena with the beautiful seriousness, eyes, beams of wisdom. So reliable, so mature. A mother couldn't have been happier with such a child. I ask to see that child one more time, to touch her blonde curls.

Love and fond regards,

Mother

Irena wonders why her mother keeps addressing her as a lover might, and her lover as a distant relative, taxed by the duty of writing? Her mother's ardent letters, like the one she received the afternoon before, display all the classic symptoms of disappointment in love: a sense of loss, a pouring out of one's heart, a desire for reunion, a flaring anger at being the party having to stoop, to bend, to offer more than the other is willing to give. Irena is used to such a relationship with Joszef, who sends a postcard now and then of Polish scenes: the river, the market, the university, a horse-drawn carriage. But a postcard for all the world to view tells the story, the empty, emotionless text betrayed by its medium. A pristine blank letter, addressed in his hurried hand and folded precisely, would have more meaning. His open missives to the world reveal there are no secrets to share, no nasty grievances to air, no touching coded reminders of the practices of love that might sicken another but tie new knots on their shared rope of feeling. "Remember when we drank all night and slept half in and half out of the bathroom, awaking with stiff necks?" Irena might ask. "Remember the first time I took you in my mouth?"

Who is this Joszef, Irena wonders, but a figment of desire, someone she has created as a mathematician does a hypothesis. Someone invented by thought, pencil, paper, air, and hope. A phantom. A walk up a flight of stairs to a dark apartment that is invisible on a map of a city that only exists in her memory. Skin touching skin or maybe only one's own skin glowing with a wish for connection. A symptom of the greatest problem on earth, worse than war, worse than death: her problem, her mother's problem. In a world of phantoms whose names we attach to our longings, we live and die alone. That is the truth. Trivial Joszef can't change it or her passionate mother, imploring her weekly to return to Poland, threatening her with a phone call. Irena is so busy fearing the possibility of hearing her mother's voice, taut with emotion beamed from another continent, that she doesn't notice that Elizabeth has muted the television.

"Calling planet earth," Elizabeth smiles, elegantly simple tonight in all-black slacks and shirt. "Guess what Adam's planning?"

"What can it be?"

"We're eloping," Elizabeth laughs.

"Adam is kind," Irena states as a corollary to her other more pressing assumption, that Joszef is not, then turns her thoughts to the situation at hand. "What can it mean, eloping?"

"We're running away together. Tonight. Will you let Jack move in with Mr. Waters?"

There is a moment of puzzled silence.

She recovers in time for Elizabeth to say, "I'm just kidding. We're planning a party for Jack. He'll be seventy-nine. I can't believe you took me seriously. You should have seen your face, Irena."

"I did not understand your meaning," Irena blushes.

"So now I know."

"What do you know?"

"You're crazy about Adam."

"I think he is sensitive man, but I do not have romantic inclinations towards him."

"Irena, what if Adam made the first move? What if you were alone and he . . ."

Irena notices another plunder, a ring, perhaps a sapphire, on

Elizabeth's wedding finger. "Elizabeth, I am not interested in this young man."

"He's a rich young man, and when Jack dies, he'll be richer."

"And why would that matter to me?"

"Don't you want to be free of this? Don't you want to stop cutting old men's toenails and be yourself again, Irena?"

"But I am myself."

"Well, think it over. I'd be happy to talk to Adam for you."

"Please do not. I have enough troubles to busy me. I do not need love. I am becoming a problem to my own mother since I left Poland. I have left a place she cannot fill."

"Tell her to get a pet. Dogs are nice."

"This is not good humor, Elizabeth. My mother sends me heartbreaking letters. If my Joszef loved me as much as my mother, I would be the subject of romantic history."

"Even if we have a party for Jack, he'll just miss Adam's father. The bastard hasn't seen him for years."

"It is true how we always think of who is missing. We look for the place in the photo where someone is meant to be. Even if there is beautiful island or blooming sunset or miraculous face, we say, 'Where is the one I really want, the one who thinks so little of me, the one I'd die for?'"

"Now you're back on track. You're some kind of saint the way you like to suffer. But you know what? I'm starting to think from what you tell me that everyone in Europe wears a martyr's badge. There are contests for the worst-dressed, the most humble, the apartment with the least heat, the poorest tasting soup, the saddest love affair, and people line up to participate."

"Only Eastern Europe, Elizabeth, where we aren't afraid to feel pain."

"You don't know how to feel pleasure, Irena."

"I think then, Elizabeth, that you should move to Europe. How do you live here? You go to stores and buy pretty things, but who is missing you in the world?"

"That's cruel," Elizabeth snaps. "You know nothing about

me. You don't screen my mail. You don't know, Irena, who misses me or who doesn't, so just shut up."

"I am sorry, Elizabeth. Your American frankness is maybe contagious."

"You think people in Europe have manners. You think you're all queens and princesses. And here you are among the rabble, poor girl."

"This is not true. I am just sorry that I offended you. Will you have some tea and cake?"

"Who can eat?"

"I have offered my apology."

"It isn't enough," Elizabeth pouts.

"I will read you my mother's love letter to me," Irena promises, feigned lust in her voice.

"I can't believe it," Elizabeth says, thick-voiced, sitting on Irena's bed in the semi-dark, shaking her head. While the dull TV hum once again fills the background, she turns the pages of Irena's mother's letter over and over in her hand. Though Elizabeth can't read the language, Irena watches her appreciating it as object. But Elizabeth is an undiscerning critic. She refuses to acknowledge Irena's mother's best moves, the parts of her plea that plunge Irena's guilt deeper, the parts meant to make Irena bleed. Unattuned to the artful manipulation of the letter, Elizabeth examines it as one might a religious relic or an ancient manuscript with beautiful engravings. Already Irena has read it to her twice, the second time more slowly, while Elizabeth shook her head and echoed phrases now and then. Maybe it is Irena's faulty ability with language that is causing Elizabeth to desire more contact with it. Maybe Elizabeth feels that Irena hasn't done it justice, that looking at the strange words or ornate script will reveal something lost in translation. "Read this part again," Elizabeth pleads, clasping Irena's arm and pointing to a page. "Read the part about the kitchen." And again Irena recites the litany of smells, the chronicle of longing her mother has expressed.

Then there is too much silence in room. It presses in on Irena, making her feel crushed by fatigue, and finally bored. She notices the old movie dotting the darkened background with bright color and occasional bursts of sound. Head cocked, Kathryn Hepburn is talking so swiftly to Spencer Tracy that Irena can't understand a word. In order for the evening to continue, Irena will have to probe Elizabeth's reaction. This woman, who alternates between saying too much and far too little, is very difficult to know.

As she turns to tell Elizabeth something that Ursuzla, the wit of their group, once said about a mother's smothering devotion, she notices that this girl's big American shoulders are hunched over and that she is crying softly without trying to shield her face from Irena's view.

"You mother is a beautiful writer."

"She says things well."

"How can it be," Elizabeth asks, "that someone can love you so much?"

How to answer such a question, Irena wonders, turning it over like a shape with too many sides to classify. On the one hand, Elizabeth means something broad and human: how can someone be capable of expressing such love? On the other hand, Elizabeth is asking Irena to assign herself value: "Say it," Irena imagines her prodding, "say that you are not worthy of evoking such deep emotion in another person. You are plain Irena, sojourning less than spectacularly in the New World, which isn't so new. You are drab as a sparrow, even after I dress you up fashionably, and your life is less than eventful. How can someone, then, feel so strongly about you?"

"This is why we love our mothers so," Irena finally responds. "They think we are wonderful when we are only ordinary. But they must," she continues, pointing her finger, "to think well of themselves." What does her mother have? The memory of a perfect child. But every day when she lived in Warsaw, there was evidence to the contrary. There was her interest in mathematics, which made her cold and unapproachable in her mother's words. There was Joszef, with whom she was a failure as a woman in her words. There were no children, which made Irena barren in her words. There were rare visits, unsatisfying phone conversations. There was annoyance and disappointment. "Long distance has restored me, Elizabeth. Like insignificant painting she cannot see, she dreams I am lovelier now. That is why I am so afraid of her phone call, which will restore my unsatisfying reality again."

"My mother hasn't written or called in ages. It's like everyone I've ever known has disappeared."

"But Jack loves you, that is clear."

"That is clearly unimportant," Elizabeth mimics. "That's like saying the medical deliveryman is interested in you."

"Cristof."

"You know his name?"

"Yes, another Polish immigrant."

"So it's not Adam that you wait to see. It's the chemical man. Irena, I never suspected. So tell me about Cristof, the chemical man."

"We attend the zoo together. Saturday we go to dinner."

"Is he married?"

"Perhaps he is, but I do not think so. He invites me to inspect his apartment."

"That's universal language for you know what, Irena."

"I think you are right, Elizabeth, but I can take care of myself in this situation."

"Besides, I think he's shy."

"What is your reason?"

"You don't want to know," Elizabeth smiles mischievously. "Do you ask him something?"

"If he thought you were cute, and his face got all red, like a little boy's. Next Wednesday, when the new shipment is delivered, I'll ask him again."

"Please, Elizabeth. He is engineer. He is not interested in childish games."

"Everyone, even Einstein, is a child about love, but I'm surprised by your interest, Irena. I thought it was all Joszef. Joszef this and that, all the time."

"For me and Joszef, there was a turning point almost three years ago. I was pregnant, I discovered, but Joszef did not want the baby. And probably I did not either."

"What did you do?"

"I did as all my friends do, as women before my friends, and women before those women."

"You had an abortion?"

"Of course."

"Well, I would keep a baby, no matter what."

"That is also fine, but in Poland, it is part of life for woman. You are born. You go to school, you grow up, you get married or not, you have profession. You have accidents and you solve the nasty problem. It is quite common here too, I think, from news."

"Sure it is, but I wouldn't do it," Elizabeth says adamantly.

"What if you were pregnant but did not love the man?"

"I wouldn't do it."

"Everyone can have opinion on this."

"I'm not talking about opinions," Elizabeth says, raising her voice. Irena fears that Mr. Waters will be disturbed by their late-night debate. "I mean I faced the problem."

"And where is your child, then, in Albany?"

"As a matter of fact, yes," Elizabeth smiles oddly.

"And who watches her?"

"No one."

"How can that be?"

"I had a baby, Irena. Three years ago." Elizabeth stops now and looks at the bedspread, takes Irena's mother's letter in her hand, puts it down, seems to check her forehead for warmth, and blinks several times. Irena walks to the dresser, and turns off the droning television. Then she quietly resumes her place next to Elizabeth on the bed. In the darkness of the bedroom, Irena looks into Elizabeth's pale face, blanched by some kind of pain she hasn't yet named.

"What happened?" Irena says softly, taking Elizabeth's

hand. Immediately Elizabeth draws back from her.

"She died. My baby died."

"I am so sorry."

"That's what I imagined you'd say," Elizabeth says caustically.

"I do not understand."

"I knew I'd tell you. I sat in the park all by myself—freez-
ing—and saw how we would talk, only I didn't picture this
room. I'd tell you Kayla died, and you'd say you were sorry. So
now what should we talk about? Your mother? Your Joszef?
Your country? You?"

"No, let's talk about Kayla," Irena says softly.

"I was living with Roger," Elizabeth says hesitantly. I met
him after high school. One day Roger comes home, and I tell
him the rabbit died."

"I do not understand."

"I tell him I'm pregnant."

"And is he pleased?"

"Well, let's just say no, Irena. He technically wasn't
divorced, and it wasn't the best time for scandals. He was up
for a promotion, and he wanted things to be quiet. But as soon
as he said it, as soon as I heard, 'You're not going to have it,' I
knew. I'd show everyone I could do something right by having
that baby, no matter what they thought."

"So then what happened with Roger?"

"Oh, he got used to the idea. He even talked about getting
married, and he bought me a necklace with my initial and a
little diamond. He bought a crib and a little mobile that
played a song. It was really sweet."

"And you were happier then?"

"It was up and down. We fought and made up and fought
some more. And the next six months passed this way. A few
times he stayed away all night at his ex's and I got mad as hell.
I'm pregnant, Irena, I'm as big as a circus tent.

"Then it was June sixteenth. There was a big bright moon in
the sky, and I was driving home from my mother's. She had a

little party for me with some of the old neighbors. I'm think-ing how nice it all is, the little cakes and the pastel paper shower umbrella in the center of the table that one of the ladies made, and punch with rainbow sherbet, the little rattles decorating packages, and all the tiny clothes. I'm at a stoplight near our apartment, and suddenly I hear *pop!* That's my water. And I go into labor. My belly's clenching like it's made of stone and I feel like I might suffocate.

"So I drag myself up the stairs shouting ahead of me, 'It's time. It's time.' But, of course, it isn't time for Roger, because he's not there. I drag myself back down the stairs and knock on a neighbor's door, and this woman, Mrs. Pidnar, who I hardly know except to yell at her teenage son and his monster friends, she drives me to the hospital.

"Four hours later, after feeling like this pain is going to rip me in half, I have Kayla. She's a big baby, nine pounds. Roger finally shows up just toward the end. I watch Kayla come out of me, she has a strong voice, and I cry, and Roger cries, and I think the doctor cries, but probably I'm wrong about that. Or else he's crying because I'm a clinic case, and he's losing money.

"A few days later I take Kayla home. Roger is in and out, at least he's supporting us, and I'm taking care of her and feeling really good. I'm walking on a cloud. I'm painting my toenails and fixing my hair and eating real good. And I'm whistling as I bathe her and nurse her and put her in these adorable little outfits and look at her splotchy skin and her big eyes that don't have eyelashes yet.

"All summer I pretty much stay indoors with her. Oh, now and then, I put her in her little carrying thing, and we go to get supplies, or Roger takes us out to eat, but we're pretty much alone in there, the two of us. I talk to her all day, and when I'm alone and think of her, my breasts leak milk. And I start believing that this is the life for me. Someone loves me and needs me. Let Roger play around. Let my friends go on with their lives. Let my mother visit or not. I have Kayla.

"Then it's September fifth, ten and a half weeks after she's born. She's healthy, she's growing, but she's not a good sleeper.

Lots of times at night she's waking up and wanting to be nursed, but she's overtired and falls asleep before she's really full, so I have gotten into the habit of taking her in bed with me for her all-night feeding frenzies. That night I carry her there and nurse her.

"I wake up about five or six hours later and it's morning, and I think, finally, finally, she's sleeping well. Roger's not home. The fucker stayed out all night again, but Kayla's asleep, so I think I'll just take a shower and eat real fast before she's up and wanting more of me.

"I start pouring my shower, but something starts worrying me. 'Why isn't she up?' I wonder. It's just maybe ten steps. Ten steps back to the front room, where we sleep on a hide-a-bed, but I already know. Just like I've known things before they've happened all my life. I'm going to walk those ten steps and look, and Kayla will be dead."

Irena watches Elizabeth's lips close. Can this be the end of her story? Surely if it is, Irena can't urge it forward, dare not say a word.

Elizabeth sighs deeply and resumes. "So I take the ten steps real slow. I keep making promises while I walk toward her. I'll take her out more in the sunshine. I'll never smoke another cigarette. I'll tell Roger to get his useless ass out of here, but I know already, Irena. Before I reach the bed and lean over to where she's sleeping on her tummy and touch her with one finger, I'm sure.

"And then I only know what I've been told. I'm standing downstairs in my nightgown looking at people on the street and not being able to speak, just standing in front of my building like that. Someone recognizes me and finds out Roger's name from the lease and calls him at work. When he gets here around eleven, I'm still just hanging around down there without any shoes or keys or anything. And when he asks me what's wrong, it's like I'm deaf. I just look past him."

"You are in shock."

"An ambulance comes for Kayla and me, but it's way too

late. It was too late almost as soon as I fell back asleep. They estimated she died about nine hours earlier.

"Now please don't say you're sorry, Irena, because I want my memory of this to be different from the way I imagined telling you at the beach, so I can remember how I told you. I don't want you to say anything, Irena. I'm going to leave now and go back upstairs and in the morning we'll talk."

"But how can I let you go?" Irena holds out her arms to Elizabeth. She imagines embracing her broad back, stiff with remorse. "Come here."

And obediently Elizabeth walks to her and stoops down so that her body folds over Irena's.

"Come." Irena, weeping, takes Elizabeth by the hand and leads her to the bed. "Rest here. We do not have to talk. Just lie here and close your eyes, Elizabeth."

Dutifully, Elizabeth does so. She turns her back to Irena, and Irena pats her softly for a few minutes until she feels a deep sigh and a slackening. She watches Elizabeth breathe in and out rhythmically. Shortly after that, she hears Mr. Waters take his nightly stroll to the bathroom and shut his door again.

Then Irena tiptoes to the washroom and sits on the toilet. She cries in the dark: for Elizabeth; for Kayla; for her mother; for poor Mr. Waters, who will die, no doubt; for Jack, who will die even sooner; for Joszef; for their baby; for herself; for Cristof's kind eyes; for Warsaw; for the lake, of which she's grown so fond; for mathematics; for the leopard in the zoo; for the faceless Holy Ghost, her favorite third of the Trinity. She sobs and sobs and runs water and sobs under its sound. She wonders what she will say to Elizabeth in the morning. She wonders if her mother cries for her at this moment, 7:00 A.M. in Warsaw.

Then she writes a note for Mr. Waters, telling him that the two women have switched places overnight. She will stay with Jack Kaufman, for Elizabeth has fallen asleep watching television, and Irena hasn't the heart to wake the tired girl.

*   *   *

A hand or a knuckle, it is all the same. The shadowy slope of the neck, a rib stirred by breath, a breast curved forward like a Christmas bell. He will notice that her tiny pink nipple is flecked by a mole at the same moment she sees the long funnel of fine hair sketched on his chest. Whatever connects in bed, so be it, Irena thinks, as Cristof hurries through the warm up—hasty kisses on her chin, her shoulder, that very breast she had considered a moment ago—and onto the prize. He is larger without his clothes, a bulky man who nevertheless moves deftly toward his purpose. My first American fuck, Irena thinks, frowning to herself that she has conjured up Elizabeth's ugly, small word. He walks her to the bed, where she lies, self-consciously cataloging her breasts, his nipples, the number of nipples in the room totaling five if one counts the covered light socket overhead. With Joszef and Chopin, there would be twelve nipples in the room. These numbers occupy her as he shifts into place, resting his full body, vibrating with eagerness, onto her small flat contours.

His buttocks raises the covers again and again but Irena, small boat adrift on a new ocean of American sex, is too taken with the entire scene to concentrate on the small, singular event. She keeps leaving her body and wandering through the room. First, she can't help but hear the too-poignant music, Barber's *Adagio for Strings*, more appropriate for a funeral. Then there's the matter of Cristof's design sense. He has furnished the entire apartment in white and gray. It is austere as a monk's lodgings, and here, on his plank bed, under the speckled comforter that resembles salt spilled on pepper, he pounds on and on. Now he is panting. Now he is finished. And all Irena can imagine is her own bedroom in Warsaw with its dark sheen and rich sense of history. Where has Irena been during this singular event, she wonders, as Cristof heaves himself to the side and settles his head firmly on the pillow. Yes, he is satisfied, though she, legs sticky and weak, has yet to consider the question of her participation.

"Now," he asks without pause or contemplation, "is there something else to add to our list of American pleasures?"

"Your apartment is very tasteful."

And Cristof laughs. He probably thinks she is a master of understatement, a wit, to be sure, but what she knows is that this is all there is to say. If life were as simple as Cristof desires, then strangers would meet on the street, rush to a room, and fall gloriously in love in an instant, like beams of light intersecting randomly in a dusty corner, like bears in the forest.

"You are beautiful, Irena," Cristof smiles.

"And you are handsome," Irena laughs softly, to which she adds her quiet resolve to leave as soon as permitted. But where are her shoes, she wonders as she notices Cristof's empty sock lying on the rug, its toes splayed out comically.

CHAPTER TWELVE

"HOW ARE YOU, Grandpa?"

"Don't ask."

"You seem kind of tired."

"It was a crazy night here. Irena and Elizabeth are playing some kind of game, don't ask me what. I call for Elizabeth in the morning, and in comes Irena with tea and pills and shots. She doesn't know what she's doing, and I have to help her with every step. 'What happened to Elizabeth?' I ask, and Adam, my heart is pounding. I depend on that girl so much, but Irena's casual. She tells me Elizabeth's just fine, like it's common practice to disappear.

"All morning I don't see her. The phone rings and Irena tells me Elizabeth will be back this afternoon. I figure it out. She's seeing some guy."

"Well, she is young."

"But you see, Adam, *I'm* her guy. I pay her. If it's someone else she's seeing and she wants to spend all night getting poked, excuse my English, then I won't keep her around. Not after what I've dished out on her. Not after what we've done together in this very bed," which he pounds with a flat palm for emphasis. "What, are you surprised?"

"Not really," Adam says, aghast.

"If there's someone else, Adam, if she can't wait, what, six, nine months? If she can't give me that courtesy . . ." and Adam sees spittle flying from Jack's lips, his face reddening, his eyes glazing over with conviction. "But that's my problem, isn't it? Your problem is what I'm going to say today, and that's no problem because I've got plenty. Remember, Adam, don't let women make you crazy. You have to save all your energy for all the guys lined up to stick it to you. That's my subject for today. Ready?"

"Just about," Adam says, watching the red light on the camera click on.

"Now after the war, this story gets a little boring. I warn you, Adam. And you know why it's boring? Because I'm respectable. I'm a big shot businessman who eats at Fritzel's and the Chez Paree. I get my nails done, I get shaved so my face is as smooth as a baby's ass. I wear gold cufflinks, 24 carat. I own a shitload of property. Essie shops at Saks, Roy goes to a fancy school, and things are quiet. That about says it all. Nobody wanted trouble in the fifties, Adam. We have a president who can't even talk; we have the Bomb, which can explode any minute; we have Korea; we have all kinds of nonsense going on in Washington about communists; but no one wants to hear of it. Leave us all alone, the GIs say. Hitler is dead. The Japs are defeated. Let's make babies and build houses and get down to business. In 1950, I'm thirty-six years old. I'm old enough to be going bald, so I'm not going to be caught acting like a punk with bets or cards or horses or some other bullshit.

"When old friends call, I'm polite, I listen, but mostly I tell them, 'It's a different world now, don't you know that? Find some greenhorns to help you.' Not that I forget my buddies. Plenty of people I owe favors, believe me, and I pay them all back.

"There's Abe Bushwitz himself. He's still around buying and selling bigtime. I see him now and then and help him when I can with the legitimate side of his business. He owns half of Skokie, some of California, and a little of downtown. I swing some weight for him with the downtown part. I can talk to

Irishmen and Italians and Germans—they're all alike in business. And I repay him real big once. He gets to build some low-
cost housing, you know, for the black people, and the government pays him in aces. I don't have to help him with this deal—
I can keep it for myself—but I do help, Adam, because you
don't forget a friend. Abe was there when I needed him. He
saved my family's butt, so I can treat him with a little respect.

"Now some of my associates, the ones with law degrees who
want to be big judges and shuffle money under the table, they
won't be caught dead talking to Abe. As they watch Abe
approach, I can see their shoulderblades hunch under their
Brooks Brothers suits and a shudder run through them. I
could die laughing. There's one named Gimble, a real chick-
enshit, who looks like he'll have a stroke when Abe sits down
with us. He twists and turns and gets all red in the face like a
boy who has to pee real bad and the teacher won't let him. Red
as a beet he sits there squirming. But what am I going to do?
If Abe needs me, I'm here. Mind you—I don't seek him out.

"Which is why I'm so offended when this small-timer
Lombardo starts making trouble for me. I'm clean as a whis-
tle, Adam. My shit don't even stink, if you pardon the expression. I could go to confession, if I was of that religion, and
have nothing to tell for the past ten, twenty years, but here's
this guy Lombardo, who starts calling and pressing to see me.

"At first I think he's some stinking salesman wanting me to
buy some insurance on my life. Everyone was buying insurance
in the fifties, like we knew terrible secrets about how long we'd
live. Everyday when I come into work, my secretary hands me
message after message all saying the same thing, 'Lombardo
called.' I start wondering whether this Lombardo has any
other clients. Later I start asking around and find out that a
long time ago, before the war, Lombardo worked for Capone.

"You know Capone, so famous and all. For what? A lousy jerk,
Adam, a small-time asshole who could only have made it big in
Chicago, which was an open market. You think it's hard to be an
actor or an artist in New York? Try being a gangster there. So

here in Chicago we get stuck with all the losers, and Capone and this Lombardo, who worked for him, are two prime examples. It's come back to me that maybe Lombardo used to be an Arny Sloan type, an enforcer that I met a few times who knows when. Now this puzzles me cause I'm good with names and faces. You have to be in this business. When What's-his-name approaches with a big cheeky grin, you have to be able to raise your arms in delight and say, 'How long has it been, Starletti?' Notice how you say his name last to give yourself a second to think.

"So it's a Friday afternoon, late. My offices then are in the Prudential Building, the tallest thing for miles. I'm sitting at my big panelled desk with my great view. My shoes are shined, my cuticles trimmed, Essie loves me, and Roy is a little prince. We're going to South Bend for the weekend, we have a summer place there, a little cottage, and the sun is shining like nobody's business. Now I just need to get out of this damn office. I ring up Lombardo from one of my message sheets. I have enough of them to paper a wall by now.

"I could tell you word for word how the conversation goes, Adam, but it sickens me. It brings me down to this man's level to repeat what it is he says to me. It's ugly, Adam, what he says, how it threatens me and my family. It makes my stomach sink to hear what he's saying. He knows a lot, Adam. He knows just about everything I've told you about me and more. He can tell me about that Sunday with the canary that I told you about. He can tell me where I was when I can't even remember it myself anymore. And worse, he can tell me about some of my property now, which worries me the most. Because, like I said, I've been on the up and up, but this is Chicago, and there are always wheels to grease if you're going somewhere.

"Now why would a man learn so much about another man, except maybe if the one man stole the other's wife? Which reminds me of a funny story. A business colleague once with a little West Side yente wife, has it in his skull that his wife's doctor, a handsome, prominent Episcopalian maybe from Kenilworth, is after his little mouse with the streaked hair and tiny tits. I see him at lunch reading a book as thick as a club sandwich. I ask him, 'What are you reading, Shel?' Shel shows me a medical book about stomachs, this doctor's specialty. 'You gotta know your enemy,' Shel whispers confidentially. And this goes on for months, Shel and his books, until the wife's ulcer is cured. Don't ask me what got Shel thinking this way. Something can plant a seed and just make it grow, no questions asked.

"Well, something's planted a seed real deep in Lombardo. He's decided that Jack Kaufman has it too good. Don't ask me why of all the rich ex-schleppers in town he's chosen me. Maybe he saw me at the baths on Division, and he didn't like how I soaped myself or got a rubdown or ate my pickled herring. Maybe I said something twenty years ago that I'll never remember but that he can't forget. Whatever. He's decided he needs to get me. It's his vocation, his religion.

"So I listen and I listen, and I tell him, 'Lombardo, if it's money you want, come right over. I'll write you a check. If it's a job, I'll find you one. I'll take care of whatever it is you need. But if it's something else that's eating you, who knows why, what am I supposed to say? That I deserve some stinking asshole trying to suck my blood? Cause if it's blood that you want, you're not going to get it. Better men than you have tried.'

"So I promise to see him the first thing Monday, and I ask him one favor. I ask him to take a weekend off from this obsession with me and do something else. It's a beautiful Friday in June. Go to the races, for Heaven's sake, play golf, take your wife to a club. Have a good steak, a martini, and consider, Lombardo, where it will get you to raise your blood pressure thinking of me. Besides, there are other fish in the sea, I finally say.

"'You're the fish I want,' the asshole replies, and we get off.

"I won't bore you with the details, Adam, but I have a hell of a weekend waiting to see him. I say nothing, period, from here to South Bend. Usually I keep Essie and Roy entertained in the car with corny songs. 'Aba dabba dabba,' 'Swim little fishie,' all the cute songs they have then. When we get there,

Essie keeps taking my pulse like I'm dead, and Roy plays in the water alone. He knows not to ask me to join him. I sit like a statue, like a tree stump, on the beach.

"And it doesn't stop Monday. It goes on for months. I meet with him and meet with him. I throw him this and that. I listen to the guy. He's no prize, and probably no one has given him so much attention since his mother wiped his little fanny for him. I'm kind, Adam. I say I have some buildings in South Shore that he can own, no strings attached.

"Then I don't hear from him for awhile, and I think we have a deal until a Sunday in early September. I open the paper and see I'm being featured, photo and all. And, of course, the information has been given to the papers by Lombardo.

"So now I'm hot, Adam. Sure, everything is true, the numbers, the gaming, the bribes, but it's common knowledge here, like the name of the mayor. The newspapermen are pretending they've discovered something? They're acting like this is Eden and I'm the snake? C'mon, people's eyes are permanently shut in this city. Try to get the cops to pursue a lead without paying them. So there must be something in it for someone to expose me now. And then I realize that Klein, who I'm building a big housing project with out in Flossmoor, he must want to get me and he's using Lombardo to do it.

"So Adam, all the time it's Klein trying to cut me down. I make a call to confirm my hunch, and I'm right. I call a Greek guy named Johnson, that's what he calls himself now, a big tall handsome guy from some island with windmills, owns some restaurants and does some numbers, and he tells me what he knows.

"And for what reason does Klein want to fry my ass? Simple greed. I let him in on a big deal that will make Freddie Klein king of the hill out in the sticks. He's no brain, but until now, I thought he was at least average. But you have to be fucking stupid to go after me like this.

"I call some lawyers and get my story moved from page one to page thirty-seven. In a week, I'm out of the paper altogether. And I take another few days to calm down Essie, who is green in the gills over this. Now mind you, she doesn't ask a thing. She trusts me and loves me, period. She's just heartsick that people are avoiding her or worse yet, calling her with disturbing questions. She's afraid to go to temple on Rosh Hashanah and see her friends. Her damn butcher is asking her when I'm going to jail, and already I'm on page thirty-seven and receding from the papers. I make a few calls downtown to investigate. 'What the fuck are you doing?' I ask a few key guys.

"'Calm down, Jack,' they say. 'If we really wanted to get you, would we leak this story over Labor Day weekend when nobody's reading the paper? We've done what we needed to do. This Klein has friends too, but just put it behind you. By the way,' one of them adds, 'how many tickets to Judge Who's-a-witz's reelection dance at the Hilton?' That's how things are downtown, a big fucking joke. The papers are funnier than the comics if you understand how it all works behind the scenes.

"'Give me ten,' I say, but I'm not laughing about Klein. I'm madder than hell. I knew the fucker from the old neighborhood. I know his homely brother and sister and pain-in-the-neck cousin, who can't keep a job, and I've helped them all once or twice. I'm the Klein soup kitchen, and look what Freddie turns around and does.

"I call Lombardo and tell him to meet me. When he shows up, my new buddy with the buildings in South Shore, I tell him I understand who he's working for. He denies it, but look at someone when they talk to you, Adam. The usual brightness is gone from his eyes. I tell him he can keep working for me and keep the buildings, or he can go back to work for lousy Klein.

"'That's tough,' Lombardo says drumming his skinny fingers on the glass of beer. But any fool can decide just like that. Does he want to be Klein's over-aged flunkie, or does he want to be a real estate executive? That's not a question.

"After this conversation, I don't hear from Lombardo again, and the story disappears from the papers. People stop hound-ing Essie. They treat her with the respect she deserves, and things get back to normal. At night we sleep again instead of lie there with our eyes glued to the ceiling till dawn. Only there's one problem. I'm building about 150 houses with Klein.

"I decide to give him a test. I take him to lunch at a club downtown. I order him a steak thick as a bible and a salad with Roquefort dressing and before that, a big shrimp cocktail and French onion soup. I order a bottle of French champagne—if it's not from France it's not champagne—and I say, 'Let's make a toast.'

"'To what?' the little beefcake asks.

"'To me. I'm a lucky man. I have a wonderful wife, I'm rich as a sultan, my child is well, kennehora, and when an asshole tries to get me, it never works.'

"'What do you mean?' he asks.

"'Don't you read the papers? This no-good-nik, Lombardo, told them all kinds of cheap crap about me. All lies. He must hold a grudge from way back. I was worried it would hurt our business relation, Freddie, but I can see you're wise as Solomon. Your faith in me is unshaken.'

"'Well, that's the kind of guy I am,' Klein smiles like the psychopath he is.

"And then he tells a story on Lombardo, like he's heard it from a third party. He's heard that Lombardo played turncoat on a man we both know named Rosetti, who killed himself. He's living in a big house in Riverside, he has a wife and kids and a lucrative racket with fake contracts to the city. He's a nice quiet guy. Then someone tells his wife he's homosexual, which any fool with eyes but his wife could tell. So he goes and kills himself over a weekend in his garage with carbon monoxide. That someone, Klein says, is Lombardo—can't trust him.

"'What did Lombardo want with Rosetti?' I ask him.

"'Some internal squabble on the Near West Side.'

"'I thought there was trouble there when my dentist, a good man, had his car taken from Taylor Street. He calls a man who explains that there are turf wars going on, like in the old days. He'll get his car in an hour. And in an hour flat it's back, and shined to boot!' I tell Klein.

"Then Klein gives me the big 'say-cheese' fake smile he's practiced for a week and eats the whole damn meal without a pause. We even have cherries jubilee for dessert. There is Klein with his little mustache blotting his upper lip all daintily. There is Klein letting me pay when the check comes, no problem. He's my buddy, right? So he thinks I think. He's sitting here the whole time thinking how clever he is, how he's getting away with murder, I'm so stupid. He's almost smirking with delight, and as we shake hands, I can see that it isn't over. He thinks he can get me yet.

"Now I want to be fair, Adam. I want you to see the whole picture here. What else could he have done? Let's put it on a point system. One hundred fifty points for confessing, but who would do that? Seventy points for picking up the check. Fifty points for containing himself a little. Would any of this helped? I could have just screwed him in business if he showed a little humility. I could have let the whole place get built and then thrown so many violations his way that he'd never have gotten his money out of the other side of the deal. You see, my money was cleared as soon as the houses were up. He needed people to live in them to realize his profit.

"But for eating my shrimps and my steak and smirking and playing me for a fool, hurting his wallet isn't enough. Remember one of the things I learned from Bushwitz? I learned to call in outside help for the worst jobs. I call a firm out of Miami. You look surprised, Adam, but there are consultants for everything. You want a golf course named after you? You want investments or a tax shelter? Done deal. So I call these particular guys only once because they have a good reputation for being quiet. By the way, those Cubans who worked for Nixon with Watergate? Some of them came from this same firm. Don't look at me like that, Adam, I know what I'm saying.

"I tell a man there that I have a little job in Chicago. It

needs to be done in a subtle way. No guns or bombs. No head-lines. It needs to look like an accident.

"It's December by now, the streets are icy, the houses are up, and Klein and I are touring a few models. We say good-bye on a Friday. Klein's chipper. He's wearing this new camel-hair coat big as a camel. Come spring, I say, pointing here and there, people will be living in all these shacks, Freddie, we'll get landscaping, and you'll be raking in the bucks. His eyes sparkle at that, like little Christmas lights in his doughy face. We shake hands and say good-bye.

"I drive home feeling real good and get my holiday shopping done. I remind myself every so often about Klein and test how I feel. I look at kids shopping with their mothers at Fields and think of Klein's own missing their dad. But whatever I try doesn't work. I'm at a counter buying some Chanel No. 5 for Essie, the biggest bottle in the store, and I'm picturing page one of the paper Labor Day weekend. I'm picturing Klein in a kitchen of the Mount Vernon model looking at me when he didn't think I was noticing him and thinking 'poor dumb fuck.'

"A few days later in my office I receive a call. Klein is dead. It seems his car went out of control on the Outer Drive, prob-ably something with the brakes. But he'd also been drinking. There was a lot of alcohol in his blood, which is how fate plays tricks. So I go home and tell Essie about poor Klein. That's the part I hate. I feel like hell lying to her, pretending I'm bereaved.

"A few days later we go to Klein's funeral. It's a day too warm for December. The sun is shining, people are leaving their overcoats in the car. It's December and plain balmy. I take that as a sign that no one up there's too upset about Klein passing. I offer condolence to his wife, who, believe me, does-n't look all that stricken. Through insurance she's a rich widow now. She's not all dishevelled with grief like I was for Essie or Essie would have been for me. Her hair is lacquered and her nails are done. I look at her and think for sure this is okay. Klein, the lousy friend, lousy businessman, probably lousy lover, is dead.

"I see Lombardo standing there. He looks like the cat who swallowed the canary. Guys like Lombardo need acting lessons. There's nothing between how they feel and how they look. It's an open book. I say to him, 'Sad. So young. Just starting really,' about this fat lying lunatic.

"'Yeah,' Lombardo says. 'A real pity for him and the family.'

"By the way, Adam, through the lawyers I throw in a college fund for little Eddie or whoever there is. That's the kind of guy I am. You can try to skin me alive, and I'll be patient. I'll give you a chance to refocus your energy, and I won't hurt your kids.

"Spring comes. Flowers poke up in the snow, spring training begins, and I sit drumming my fingers, waiting for repercussions. Every morning I rush into work. I read papers all day—there were three dailies then—for signs of trouble. But Klein has blown off the earth like a speck of dust. Good-bye.

"I take Essie and Roy to Acapulco for a week. The flight, in one of those big old propeller planes, takes an eternity, but we're finally there.

"Even as we plop down on the runway, I can feel something receding that I admit is fear. It's an unhappy word to mention, a sad thing to feel, but believe me, Adam, it's no shame to be afraid. It means you're thinking, that your mind and heart are connected. It's the ones who don't feel it who are scary, the ones who can slit their own mothers' throats, then light candles in her memory. I feel a lightness, almost glee. I catch myself smiling in mirrors I'm so relieved at being home free. I eat and drink like a horse and soak in the sun. The water's fantastic; I toss a ball to Roy; no one gets sick from the food.

"To all the world, I look like a happy man, but I realize something important, Adam. All this relief is just a sign of weakness. I've lost my nerve for this business. I have too much to risk to stick my neck out so far. I give up some old connections, and I vow never, never to need a consultant again.

"So that's almost my last gangster story. I wasn't a gangster anymore, Adam, except in your own father's eyes."

CHAPTER THIRTEEN

A T TEN IN THE MORNING, pale young Dr. Nudelman had posted Jack's record loss, seven more pounds. The CAT scans, x-rays, and ultrasounds were further evidence that the disease was spreading. The visit had ended with one of those moments that, Jack knew, must mortify doctors for whom death is a personal defeat, like bankruptcy for a businessman. In a world that values bounty, Jack was turning into nothing. Looking out of Nudelman's window at the pale gray sky, Jack thought of Adam's tapes, what essence of him they held; how they would survive him as something real, more real than what most of his apartment closets held: counterfeit, poor forgeries, stolen securities, compromising photos of former enemies, what have you.

Meanwhile, he had immediate business to attend, the compelling embarrassment on Dr. Nudelman's face as he was about to begin his concession speech. Sitting behind his doctor's desk with its green-shaded brass lamp and photo cube of his tanned family in a tropical locale, he leaned toward Jack and spoke his name faintly. Nudelman's light lashes fluttered over nervous, pigeon gray eyes. His gentle, ordinary face barely moved under the message he was to deliver. "I think we're making you sicker and nothing else with all these chemicals, Jack. The cancer is spreading."

"Where else can it go?"

"You need to think about making plans," Nudelman grave-ly continued.

"I think I'll get a new body," Jack proposed. Then, blinking squarely at the beautiful cross-sectioned heart and lung chart, Nudelman's profound discomfort, the strange green light bathing the desk, the happy Nudelman family encapsuled in their photo cube for all eternity, the dappled gray sky of December, he paused. "How long?"

"Two to four months."

"Sixty days?"

"Possibly."

Jack's now grim-faced former cheerleader, the man who had urged him to keep fighting for three years, was quietly asking him to stop. It had to happen sooner or later, so why did Nudelman seem so disappointed? Maybe doctors, like par-ents, believe they can protect their charges from harm, extending their hands to create a charmed circle in whose shelter a person can safely avoid his fate. "And what will those days be like?" Jack asked, feeling duly obliged to follow the Nudelman script, lest the moment become more excruciating.

"We can control the pain, but by the end pain control gets difficult."

"What do you mean?"

"It's a fine line. We can give so much that you'll feel no pain at all, but you'll be unconscious with that dose."

"Or?"

"Or you'll be more alert and suffer."

"Nothing's fair or easy, Doctor Nudelman."

"I'm supposed to tell you that, Jack." Then Nudelman cleared his face of grief, erasing its weighty sincerity. Partially recovering his blithe bedside manner, he offered Jack a conso-lation prize. "Please call me Harold," he said soothingly.

"Harold Nudelman," Jack began, "a colleague is being honored next month in Warsaw, a great jazz musician from my day named Harrison Waters. Since my mother was born in Poland and my friend Irena's from Poland, I was thinking: maybe I should take one last trip. Surprise Harrison. See the place my mama, smart girl, left to come here. Maybe see some long-lost Nudelmans. Celebrate my seventy-ninth birthday in the Old World."

Nudelman, Harold, smiled warmly, as each man stoked the other's sinking spirit. "Jack, I think that's a great idea. I can give you what you need, and I can arrange for a doctor in Warsaw to take over your care. If that's what you want."

"I'm taking my grandson too. We have a big project that needs a new location. He's making a film about me, and Poland will be perfect. Besides, who needs another winter in this crummy town?"

"You might go somewhere warm then."

"There's plenty of heat in Poland."

"When will you go?"

"January twelfth is the festival."

"That's great," Nudelman declared. "So I'll see you one more time before you take the trip?"

Jack watched Dr. Nudelman's sad glimmer of a smile. "C'mon, pretend it sounds good. I want to stop making everyone so uncomfortable. The facts are this. In my mother's day, death was a mystery. One day you were healthy. The next day there was maybe a tickle. Then you were coughing and coughing like a horse, and then you were dead. Every day the doctor came with his little bag—what the hell could be in it back then?—and every day you got worse. It took a matter of weeks. There was no hope, no blame, because it was life. Today people think with the machines and the chemistry and the million-dollar gadgets, they'll live forever. You've done your best—Harold—" Jack declared, patting Nudelman on his narrow, freckled wrist.

"And so have you," he returned, clasping Jack's hand.

"So it's official. We've both done our best, and now I'm going to Poland."

He was proud that he hadn't broken down with the news. Still, it was a relief to be out of the sweltering, doom-filled office and shivering into an anonymous cab with Elizabeth. Seeing his breath, Jack thought, "I'm still alive but not for long," and immediately adopted the habit of the dying, bestowing poignant labels on their experience, claiming the world more dearly for themselves than ever before. The Christmas lights on Michigan Avenue were candles of hope and regret. The women in furs, who strolled along despite the brisk wind, seemed uniformly beautiful, brave, and worthy of love. Drab pigeons made dovelike shadows on the street. Light itself shimmered soberly in the hollows of buildings, stoking images. How could it be, Jack wondered, that we are born into a world of such admitted beauty that it goes unspoken?

Elizabeth, who sat stoically beside him on this suddenly historic cab ride, glowed with the unquenchable spirit of youth. Jack could testify that it flickered all too soon. How could he have begrudged her an evening away from death and disease, poor girl, who had soothed him and clasped him and let him inside her whenever he'd wanted? No, he wouldn't ask her a single question about last night, this clever girl, whose eyes were so alert, like little foxes. Her incidental movements were graceful, and her neck an apparition as she unwrapped it from its aqua mohair scarf. For a moment he confused her with Essie, who should in all right be accompanying him now, Essie of the noble chin and black-brown eyes filled with deep and generous wisdom. He could squint and envision her next to him. He was talking softly to Essie when someone interrupted.

"The doctor gave you bad news," the voice left off.

And he blinked several times to confirm his whereabouts. In his current phase of decline, he would require more custodial care. Maybe Elizabeth relished it, Jack reflected, as he tried to respond to her prodding expression of concern.

"It's not news," he finally quibbled, trying to abandon the moment with a deft stroke of language. Closing his eyes, he anticipated Essie's return. Maybe if he fell asleep he could dream of her again. So many times after she'd died, there'd be dreams in which Jack had two sensibilities. Jack, the actor in the dream, had kissed her friendly lips, while Jack, the dream producer, warned she was a phantom.

"Your face is flushed," Elizabeth intruded again. Putting her hand on his forehead, she said, "I bet you have a fever."

Jack shrugged. News of his body was useless. Didn't Elizabeth understand that he needed to ignore his failing foundation and concentrate on the windows, where each remaining leaf quivered, and the yellow of their cab mirrored the most ravishing colors he'd ever observed? Impatiently, he waved her concern away.

After Jack crawled back into bed, Elizabeth gave him a shot. He needed them more frequently now. And then he had a long and simple dream about California. He and Essie were running a dry cleaning store on Wilshire Boulevard. It had bright wood panelling and a rotating fan on the saffron-colored counter and a big wall calendar from Chinatown with bold, curvy numbers. Jack was operating a conveyor belt powered by a wall switch. Essie and Jack smiled as all the clothes they'd worn through the years—wasp-waisted pinafores, pleated flapper dresses, pants without zippers, double-breasted pinstriped suits, Hawaiian muumuus blaring with color, sky-blue leisure suits with wide, cuffless bottoms—paraded past them.

"Elizabeth!" he shouted as soon as he woke from his sweaty dream shop. "Did Adam call?"

"He'll be by later." She peeped her head into Jack's room and waved. "He had a few appointments first."

"Have you ever travelled?" Jack asked sleepily, taking a sip of water. His dog-breath reminded him how terrible it was to be an old smelly, dying man. It was enough to make him sick, he thought caustically.

"Sure, a little. We went to Niagara Falls and the Poconos."

"Never been abroad?"

"Is Canada abroad?"

"You're going to need a passport." .

"Why, Jack?" Elizabeth smiled curiously.

"We're going to Poland."

"Why would you want to go there?"

"We're going to see Harrison play, only Harrison doesn't know it yet. He's winning a big honor. We're also taking Adam, only he hasn't heard."

"My lips are sealed." Elizabeth placed her index finger square on her mouth. Then she tiptoed to the phone and dialed Irena.

When Adam finally arrived that evening, Jack was too tired to work on the video. While anticipating his arrival all day, fears of his death had materialized out of thin air, like shadows on the wall of a cave. They intruded on the procession of visitors he had conjured with his best efforts: Bushwitz and Essie, his mother and Arny Sloan. Even lousy Klein's wife, happily remarried and swathed in mink, had approached his bed and shared a moment's conversation. His poor old father, looking like a sack of potatoes in ill-fitting clothes—and with the same dirty hands—had appeared and kissed him warmly. His brother with the checkered pants and cinched-in belly had sauntered in, tan and tall and prosperous, fresh off the 18th green. Roy had arrived. Pale and contrite, he took his father's hand and pleaded for forgiveness. Jack gave him a key and showed him where in the closet he'd been stowing a gift for him. When Roy tried on the ring, it glowed brighter than any real bauble Jack had seen in his life.

At the end of each interview, Jack had informed his guests that he was dying—but not before he went to Poland. Twice Roy had stopped him, refusing to hear the news. He'd told Jack that it was all a mistake, that those were other people's tests, that doctors were routinely wrong, that such a father—albeit they hadn't always seen eye to eye—would live forever. Then his son's eyes had grown desperate, imagining a world devoid of him. But Jack had reassured him. He wasn't afraid of dying, wasn't afraid because Essie would meet him, that he could guarantee. Now that his real grandson stood here, there was nothing much to say.

CHAPTER FOURTEEN

Poor irena, hearing first from Mr. Waters and now from Elizabeth that there was no way to avoid her appointment with destiny. "My mother will be so happy. What luck," she repeated with resignation, as breathless Elizabeth told her the news she'd received from Jack, that Harrison had been invited to Poland. Irena had been gone less than a year from a place she'd hoped to leave forever. But surely she was not thinking well in imagining she'd never return to Poland. Some day, surely, her dear difficult mother would have died, and Irena, dressed in mourner's black, would have tearfully returned. Or maybe Joszef would have written the message she'd waited forever to hear: "Irena, I can not live without you. Second to my mathematics, you are the animating force in my life. You must return to this emotional battlefield, where I stand naked as a general deprived of his army." Instead, head hung, like an insolent girl kept after school, she would return to her mother's schemes and Joszef's ambivalence, and to a Poland that according to Urszula, was becoming so cheerful, so full of commercial intent, that its soul was vanishing faster than its problems.

That morning, before Elizabeth's call, she had walked in on Harrison, seated at the piano-shrine he never approached.

What was he thinking, her kind old man, about the invitation to Warsaw, the Paris of Eastern Europe, where, against all odds, jazz is adored and worshipped more ardently than any little god? How strange to be honored by Irena's countrymen, who had written him in formal English, eager for him to attend "the celebration of his talent." Irena knew that Harrison considered his talent a relic, and so he had wondered if they understood how little he could offer The Society for the Preservation of Chicago Jazz. They'd already done Art Hodes, Harrison had observed sadly about his departed friend with the magic hands. "Art Hodes," Harrison had added, "was a genius. He could swing you into bad health. What do they want with me?"

But he'd agreed to pack his bags and gather his medicines and accept the complimentary tickets for two. What a great relief it must have been when Irena had politely consented to accompany him. From the length of his preface to the invitation, she could tell how well he discerned her complex feelings about the trip. For this generous man she would banish her apprehension and offer steady, banal, and helpful reassurances. She would push the fish-eye lens image of Joszef and her mother to a remote and bewildering corner of her mind and begin reassuring herself that since she would be accompanying Harrison, she could relax. There'd be a human cushion to her visit, a strategy to deflect the emotional bullets that awaited her.

Surely her old man still worried about Irena's vulnerability. What if she elected to stay? Sensing this, she had offered reassurance. She would accompany him. She would return with him. That was the promise she'd also present to her mother like a sealed contract, her zealous mother, who would ignore her words, despite their firmness, and expect her to stay. She did not mention Harrison's own heart, erratic drummer, subject to laziness and short irregular solos, a danger for a man his age anywhere in the world. Still, he was as likely to take ill at home sitting and watching the news.

So reluctantly, with many qualifying clauses but finally great pleasure, Harrison had timidly asked Irena to call and accept the invitation in her flawless Polish. She'd told the jazz society that Harrison would be delighted to attend but had heeded his urging to stress the whole truth: that his health was precarious, that his hands no longer played. Were they sure they wanted him? When they'd relayed their immediate assurances that his presence would sweeten this already glorious event, he had taken to the piano—which she kept dusted for this auspicious occasion. Irena knew that Harrison's strength had been legendary in his two-fisted piano days. She imagined as she stared at his swollen, humble fingers, that he could still hear the music play in his head. Every so often, as she performed her tasks that morning, he'd pick out a few notes by bending his fingers slowly and making them land on the proper keys. For a moment, painfully prolonged, he had plucked the melody to his version of "Nobody's Sweetheart," arthritic syncopation. It was the same song she'd heard Marian MacPartland play with great flourish on *Piano Jazz*. As the notes emerged one by one, each separate and slow, she could feel them in her throat and on her tongue. As he urged his hands to work more smoothly, she knew that the sweetness had never left him. Harrison wasn't old, and all the people he loved most—all of the musicians he had ever played with— were still alive. She knew that their pulses and breath were in his memory of playing in the dark, smoky clubs when his hands were reliable machines, deft little prodigies. Shortly before noon, when Irena was scheduled to leave to run errands, Harrison slowly stood up, straightened, and crept to his chair, where his newspapers awaited him. Then he'd asked Irena for lunch. And Irena, dutifully walking to the kitchen, having observed something she knew was private and sacred and distinct from any other morning of her life, had subdued her desire to comment or applaud.

*   *   *

The pin stuck into the map at Chicago secured many objects. It fastened a school ribbon for spelling; a photo at age three, where Irena sat upon a stuffed black bear and smiled into the glaring sun; a postcard of a turbulent lake slashed with red letters spelling its American name; and Irena's miraculous letter, which said she would be in Warsaw around the turn of the year. Lina had dragged an ottoman in front of the map on the bedroom wall and draped it in assorted doilies. The remaining days of December, she would light a votive candle and say a casual prayer at her shrine: to the memory of the Professor, who would have his daughter on home soil again, to St. Christopher—may engine trouble be banished and airline terrorists writhe in hell—to her mother, for bringing her into this imperfect world and giving her a daughter to love. Husbands were fine, but they died too soon. Religion was useful, but just as a garden, there was upkeep and labor. There were seasons of disappointment. There was occasional blight. But faith in a daughter never could die.

Irena would return, to be sure. What had Lina been thinking those dark, doubting mornings when her mind zigzagged with worry? Irena was coming home to her. Her daughter had devised a scheme to trick her wealthy old man to come all this way. He would even pay for her visit! How clever her Irena, how shrewd—but no matter her intelligence, a long-established fact. She would see her Irena in only a month. Filled with the news, she spent her early morning telling Chopin's double, who had taken to coming in from the small garden with feathers in his mouth; and her poor daughterless friends, who were already envious of her; and the vegetable man, who bestowed the usual cabbage and carrots with new esteem; and the eggman, whose eggs were robustly brown this fine December morning. Her daughter was coming in less than a month. There were so many things to do. Her house, untouched since the Professor's untimely death, still reeking of sadness, had to be dusted, the walls and floors washed with pine soap, the paintings and mirrors shined. It was fine for

Lina to see herself through a clouded lens but not Irena. She would maybe add a few new pillows, a decorative touch here and there. And she would fill the rooms with flowers, how Irena loved flowers. She would go to the market and buy them off-season, no matter their expense. Where did they come from? From Southern Italy or Turkey, where the sun shined all year? Where fields of poppies bloomed, and roses, in profusion, climbed trellises towards the sun? She would purchase a new dress. She had seen a good black one with a flowered sash in a display window—it looked large enough—and she would cook! How she would lay the table. Duck and red cabbage, pirogi and sausage, wonderful potatoes floating in cream and buttery dill weed. The best vodka money could have. Sweet tea with honey. This and more she would procure for Irena.

Maybe the university would have her back, her brilliant daughter who had scored higher than any woman in recent history on the rigorous exams. Her daughter, whose head was filled with numbers and angles and abstractions. Her Irena was returning to her now—by means of a diagonal, the shortest distance between two points. Lina pictured a small luminous plane bisecting a puffy cloud. Of course, she would call Joszef later, but first she wanted to bask selfishly in the knowledge. She had been the first one in Poland to possess the news. What did government officials, poring over their musty files, know compared to her? What did the Pope know in his posh Roman villa so distant from home?

She watched her breasts heave under her dress as she pinned back her hair. Maybe she would go to the beautician's as well. How long had it been since someone had touched her? Months, she guessed, with Irena gone. She'd sit in a fine cushioned chair and lean back and relax as the girl's long fingers massaged her scalp. "Is the water perfect?" the girl would ask and then gently lather again and scrub. Maybe she'd have curls. She hadn't had curls in twenty years.

In returning home, Irena would surely concentrate on the familiar, her mother's warm home, her hospitality, her ability to feed and soothe and offer sound advice. And well Lina could imagine the splendid visit. "My mother's house near Lazienki Park is very comfortable. It is a bit yellow and frayed but full of wonderful smells. I know you will be satisfied," her charming daughter would assure her companion. Her old man would heartily agree that it is more satisfying to stay with Irena's mother than at an anonymous hotel.

While inside the curtained window, Lina, with the care of a navigator in difficult waters, will ready herself for the visit. She will slick down the bodice of her new, too-shiny dress (she really must lose some weight!), run her plump fingers through her bunched gray curls, and wet her lips in anticipation. Then she will appear in the doorway, her mounds of cheeks smeared with tears. Peremptorily assessing and hugging her daughter (how skinny she's grown!), she will turn her attention to directing the arrival. The driver will be dispatched with a few Polish witticisms, their luggage maneuvered onto her square of land. "Please," she will insist in her halting English, "I take."

What will Irena be able to do as her mother vigorously shakes Harrison's hand, then wrestles them for their luggage? It will make Irena feel secure to see what Lina, an army of one, can accomplish with her superior strength and supreme sense of mission.

"I am Lina," she'll repeat warmly, as her guest, a bit faded and confused, finds a seat in her crowded front room. While the burden of hospitality takes Lina's complete attention, Irena will settle herself unobtrusively in her usual corner, from which she will survey the new scenery.

Who is this mother of hers, who has zealously made everything sparkle and reek of pine? Lina's small collection of folksy pillows have reproduced overnight. And all the flowers, Irena will think with admiration, as if someone has recently died or been gloriously wedded! Not in her life has Irena seen such a collection. Crammed on every table will be vases of roses and gladiolas. A willow basket of orchids will provide a centerpiece for the crowded coffee table. And when her mother runs out of vases and counter space, she'll engineer a small miracle, a precarious arrangement on the narrow mantle. Twin drinking glasses hold the longest, strangest blossoms Irena has ever seen. Save for their brash purple fringe, they are phalluses, to be sure. What has her mother paid for this winter garden?

Then Lina will busily lay out endless provisions on the coffee table: tiers of home-baked sweets delicately dusted with white powder, charming teacups spotted with orange pagodas, her familiar stubby-legged teapot, and a lacquered bowl of large yellow apples tinged with faint bruises.

But now something has gone wrong with Lina's vision of the homecoming. Her heart will thump when Irena spots Chopin, who rubs against the legs of both guests in equal recognition. How is it that Irena's cat has become so democratic? How has he ceased to resemble his former self? His dappled legs appear longer and more equine, and when she picks him up to stroke him and whisper how much she has missed his insistent purring in her ear before dawn, he replies curiously with an elongated, doglike yowl. Reaching down to cuddle him, she notices how thinly muscled, scrawny, really, he feels in her hands. Irena will fling down the proplike cat and stare at her mother.

"Mother," she will finally say, her voice thin and contemptuous, as Lina brings more bounty—pomegranates and figs, and a particularly fragrant wedge of Danish cheese—"this is not my Chopin."

Smiling randomly, a searchlight beaming in countless directions, Lina will ask her guest what his pleasure will be. Quietly the bleary-eyed traveler chooses from the assembled riches. When Lina gets to Irena, she replies in Polish, "Sometimes our memories play tricks. You, too, look different from before, perhaps softer and a bit older, my little dove, but I still know that you are my Irena."

"This will not do," Irena says in their adamant tongue. "This cat," her stubborn daughter will say, "is a fraud. I will have you arrested for this."

"How can this be," Lina will ask, "when I have done so well? The flowers, the fruit, the cakes, Irena, do you not see that I have done my best?"

"I will file a report at the station, Mother. I will have you written up for this. Oh, how our family file will grow! So many disgraces attach to our name! Thank God father isn't here to see this new outrage!"

No, this will not do. Before Irena's return, Lina must find the real Chopin. She must restore the cat or her daughter's discerning eyes will name the fraud and berate her for it.

Each day Lina will look for him. She'll visit animal shelters, parks, laboratories, ladies societies, and merchants. Somewhere in Warsaw the real cat must live, the plump, short-legged male that stupid Joszef lost last October. And if he's nowhere on earth, Lina will cast out this foolish new stranger and make a marker in her yard. "This, I am sorry to say, my child, is where your cat now lives. If there is a heaven," and she will cross herself sincerely, "your sweet Chopin is in it."

To banish this thought, Lina directs her attention elsewhere. "Joszef must know," she repeats as she walks to the phone, picking up items along the way—an old newspaper, a yellowed doily that has slipped from its arm on a chair, a speck of debris formerly attached to the cat—and, reading her ancient address book, dials his number.

"Joszef," Lina says when he answers with a strangely droll hello. "I have wonderful news."

"Who is this?" the man is asking.

"This is Lina, the mother of Irena."

"Lina, how are you?" the voice continues without affect.

"I am wonderful, Joszef."

"And why is that?" the apathetic voice asks.

"Because," she says, thinking poor dumb Joszef, dull as a stone, hollow as a bell, "our beautiful Irena is coming home to us."

"What?" Joszef gasps, as if the air around him is being forced down a tube. "When?"

"She is coming in less than a month. We must get ready, Joszef. We must make Warsaw new to her so that she will never leave us again. You will help me then?"

"I will call you in a few hours, Lina. I am still in bed. It is Saturday, is it not, and I was hoping to get a little more rest. I have been too busy lately."

"I am sorry to disturb you," you terrible selfish man, you dolt, Lina whispers to herself. She feels anger heating her chest like a bonfire. "It is important that we speak further. Please call me at your convenience. Do you have my number?"

"I do, Lina, and I will call."

"Good-bye then."

"Good-bye."

Wearily, Joszef hangs up the phone and looks at Urszula, who is staring, goblet-green eyes up at the ceiling.

"That was Irena's mother?" Urszula asks.

"Yes, it was Lina."

"Is everything fine with Irena?"

"It is fine, I suppose," Joszef says, distractedly lighting his first cigarette of the late morning.

"What did she want?"

"She wanted me to know that Irena is returning."

"What?" Urszula laughs. "Our little voyager coming back home so soon—how can this be?"

"Lina has wished this for months. She has prayed and conspired and connived, but I cannot guess how she's arranged it."

"Joszef," Urszula teases, massaging the area between his navel and pubic hair, moving her hand slowly toward his slouching penis, "what does this mean for us?"

Joszef closes his eyes with pleasure and concentrates on the hum of Urszula's playful voice. Why was Irena always so serious, so sober? Why must she return? He can smell that Urszula's already been out of bed and put on coffee. He inhales her talcumy, clean fragrance. "I'm not sure," he says with amusement, "that it means much."

PART THREE

CHAPTER FIFTEEN

I DON'T UNDERSTAND the whole Elizabeth phenomena," Adam told Irena.

"It's a puzzle," Irena agreed.

"She says she is coming to Poland next month with Jack. Now she is missing."

"She came, she saw, she conquered," Adam smiled.

Irena returned his look, lifting her coffee and taking a delicate sip. They were at their favorite booth at the coffeeshop, the same booth where they had discussed American television, gambling, love, and movies. Before Elizabeth had disappeared, before Adam had moved in with his grandfather, before the new trio of starched nurses was rented from the agency. Irena was amused that even with Elizabeth gone, she still could hold sway over the conversation.

"What does Jack say about Elizabeth?"

"Not a word." And he stirred his coffee, thoughtfully balanced a question in the air, withdrew it, dared to offer it. "Was she a golddigger?"

"Please explain."

"Did she use my grandfather?"

Irena had great trouble interpreting his exact question. First, there were the emotional distractions. Adam, whose eyes were beautiful blue marbles, had asked her to lunch. Second, he was so young—so earnest in his quest to make everything understood—and so American—he must resolve the issue quickly. He surely didn't understand Irena's mind, where truth was a remote, beautiful spire on the tower of precision, accessible only with patience, virtue, and labor. How could he expect her to be so hasty? How could he demand so mechanical an analysis of human relations? Was it theory he wanted? Had Elizabeth had a scheme all along? Had it been in place when she arrived, or had she invented one to account for the advantages she found? Were her actions initiated by her own desires? Was she merely attuned to the moment? All of these questions were access roads on Irena's approach to truth. They must be explored before a response was attempted. All the while that she thought, Adam was observing her. It was clear that he was puzzled by her silence. Why can't the mind signal action louder than any siren? Why does it present a dumb show to the world while it performs its most vigorous tasks? Irena was becoming more and more conscious of Adam's need for an answer, but one single sentence wouldn't come to her.

"I don't know," she smiled uncertainly, and they both laughed. All the extraordinary work for this crumb of an answer! There should be sweat and blood to honor such thinking. Instead, a fine nervous laughter fell like confetti from her mouth—and then his. It embarrassed them further to share their mutual embarrassment. They were mute. They were dumb. Each felt a slight tug of longing toward the other that must be privately acknowledged, since they were, after all, honest people. But since they had come together for the good of mankind, since there must be nothing selfish or grasping about their plans for the trip, since there would be injunctions against their intimacy—their feelings must not be spoken. The moment, both dreadful and promising—hung in the balance as Irena took a fierce bite of her turkey sandwich. Adam moodily added sugar to his tea and picked bacon out of his bacon and egg sandwich. Food diversions busied them. The drumming of fingers was contagious. They did not look into each other's eyes. The urge to say something more passed like an unexplained flash of light on the horizon.

"However," Irena finally continued, "Elizabeth was not a fool. She knew of advantages. Perhaps you are asking if she had them in mind all along."

"And there's no way of knowing that."

"Exactly."

"For instance, did she have to accept every gift?"

"We only know of the gifts she did accept. Perhaps she refused others."

Adam smiled in appreciation of Irena's sound reasoning.

"I will say this, Adam. She was good to Jack. She was kind. She accepted his love. But a woman in her circumstance, so distraught, may go to great lengths to get what she needs. Which reminds me of a story I read as a child," she continued. "A bird needs to make a nest in a cold spring. The world is frozen. There are no leaves or twigs. All of what she needs is not available. So the bird makes a nest of snow. She lines the snow with feathers."

"Where did she get the feathers?"

"She pulls them from her very breast."

"Then how did she stay warm?"

"She is unable to stay warm. Worse, she is unable to fly."

"That's a terrible story."

Irena smiled and quickly continued. "She stops being a bird."

"How did she do that?"

"As she is dying, she becomes a flame. She defrosts the whole world."

"And what about her eggs?"

"We never hear of her eggs again, I am afraid. But other birds make their nests, and spring is able to come."

"So Elizabeth did what she had to do."

"Exactly." Biting into her sandwich, Irena felt very wise. "She was alone. She had to provide somehow for herself. She found a way. And maybe Jack is the first man who is kind to her. Living in Albany, she did not experience kindness. I know this from her story. It was tragic thing. She left her home, came to Chicago, and found Jack."

"Which is my point, Irena. Did she use my grandfather?"

"No more than he used her. No more than people do always. She listened to him. She cared for him. She gave herself to him. This gave him hope, for which she received rewards. Remember, Adam, you were not always there. She was all he had for several years. But what is worrying you? Has she taken some possession of great value?"

"Not a thing, but I wanted to do more for him."

"You have done so much."

"I wanted my father to come back, but that can't happen."

"Jack understands that. He is happy with you. He would not let Elizabeth go like this without you. He does not expect miracles."

"He let her go? He knows where she is?"

"Of course, Adam. This is all arranged. He does not want her to have to see him die. He is sure that will happen soon."

"How do you know this?"

"I just do."

"Did Elizabeth tell you?"

"She did not need to tell me, Adam."

"What do you expect to find back in Poland, Irena?"

"I am less certain of that, Adam," she said. "My mother, of course, who is like Poland herself. No matter how it changes on the map, there is always the same Poland."

*   *   *

"Now don't say anything," Elizabeth had told Jack impatiently. "Don't help me tell you." Standing curbside, waiting for her cab to the airport, she imagined herself back in the close air of Jack's sickroom: the view from his bedroom with the moon angled in a corner of the sky and the black water of the lake, lit by long amber strokes of light. She had kissed Jack good-bye, a small friendly kiss—minor, considering their history—and had promised to write, but when had she ever written letters? She couldn't write like Irena—her friend who used words more precisely, who knew how to make things seem momentous with her voice, her hands, her eye blinks. Of course she wouldn't write. She'd call Jack as soon as she found a place for herself. He would want to know that she was safe.

Elizabeth couldn't understand how Irena had come to possess the world she simply visited. It was as if her friend dignified the moment when she took a comb to her hair, when she pulled on her brown tights with her thin, proficient hands, when she ordered tea with extra lemon. Each act was a gesture of self-regard, as Adam's movie had likewise been. Why couldn't Elizabeth adopt this same assured pose, she wondered, as she watched a child pirouette on her stocky little legs wrapped in red tights?

Now the child's mother, a tall woman, dressed too lightly for cold December, shouted warnings. "You're getting in people's way. Stand still, for God sakes, before you fall over."

And knowing her small, contingent place in her mother's regard, the little girl instantly obeyed. Standing soberly beside the doorman, she faded into the scene, just as Elizabeth had always done when her mother's withering gaze landed upon her. Why did so many women move warily, like trespassers, through life? That was what Elizabeth had feared most for Kayla, that despite her vows and resolves, Elizabeth might have seeded the same garden of insecurity her mother had planted in her. That child standing so still, knowing what little concern the world had for her, might have been Kayla.

But if Kayla had lived—and here Elizabeth always sighed deeply, feeling a resonant wave of self-pity—things would have been different. The night before, after she'd reserved her plane ticket for California and packed her belongings, she'd explained to Jack that Kayla had been her one opportunity in life. She was comfortable admitting this to him. For all of his posturing, there was nothing that didn't get under his skin. That he was defenseless, like Elizabeth, and pathetically brave, tied a final knot of sympathy between them. Elizabeth felt ashamed about ever having doubted him, as she had that day at the frozen beach. It was Jack with his crude emotions, who was qualified to know more. Irena could be trusted with the easy part—about the baby—but Jack deserved the full story. And so, before the long day had closed and she had served him his usual tea with the extra sugar cubes, she had pulled his door tight.

"Jack," she had said in a hushed voice wobbling with fear, "I need to explain some things to you, but I'm not good at this. Irena and Adam, they use words well. Irena, with her broken sentences, can talk me into a corner. I wish there was some other way, but I need you to know this, Jack. I wish we'd been together for a long time. Then you could have watched me grow up and understood me better. I wouldn't have had to have said a word then.

"Sometimes I imagine that you're my grandfather. I do," she reaffirmed into his bemused face. "I wouldn't have disappeared for years like the others if I had been, I can tell you that.

"I wasn't good in school. I bet you were, so maybe you would have done something different. I never had a job or a man that mattered, until you Jack, so when I got pregnant, I was doing something important.

"I loved Kayla. You should see how I'd dress her in her little outfits and play with her all the time. Sometimes my mom would say that I treated her like a doll. 'Wait 'til she gets a mouth!' Mom warned. 'Then we'll see what you're made of.'

"That was the problem with my mother. She was always looking for a way for me to lose, even when I was winning. She was always there to point out the thorns. I know you weren't that way with Roy because I never see you act that way to Adam.

"With Kayla I felt confident, like the world didn't matter for once. I was so good with her that I mattered."

She had paused then and breathed deeply. She had left the room, brought them both more tea, smoothed his bed, and studied his eyelids to see if they were flirting with sleep.

"Now Kayla's like a tatoo. I can't look at the world without seeing Kayla. I can't be with a man. I can't be alive because I lost her, Jack. Those nights we were together, I wasn't with you. I was cheating because I was with Kayla."

"What you gave me was fine, Elizabeth. I'm just sorry you're so unhappy."

"Everyone's sorry. So what good is it?"

Jack had extended his arms to her, and Elizabeth had curled up beside him in the bed. "You're good, Elizabeth," he'd said, stroking her hair. "You're my girl."

"But my baby."

Jack stroked Elizabeth's hair as she wet his pillow, his scrawny arm, his shoulder, his old man's woolly ear with tears.

"It's okay," he whispered.

"How do I live, Jack?"

"Forget her, like you told me about Roy."

"And did you?" Elizabeth asked, sniffling bravely and blowing her nose.

"Of course not," Jack shrugged, smiling absurdly. "But we're both survivors, Elizabeth."

"How can I leave you, Jack?"

"I'll be all right. Adam's a good boy. You've taken care of me fine, but this is no way for a pretty girl to live. You have your whole life, sweetie. C'mon, let's get some rest."

She had spent her last night in Chicago in Jack's bed, thinking how comfortable she felt sleeping next to a man who had killed and comforted people with the same mind and the same heart.

California did make her feel different. Maybe it was the simple and immediate change in the weather that altered her perspective. Rubbing her wrist along her damp hairline, she observed how even the metallic airport world seemed brighter, more vivacious than the one she had left. Heat throbbing off the tarmac didn't obscure her vision of everyone's tanned, permanent youth. Old people in wheelchairs were healthier than their Chicago counterparts. Steel glistened. Floor tiles glowed like Christmas bells. The sky, a gauzy gray-blue, seemed soft and welcoming.

And, of course, there was the excitement. No one else in the airport lived such a glamorous life. Just the thought of the thin envelope with the huge check made her dizzy. How much would it be in singles? Maybe if you stacked it up, it would extend past the palm trees she saw in the distance. She had never seen a palm tree on a boulevard before, odd improvisation on plant life. They were part of the new state of mind she couldn't describe except for its lightness. It made her think of herself in possession of possibilities and hope: beautiful hair, shiny teeth—a confident gaze to hold people's attention—like those people on game shows who are destined to win.

Maybe all those months with Jack had been harder than she'd imagined. Now that she would sit by a pool and close her eyes, different aspects of herself might become more pertinent. She was young, she was pretty. She had $50,000 for herself and tons of jewelry. That and more to come if she just asked, and Jack was just a phone call away.

When she saw the pool in the courtyard below her hotel room, she thought she might like settling in California. She could always get some kind of job and make her resources stretch. And lots of inexpensive low-rises had bean-shaped pools like this one, which reminded her of her fourteenth summer, the one before high school. Johnny Reardon with the high bridge of freckles on his nose; Brady Digges, with his swoop of blond hair; Harry Pelankis, of the cavernous eyes, who'd played minor league baseball after high school—countless boys had thrown her through the high sun of June into the blue water of the Rangle Park Public Pool. Her naked legs had ringed their necks like a wreath as they chicken-fought in the shallow end or prepared to toss her toward the deep. She had admired her own lithe body as she danced to disco music in her fishnet bathing suit on the slippery salmon-colored deck. She was young, boys' lips were ready; everything glimmered and shined irresistibly.

Friday nights all summer, she and her crowd of girls would head to the mall to watch *Saturday Night Fever*. There, they'd be inspired by this hopeful, mundane tale of American possibility. Yes, talent did count for something. Someone's feet could win him a place in the world. For several years that movie developed her concept of how she'd make her way. It was the closest the world had come to giving her a clue. Who else was supposed to teach her? Not her family. Her sisters, older by ten and twelve years, had married after high school, had children, gotten divorced or not—it didn't seem to matter either way. Then they'd zigzagged back and forth from her mother's gloomy kitchen with their babies, cigarettes, odd jobs, food stamps, black eyes, tears, court orders, reconciliations—an endless cycle of exits and entrances. Long cigarette ashes accumulated. Curses were shared and improved on over the years. All of them drank some, talked too much on the phone, cooked indifferently, streaked their hair, ignored their bills, lost their electricity; all made promises they never kept, to leave the sorry losers they'd met on assembly lines, in country & western bars, at the Dairy Queen or midnight weekend candlelight bowling. But each man was a new chance. Each time they were infected with something close to religion. Each time didn't seem like the last one.

During their stints at love, their own futile trails were dogged by the memory of their father, Clark O'Conner of Elizabeth's childhood photos—hair combed in front like a surf wave, thin chest sprouting fuzz around the shirt collar—looking lost in a sea of girls. Their model of male behavior had simply snuck out one night after he'd been laid off from his job as a beer truck driver. He was too ashamed, their mother had explained. He was a proud man, she said for awhile. He was a fool, a mean, drunken bastard. "Sometimes he hit me," she repeated with more fervor as his departure created a decade-long habit.

They became a family utterly suspicious of men. There were special sayings around the house and looks they shared when they noticed possible signs of treachery in strangers, in the husbands and lovers of friends, in characters on television ("What damn fool would think of trusting J.R.?"). To accompany their derision was a litany of sayings: "All men are alike"; "They screw you, then they *screw* you"; "Men—can't live with them, can't live with them"; "Don't make my brown eyes black and blue." And there was advice: "Keep your legs together"; "Take the money and run," though her sisters never had the chance. Elizabeth was surprised they didn't have kitchen samplers embroidered with their slogans.

So many times at those Friday night features, Elizabeth had vowed that her life would be different from her mother's and her sisters'. Like John Travolta or like Sissy Spacek in *Coal Miner's Daughter*, she'd find a talent and pursue it. Like Debra Winger in *An Officer and a Gentleman*, she'd find a decent guy who'd carry her out of her surroundings to a better place, and she'd go willingly. She'd find a way out and she'd find love. The two might be synonymous for all she knew. Maybe her house was an aberration and the rest of the world lived by other more forgiving rules.

At first Roger's kitchen, shinier than any white she had ever seen, had been her evidence. She'd sit at a butcher block table in a tan barrel chair and think how free she felt, how she had already surpassed her rather listless high school career by meeting a man ten years her senior and living in The Oaks Apartment Complex on the side of town where so many things were new: strip malls with shiny green cupolas, windows framed by franchise neon, mazes of fern bars, trays of appetizers with Oriental names, fake Tiffany glass, collector mugs for every television promotional occasion that was invented.

But Roger wasn't so new. He still had a wife who sometimes called; who had a name—Jennifer, who'd given him a son—

Peter, who was seen on Sundays without fail. It was Peter's funny mouth and winning way of accepting things without question—"I want soda," for which Elizabeth could provide any liquid response—iced tea, milk, grape juice, orangeade—that had begun to make her a little careless with her diaphragm. Now and then, she was too tired to get it. She'd run out of the gooey cold gel used to coat it. She'd want Roger just at that moment when he came out of the shower after work, and his long body glistened with moisture.

Now and then became mostly. Six months and three days after they'd moved in together, she'd taken the home pregnancy test, the cheapest one she could find. All day at work she'd thought about the miniature cup of urine in their refrigerator behind the orange juice and Coors. She'd raced home before Roger and tested it out, and yes, the indicator was positive that she carried Roger's baby.

"Guess what?" she'd asked between bites of a cheese omelette they were sharing at dinner.

"You're pregnant," Roger smiled.

"How did you know?" she smiled back.

Roger put down his fork, turned in his seat so his long knees faced away from her, rubbed something invisible from his face and hands with the red cloth napkin she'd placed on the table to be festive. "Do you know what this means?"

"It means I'm going to have a baby."

"I thought we were being careful."

"We were, but not careful enough. The test is never wrong."

"I'm up for a promotion."

"Good."

"I mean, there are certain standards where I work. It's okay I'm not with Jennifer, but we're not married."

"So?"

"What will Jennifer say?"

"Why does that matter?"

"Why do I work at Martone's?"

"You like to sell cars."

"Jennifer's uncle got me the job."

"So you can have a life."

"I know, but I never asked her about children."

"Jennifer, can I have sex? Can I have children? God, Roger. She left you."

Recalling this moment with almost a laugh now, a moment that used to require some of her family's more malevolent sayings, Elizabeth understood that it was her relation with Jack that was the turning point for the O'Conner women, who had heretofore unhappily married Maginneses, Laskowskis, Desmonds, Dukes—men of their age, their religion, men from the streets of Albany, the products of the same dismal kitchens—all adding another like note to the chorus of failure. Someone had finally done something different.

Yes, her time with Jack—not her fourteenth summer, not her months of presumed happiness with Roger—had been the best. His trust in her, his kindness, the patience of his old man's body, his willingness to please her, to speak to her when they made love, to share his memories, his stories, his ghosts—those were the best things that had ever happened. She closed her eyes now, warm and sleepy from the long day. Jack's reassuring arm, its sinewy flesh and forest of white hair, was the last thing she remembered before falling asleep.

CHAPTER SIXTEEN

RENA, I WISH you had seen me back then," Harrison sighed. They were playing at being comfortable in their posh airline seats. Harrison stirred his second Dewars. He had convinced Irena to try a Bloody Mary, which she was using more as a prop than a drink. What is it about airline travel that makes people more forthcoming? Her reserved companion was suddenly full of information.

"I could make folks draw a breath. They used to tell me I was real, I was cuttin'. That's how we talked then. We talked the talk and walked the walk. We cooked back then."

"You cooked?" she smiled.

"That's right," Harrison continued. "And all the time Gwen was there like some guardian angel, smiling at me from her seat at the bar or at the nearest table. She just loved me when I played.

"When we traveled like this together across the Atlantic, I held her in my arms on the deck of a ship. I couldn't believe my eyes, how everywhere was water, and me and Gwen, two little people from Chicago, were floating into that nothingness with so much hope in our bright heads, hope percolating and giving off heat. It's like that when you're young, Irena. Everything can and will happen tomorrow. And damn you're good. And damn you deserve it.

"I held Gwen on that big white boat, bigger than a building, and I made promises. I couldn't promise her money—she already had that—so I promised her children. 'We'll make babies and more babies, as soon as we make Paris,' I told her. 'Now,' she said, 'on the ocean, Harrison.'

"So we got to work, Irena. We worked at it like I used to practice my piano way back in church when it was closed from religious business and my mama would sit and listen to me for twenty minutes daily, doing my Chopin and my Bach. Then as a reward she'd let me rip, and I'd slide into a song like you slide into mud in the rain. You slip and let go. You fall and let it cover you whole. You don't care how you sound. You don't care how you look or who's looking.

"Then, all of a sudden, I'm making sounds no one's ever heard before. People are coming to church all hours just to hear me play. The neighbors are bringing their grandbabies. My old teacher is coming with her older mama. The reverend's dropping in to listen after leading Bible group.

"Then Mama's taking me to shady places I don't expect she'd otherwise go. She's a good, God-fearing, honest woman, but she knows I have the gift.

"Fourteen years old, I'm there standing in front of local giants holding their horns and their bottles and joking with no let up 'til they hear me play. Then there's silence way after I'm done 'til one of them says, 'You're right, lady. This boy can wail.'

"I don't see faces anymore, Irena. I just see a glow, like I'm looking at something through rain or sweat. I'm seeing something that won't focus before my eyes. The piano is all liquid, their faces are wet flowers, and I know I have it, yes, I do.

"Now, wouldn't it be great if other things worked so smooth? All the time on the ocean, all the time in Paris and back, Gwen and me went at it like crazy, like we were inventing new forms of music, like we were learning new instruments. I won't embarrass you with the details, but the lesson's this, and this is why there's sadness, Irena. This is why good people cause each other pain," and he reached to adjust his pillow and pull the shade to block out their first-class view of the gray Atlantic as evening fell.

"The thrill is easy, but it's not the thrill that finally counts. It's the result. If all the music in the world can't get you the result, then you're lost.

"'No baby!' Month after month, I'd hear Gwen howl with rage. I watched her beautiful eyes turn mean. It wasn't going to be. And even when we'd gotten used to it, when we'd decided it was for the best with me always traveling, on the road all over hell and back for years, even when we'd made our peace and said we were content, I could say one word—Paris—and all the tears, all the anger, all the tortured love that we'd brought out of ourselves to yield nothing, would flow again.

"'Like the Bible,' Gwen would say, 'like a voodoo curse, Harrison, like the empty womb that is a punishment for sins. Whose sins?' she'd moan on and on. She'd nearly spit at me as her whole body would rise with her voice. 'Never say *Paris*. That place robbed us of the real music. All your playing, all your drinking, all your concentrating on other things stole babies from me, Harrison. Now when we die no one will carry our names. No one will miss us.'

"'Won't you miss me?' I'd smile best I could.

"'Look at him!' she'd shout at the walls. 'Thinks he's better than me. Mr. Only-The-Good-Die-Young thinks he'll go first.'

"So that's how I got together with you, Irena, why we're on the road together at this point. And now that we're all alone on that same ocean, I have one question, which you don't have to answer. But what I want to know, what Gwen was asking—and I think she was right to ask—is this: Who will miss me?"

What can she say to deflect his loneliness? Maybe the trip to Poland was a foolish idea for such an old man. Maybe the darkness over the ocean, like a cauldron of troubles, conjures fears. "Many people love you, Harrison," Irena reassures softly, trying to push her own dread of arrival out of her mind. As she pictures the stifling kitchen of her mother's house, she feels Harrison patting her cold and reticent hand.

*   *   *

What a terrible flight Irena had already endured and now this day! Her nerves were raw and trembly. Though her mother was overheating the house for her American guest, she couldn't stop shivering. Then her mother's kindness to Harrison had made Irena feel cruel in her judgment. Lina was, after all, a good person whose daughter felt too little appreciation. And this strange turn of events: that her mother, who had never betrayed the slightest interest in anything outside of Irena and the professor, was suddenly showing Harrison a formidable collection of jazz records. Shiny 78s in hefty gray boxes had supplanted the crystal candelabra in the dining room. Huddled around the old phonograph like conspirators, Harrison and Lina listened to a scratchy sweet voice launching "Blue Moon" into a shiny new heaven. Though her mother spoke little English, she and Harrison were exchanging warm smiles and excited phrases that included "Ella," "Armstrong," and "Bix."

"Why were you keeping your mother a secret? She's a national treasure," Harrison remarked to Irena as she knotted his tie.

"What?" Irena asked puzzled.

"Your mother's a fan," Harrison smiled. "Mr. Majewski's real pleased that she thought of bringing me here."

Irena stored this odd new fact along with others that she would share with Lina when time permitted. Meanwhile, she tried to interpret her new information with the zeal of an anthropologist. She fingered the records in their brown and gray sleeves and wondered when her parents had pursued this avocation, obviously in some twilight past before Irena's existence. She had seen pictures of them in the late 1940s when they were first married. Her dapper father was dressed in a suit with broad shoulders. His love for Lina was captured in an airbrushed palette of pastels. Lina wore a fox stole, its pointy little head facing toward her short slim legs. Irena had always suspected that her preoccupied smile revealed her hope for a child, and Irena imagined herself, invisible in the photos of her parents' first fourteen years of marriage, as the beacon which they were approaching over a course of years.

But who knows, Irena suddenly thought. Maybe her mother's look was anticipation of an evening of American jazz, a secret pleasure that must have sprung from the rubble of the war. Her look had everything to do with the present and nothing with the future. With Warsaw in ruins and the Soviets claiming it as their own, her parents had fashioned a better new world. Only years later had the idea of Irena even occurred to them. Maybe Fats Waller was playing his seductive dreamy notes at the very moment Irena had been conceived! Were it not for Fats Waller, perhaps she wouldn't exist.

So when Lina had wanted Irena to postpone her plans and keep her company, Irena had pursued Harrison's lead. "Mother," she smiled ever so slightly, "You never told me about your interest in jazz."

"Your father and I were great fans."

"And why didn't I know?"

"Irena, there are so many things you do not know about me. Your father and I were young once. We had our enthusiasms, our pleasures. We ate at odd little restaurants owned by foreigners. We loved American jazz. On weekends in summer we hung Chinese lanterns all around the yard and had music festivals right here. The phonograph would play all night, and our friends would dance right under the window of your future nursery.

"Don't look at me that way, Irena. All that I tell you is true. Is it so hard for you to imagine that I was young once? During that time we and our friends were very daring. We would go to secret art exhibits that the government had banned. People showed art right in their homes. In many unassuming parlors, we saw fine European paintings. It made us feel connected to the rest of the world, less troubled about our possibilities here. It was consolation, this music and this art, that told us about freedom. When the Russians presented Warsaw with our hideous Palace of Culture, we protested; secretly for years, we boycotted it with our jokes. 'Stalin and culture are a contradiction in terms,' your father always said. One would have done culture a favor if a small bomb had been detonated in that building.

"Yes, I was young then, Irena, and as thin as you. I wore hats with ostrich feathers, which are gone now, but I have these old records to remind me. I never considered my dedication to that era until you mentioned Harrison."

"And what is it you did then?"

"I uncovered the record player and listened to some Louis Armstrong and 'Fatha' Hines. They were my favorites. Then I looked in your father's drawer for the number of Mr. Majewski. Anton Majewski has been an acquaintance for forty years. He is an unattractive little man who resembles a rat, but he is very intelligent. I told him how much your father and I had always adored Harrison Waters' music. I told him that your Mr. Waters would love to visit Warsaw."

"But, Mother, you never mentioned in your letters that you and father knew of his music. You never acknowledged knowing Harrison. 'Tell your black man this. Tell your black man that,' you wrote so many times."

"Truthfully, Irena, we did not know Harrison or his music. It was you who told me of his reputation. It was a miracle when it turned out that Mr. Majewski knew of your Mr. Waters. He is a celebrated man. When I explained that my daughter had a connection, he took it from there." Lina's face shone like a trophy.

*   *   *

Three times, Irena had counted in the cab to Joszef's, there had been the small matter of cat phantoms. Irena had thought she'd seen Chopin first as she arrived at her mother's house from the airport, later, out the window that faced her garden,

and now, driving in the Old Town in the bluish late afternoon
light. Why wouldn't she accept what she'd been told, that
Chopin's narrow grave was in Lina's yard?

She had closed her eyes to the city that was changed for her.
Sleeker foreign cars lined the streets. Tourists gathered in
front of hotels with large decorative awnings and international logos. Even the old drunks waiting for trolleys seemed
somehow more deliberate, more crisp in their steps.

How strange now, after the dreamy ride, to be walking as a
visitor up her familiar old stairs, dank and steep and musty
with winter air. The hallway was the same unperturbed
brown, the manager's name was the same; the wall sconces
flickered as they always did at dusk. All these mundane facts
struck Irena as a revelation while she stood for what seemed
like forever pressing on her poorly wired former bell.

"Irena!" Urszula shouted, wrapping her in a dizzying
embrace. Irena thought she smelled the perfume she had left
behind with Joszef for fear it would have shattered in her suitcase. Her old friend looked radiant in her soft gray sweater
and jeans. That she wore no shoes but dark thick socks struck
Irena as shameful by Polish standards. Though she had accustomed herself to going barefoot on Harrison's plush carpeting,
shoelessness still seemed an aberration on native soil. And
why Urszula, her most sophisticated friend, would adopt this
habit, Irena couldn't guess.

Shaking her head with authority, Urszula explained to
Irena, who hesitated at the threshold, that Joszef had gone out
for coffee. "But he was coming to see you later!" she added
quickly.

"I arrived late last night," Irena stated, looking past Urszula,
whose body was effectively denying her the opportunity to
scan the horizon of her apartment.

"I know. Your mother called."

"And I was eager to see him."

"He will return soon," Urszula smiled nervously.

Irena walked forward, more aware of the combination of

apprehension and anticipation whistling in her ears than the familiar place she was reentering.

"Please, sit down," Urszula said softly. "Let me get you some tea."

She came back holding one of Irena's favorite old teacups, the violet-covered one. "I am surprised, Irena," she began, offering her cubes of sugar from Irena's old sugarbowl, "that Joszef has told you nothing."

"I am not understanding," Irena said quietly. Judging from the luster of odd objects—her former tea kettle, the silverware draining in her old tray, a brass doorknob she must have touched thousands of times—she might lose her eyesight before she did comprehend.

"Joszef and I are together now." Urszula paused. "We did not mean this to be, but coming together, God knows how, we found ourselves compatible. It was a small miracle."

"You live here with him?" Irena gulped in air but was otherwise immobile in her former chair.

"I am keeping my own apartment, but, yes, I do stay here much of the time."

"Then perhaps you know this, Urszula," she said, voice lifting with purpose. "What has become of my cat?"

"Your mother has him, so to speak."

"She says my cat is buried in her yard."

Urszula served up a wry smile. Her gray eyes grew tiny and winsome with knowledge. "This is an unbelievable story, Irena. Joszef was bringing your cat to Lina's house on a bus, which, as you know, is a very long ride. It was October, the bus was sweltering, and Joszef fell asleep. While he slept, the cat disappeared, carrier and all. Joszef was frantic and confused. When he told Lina the sad news, it was her opinion that a new Chopin needed to be located so that her descriptions to you could be vivid and realistic. Joszef found a good match, but as your arrival grew closer, there were more calls. Lina began to believe that the match would not satisfy you. She must have given the cat away and dug the grave quite hastily since you have appeared earlier than expected. I have no idea what is buried in her yard except her fantasies."

"I am speechless," Irena murmured, "about so many things. In all of our years here, Urszula, you never indicated an interest in Joszef. You led me to believe that I was not to be envied for having him. You would even mock us."

"Isn't it strange, Irena? Joszef at a distance seems lacking. Observed more closely, it is a different story. I am happy with him, Irena, though we are opposites. You know how I am often amused? I think, perhaps, you and he were too much alike. You duplicated your troubles when you were together, and so they weighed you down. I can laugh at Joszef to console him."

Irena closed her eyes and thought of consolation, which appeared in the form of Harrison, with his jaunty fez and mild eyes. She thought fondly of Cristof and his solitary bedroom zeal. Elizabeth, for all her complexity, took on the redemptive singular glow of memory. The general kindness of her American friends was uncomplicated and tender. Its value grew as she considered how everything about Poland was lost to her. Standing at her mother's threshold upon her return the sky had been the imprecise hue of a lost letter. Drab birds sat on motionless trees. There was no lake to offer a lulling backdrop, no wind to urge them on. The entire landscape was listless, fixed in Irena's critical eye. The city that Irena has craved like a lover's fingers was a staid portrait in grays and halftones. The newness she had fought in Chicago had been her own fear of giving up Joszef, but now she would give up Joszef along with her fear, which had fused in several places.

"Tell Joszef he is not to visit me at my mother's. Thank him, too, for being so thoughtful about my Chopin. It is funny how people are fooled only briefly. It has taken me so long not to be fooled by Joszef, however, that I doubt my own intelligence."

"I am sorry you feel this way."

"I have one more request, Urszula. If you would be so kind, please discard my old perfume. It doesn't suit you, I am afraid."

*　　*　　*

"Chicago Jazz: A Tribute to Harrison Waters" was having its dress rehearsal at 8:00 P.M. at the Marriott. But before Irena would join him there, as she'd promised, she needed to return to her mother's house.

Lina was waiting for her at the door. "Three young men came for your friend in a car. Mr. Majewski has phoned for us twice. He hopes to see us soon."

"We must talk, Mother."

"I'll make tea," Lina said brightly. "Yes, there is so much to say," she added.

"This afternoon, Mother, I went to see Joszef, and I found that he is living with Urszula."

"No!" Lina frowned.

"When I heard this news, I wanted to leave very quickly, but instead I asked Urszula one thing. I asked about Chopin."

Lina blushed. Her empty mouth nervously chewed air.

"I am surprised that you can still blush, Mother."

"I thought maybe it would hurt you less, Irena. I thought it was best for you not to know."

With Irena silent, Lina continued.

"And remember, please, I've told you about Joszef again and again. He is a selfish man." She shrugged and smiled slightly as her voice took on power. "But you were always headstrong, Irena. You would not listen to me."

"But Mother, when you heard I was coming, how could you have imagined I would not know?"

"It was my hope, Irena. That is all."

"And now?"

"And now I am fond of the little cat, which is useless to you. I will keep him—he is staying with Jadwiga down the street— but give him a new name."

"Mother," Irena said, tears for the whole foolish day pooling over, "do you think I have returned to you?"

"I am hoping this, but I do not know, Irena." And in haste

she opened a drawer. "Here are some small things," which she removed quickly, "that I have saved, insignificant but carrying so much of father. Mostly useless to others, I would expect. Some letters," she says, holding out a thick packet tied with twine, "and a manuscript I could not risk sending. I can not judge its value, but you are more clever, Irena. I give it all to you. Coins not worth much, I have discovered since last I wrote, but still you must have them."

Irena watched her mother's plump fingers fumbling in the pile of paper. She covered her mother's hand with hers. "Do you understand, Mother?" she asked softly.

"Harrison tries to explain that you probably will not stay, but I do not know besides that."

"What did he say?" Irena asked with alarm.

"He says that there is a Polish man in Chicago. He maybe needs you? This sounds very promising to me, Irena," she smiled. "He is a handsome, polite young man?" Her voice was pumped with optimism as she continued. "Thank goodness that Joszef has Urszula. I gave him a hot water bottle for sleeping, but Urszula is a little better, perhaps."

*   *   *

The Marriott was filled with Polish jazz enthusiasts with various beards, berets, suits, turtlenecks, boots, satchels, and blue jeans. Here and there an intense young woman, who reminded Irena of herself or of photos of her mother in her twenties, could be spotted in a small thicket of men. On the stage a young man with an earring was droning in thickly accented English. Irena heard various familiar words again and again: *Harrison Waters, Chicago, Prohibition, two-fisted piano.* Otherwise, she was not listening. She was straining to see Harrison and simultaneously coaxing her mother along. Lina was plodding behind her, thickset and slow, in a brown woolen coat and matronly shoes, observing her feet as she walked. Irena remembered the many rooms she had awkward-

ly entered at her mother's side. A force in her own home, Lina
had always been reticent in public. Irena was whispering reas-
suringly and pulling her forward by a coat sleeve. "Please,
Mother, come along with me," she urged. "We are late. We
must find seats."

Finally, she took her hand and led her as one does a child.

"Look!" Lina pointed. "It is Mr. Majewski. Do you remember him, Irena?"

Irena saw an old man with a rather long red goatee. He was
her mother's age, at least. As she looked his way, he threw
Irena, or was it Lina, a courtly kiss.

"Mr. Majewski," Lina whispered and nodded in his direction.

Now in the pink-and-purple room that looked so American
with its new vinyl seats and bright track lighting, Lina was
pointing. She had spotted Harrison, dapper in his camel-hair
jacket and lovely songbird tie that Irena had knotted for him
earlier in the day. Irena and her mother walked slowly toward
the front of the auditorium. She noted on the walls, which still
gave off the sheen and aroma of newness, poster-sized photos
of Harrison seated behind countless pianos. At the center of
the stage, he was pictured at a table, joking with a woman
whom Irena recognized as Gwen, beaming his benign
approval at the world.

Irena moved with more conviction toward her destination
now. "Come, Mother," she whispered to Lina, who had fallen
behind once again. "He is beginning."

Irena and her mother stood in the aisle listening to the
announcer say into the microphone, "Good evening, Ladies
and Gentlemen. Mr. Majewski, Vice-President of the Warsaw
Jazz Society, wishes to extend a welcome to all of you here,
and especially to Lina Bozinska and her daughter Irena, who
have made it possible for us to host Mr. Harrison Waters. We
are very grateful and hugely honored." Irena blushed warmly
as the audience applauded and she heard the announcer continue, "Live from the Dreamland Cafe, formerly appearing at

the Zeppelin Inn and the Platinum Lounge, Ladies and Gentlemen, Mr. Harrison Waters."

"Excuse me," she whispered in English as she made her way down the long row of plush new chairs. She smiled at the vow she had just made, to begin dreaming in English, the language that had comforted her without her knowing. At the same time, the stage was ignited by sound from two echoing grand pianos.

CHAPTER SEVENTEEN

WHY DID AIRPLANES have to fly in the dead of night when the unlit world swirled into obscurity? Jack wasn't able to see the Atlantic, fickle ocean, which had christened his parents' steamer, then imperiled its voyage west. The main character in his mother's favorite saga was invisible; he wouldn't see the water where his mother tasted her first banana (*"I thought I was supposed to eat the skin!"*), or (and here the mood always sobered), strained to sniff the unsullied air of the New World. How could it be that the irregular coast of her beloved America, which had offered a general taste of freedom and mostly little else, was slipping under Jack, unseen?

While the other passengers were sleeping, Jack savored the isolation that night afforded, a time when the fear of death used to hound him. Now that he was dying, he could use these unobserved hours for philosophy. In Jack's metaphysics, the sky was a mine. He had come with his pick axe and shovel to sound its walls and reveal traces of precious stone. In the padded seat, where his body took up so little room, Jack observed Adam beside him, the kindest, gentlest boy he could know. He had to give Roy some credit for his gift of Adam, who had a way of amorphously dispelling fear. With Adam, Jack wouldn't die, at least not for now. And maybe never, he thought, suddenly animated by the soft hum of his grandson's breathing.

Just then, his thought vanished as the plane caught an air pocket, punctuating his euphoria with proper respect for natural forces. He supposed that for Irena the trip had been different. She had headed into the darkness toward home, a place where intimate connections obscured the historic context, a home older than anything that had ever surrounded Jack. If his parents had stayed and somehow survived the war, Jack might have lived there comfortably, but he rather doubted it. He needed the impromptu nature of Chicago, a city that had blown across the map and stopped a moment before drowning, a city where anything was possible. Sure, there was already an aristocracy when his family had arrived, the Pullmans and McCormicks with their beautiful stone mansions, people whose wealth was old by local standards, fellow greenhorns by Old World appraisal. Nothing was indelible about his city; history books could easily be changed when the subject itself was flux. But Europe—Europe with its castles and coats-of-arms and decaying manuscripts written by candlelight, with its kings and serfs and tapestries and famines and Chopins and cathedrals and pogroms and nights of shattered glass—how could little Jack Kaufman have swum in that sea?

The plane plowed through the sky all night, bucking air currents that fought to subdue it. It moved by faith alone, Jack was certain. He remembered how Essie would clutch his forearm on flights and open her worried brown eyes wider than wide. She was sure they would die, but she could never speak it. She had learned from her mother, mistress of dread, that words were charms, and luck was something for which a person bore ultimate responsibility. "What you want to keep," the small lady with the somber eyes would warn in Yiddish, "people take from you. What you don't want, they throw back in your face like cold water." Confusing your enemies had been Ida's strategy, Ida of the curses and salt over her shoulder and spitting into her palm to ward off Eastern European harm.

According to Essie, there were no evil eyes here, Essie, the all-American. What did Jack and Essie, babes in the woods, know of pogroms? How *could* they know, Ida shouted, while she chopped eggs and onions in her old scarred bowl. It was true that compared to their parents' troubles and terrors, the Depression was a small economic blip. Jack remembered how scrawny, irascible Ida would stoke her apprehensions: by finding coins and stealthily hiding them; by buying rotten fruit from Mr. Bruno, who sold it dirt cheap; by warning Jack to beware of particular strangers on the street, as if she knew his real business and its unforeseen perils. "Look what a good thing I've found!" she would announce to her New World daughter, a discriminating shopper, before revealing a bedraggled scarf run over by a trolley car, or a single earring missing some essential bead.

Having taken their first breaths in America, Jack and Essie were strangers to real trouble. And all of their adult lives, they'd never chosen to travel back to its demarcations on the map. For them, the Old Country, renamed by their parents' bitter stories and their sense of relief at having escaped their unspeakable conclusion, bore a warning label. He and Essie had been all over the Caribbean. They had swum in the bluest, clearest water on earth. They had visited Cuba when it was livelier than Miami and Las Vegas put together. But they'd never reversed their parents' journey.

Jack had been swimming inside his mother when she first laid eyes on New York, where no one had been kind except the Irishman who'd put them on the train to Chicago. Now, through the blackness of the sky, he was returning to the country that his mother discussed with trepidation and his father waved off with his hand like so much bad produce.

Now, likewise, he waved off the thought of his earlier voyages to concentrate on Essie. Soon he'd take up residence beside her in the Poppy Section of Westlake, a cheerful cemetery on the unhistoric western outskirts of the city, where most of Chicago's Jews were buried side to side like former tenement neighbors. His mother's body was there, but her little apartment in the Jewish part of Warsaw? Graves in the air, he thought, for those like her, whose place in the world had passed brutally in his lifetime. An atrocity that couldn't be comprehended swallowed up the simplest request of a man— to see his mother's birthplace.

And he smiled sardonically to think that in Chicago, such a place might have been cleared away long ago by a person with far more trivial motives, a person such as himself, who erased history through enterprise, then mooned through the night for its return. But if nostalgia were to dominate, Jack chuckled, we'd be sitting on a dung heap, our beautiful heads filled with tender ideas.

It amused him how his imminent demise fit into the plan— the small matter of his obituary, for instance. Would he be remembered as someone who plowed up sacred places, who obliterated the story of anonymous citizens? To what shopping mall would a sorry guy go to pay his last respects? What shoe store? Could memory mediate a truce between progress and nostalgia?

But it was more than nostalgia, Jack knew. It was everyone's birthright not to be plowed under. It was our small consolation to build houses of memory and to travel through the windowless night to arrive at them. He'd share this idea with Adam once they reached Warsaw, but for now Adam could sleep, unaware that an address that no longer existed, tied them both to this earth and to its obligations.

CHAPTER EIGHTEEN

*D*EAR CRISTOF,

*This will be an easy letter to begin because so much has
happened since I arrived in Warsaw. I can start with
any fact of my trip, and the news is startling, even to myself.
First, I must tell you about Jack Kaufman, who was not able to
visit his mother's birthplace, as was his wish. He did board the
airplane and fly across the ocean, but soon after he landed, he took
ill, and the best doctors could not save him.*

*Adam and I are certain that Jack knew he would die very soon.
That is why he had sent his young woman away and why he flew
all night to a country he did not know. It was better for him to
die here, I think, where he has no history but "a clean slate," as
they say in America. I was able to smooth Adam's way with the
Polish officials in this regard. "He was a very important man," I
insisted, suffering no delays with their endless forms and
inquiries. Finally, Jack was treated with the anonymous dignity
that state officials are so adept at bestowing upon the living and
dead alike.*

*Before I helped Adam reserve the plane home, an epic struggle
that lasted five days, I held his hand while he selected his grandfather's plain pine box. At the airport, each of us—Harrison, my*

mother, and I—kissed Jack farewell, peering inside at his smooth, peaceful face. Harrison was especially moved, and his sadness brought me to tears. There we all stood, huddled together in our grief like castaways in a storm. When it was my time to leave, I pressed a small token upon Jack, one of my father's letters, which is very dear to me. My mother enclosed an old jazz record, a shiny 78, brittle as an old bone, on which Miss Ella Fitzgerald sings her tunes. It is so strange to imagine my parents listening to jazz before my birth. I had been like a child in this regard, believing the world began when I took my first breath. Yes, there is much I never knew about my mother. To think, Cristof, it was her doing that brought Harrison to Warsaw. So little did I understand her connections to the larger world, her interests beyond me and Father and our little house. But my mother knows far more about jazz than I or perhaps you. Now, while cooking, she plays records for me. I hear Fats Waller sing "Rosetta" and wonder why it took so long for her to reveal her past. Perhaps she thought it irrelevant to me, pragmatist that she is. Now, after dinner I often fall asleep in my father's old chair listening to her American music, and when my weary eyes blink open, she is saying "Charlie Parker" or "Billie Holliday" with the zeal of a young girl who has a new suitor.

When Adam boarded the plane, Mother and I presented him with roses to sweeten his journey home. Then she and I lit many candles and said countless prayers and hurriedly baked cakes and tortes to share while we basked in Jack's memory. I am convinced that my mother, who did not know him at all, believes that she did, having heard so many tales and having witnessed his end. She is officially mourning, she tells our neighbors, who see her draped in black, conspicuous in her sorrow. I have told her that Jack was terrible in some ways, Cristof, but in the end he was a kind, brave man. Whatever the world thinks, I cannot forget his patience with Adam and his generosity to Elizabeth.

With Elizabeth and Jack gone, all that remains of my cozy Chicago retreat is Mr. Waters and me. Please be assured that we are alive and well. My own life is not prone to new starts but *rather to long, symphonic conclusions. In Warsaw I have learned so much about my father, who left pages of remarkable notes, now in my possession. Though what he says is merely historical now that our country has become another thing altogether—so bustling and confident, almost like America itself—it is of interest to me. Reading what he left behind, I can still hear his voice, his fearless civic urge, that often exceeded good judgment. You could say it was his words, so open and bold, that directed me to my new home. Though I didn't travel by balloon, it would have been a proper vehicle for his fragile, inflated dreams.*

Still, his legacy of truth has led me to explore what would perhaps be better left alone. My mind takes more than it needs from this world. Irena, the glutton, has a full plate of knowledge. She wonders what is left for others, and she is a bit embarrassed with the irony that her knowledge has left her somewhat poorer. She should be more like her mother, who conjures up lost pets and makes them reappear, who relies on her old phonograph records to summon a past I never knew, who speaks at night to her husband as if he is present in the room, who mourns deeply for strangers, whose little shrine shows no penchant for reality with its timeless icons and cheap store-bought charms.

Perhaps numbers are better for me than human affairs, Cristof. Take the new sum, for instance, of my trusted friend Urszula and my Joszef. Some day I will master neutrality, which I was hoping distance would award me like a prize.

My mother's tricks turned out to be mild compared to my former lover's larceny. In putting a brave face on my departure, she says her few days with me are enough. She presses my hand and smiles like a child into my face. She doesn't ask for more. She knows that I will be leaving after Harrison returns from Vienna, where he has been ferried by his young admirers. Yes, he is thriving here, evidence that we should all change countries at least once in our lives.

I have phoned Krakow for you, and your sister sends her love. There was much she wanted to know about your life in America, and I tried my best to inform her. Sometimes I improvised,

Cristof, yet she seemed satisfied with my description of our new city and your work there. She insists on one thing: that you must send a picture of your new silver Chevy Lumina, which she says has a lovely, mysterious name.

Meanwhile, I am trying to contrive some answers for myself since the Warsaw of my past, the one in which I invested my faith, is lost to me. I am not despondent, having anticipated this conclusion, yet it is difficult to accept the upheaval. It is as if a huge oak tree has been uprooted and fallen, and the ground on which I stand is vibrating with the aftershock. No bruises are visible, but my hands still tremble when I pick up my teacup or hold my pen to write you these lines.

But I will be fine, you should be assured. When Harrison and I return to Chicago, you will see that I am, if anything, less burdened, more free. I will be able to joke and smile, perhaps more readily, knowing what I do. We will share a cigarette and admire our new lake and laugh at the course of events. We will drink some wine as I play Harrison's music for you from his new Polish jazz tape and CD. What can be more amazing than that? Perhaps the fact that my mother has requested that I send her a CD player so that she can listen to Harrison as well.

But as my life in Warsaw draws to a close, I hesitate just as I do reading a book that I love. I pause with regret before the final pages when the beautiful world I have come to require will disappear forever.

I will use my last days in Warsaw to say good-bye to the Old Town with its maze of roofs. I will wave farewell to the Vistula and Syrenka's intrepid sword. I will touch the ornate walls of Lazienki Palace. Then I will order some bitter coffee with formidable lumps of sugar at my favorite cafe and throw a few crumbs to the pigeons, who will always welcome me home.

Now I see that my mother's small garden, covered by leaves and snow, is showing its first signs of spring. I am tempted to linger here and watch the season change for the last time as crocuses push toward the light and wrens collect twigs for their future homes.

What am I returning to, Cristof? My answer is always the

same: to Mr. Waters, who needs me at present, and to a future I still must meet. Whatever it holds, I resolve to know it well for it must suffice. I will make it as precious to me as my childhood bedroom under this old, ivy-covered roof, where my mother remains with my father's dear ghost. Sometimes I think that if I listen closely, I can hear him too in the corners of all the rooms that he inhabited.

Some day, Cristof, when this residence is mine, I will have to decide if my heart will pull me back. Though much is to be cherished here, I will welcome the sight of my new city when I return. From Mr. Waters' window, I can not see the stars at night, but I know that they are there just the same.

Fondly,

Irena

COLOPHON

This book was designed by Allan Kornblum, using Adobe Caslon type. All Coffee House Press books are printed on acid free paper, and are smyth sewn for durability and reader comfort.